The Mirror of Ashes

A FORGOTTEN RELICS NOVEL

Ellie Di Julio

ELLE BELLE MEDIA

The Mirror of Ashes

A Forgotten Relics Novel

First Edition

Content © 2015 Ellie Di Julio

Cover image © 2015 Desiree Kern

ISBN-13: 978-0-9936290-7-5

Published by Elle Belle Media

for the Region of Love –

here there be monsters

PART I
BAH, HUMBUG

ONE

Just four hours, that's all I need.

The sleeve of my black parka makes a great sleep shade as I lie face up on the couch. I flopped down ten minutes ago without bothering to take off my muddy snow boots and haven't budged since. Too tired. You try working twelve hours on, six hours off and see how you feel.

Hard to believe that two weeks ago I was raring for action, desperate to start work as a full agent. Now I'm lucky if there's time to breathe between assignments. After the Faerie case, Agent 99 not only changed his tune about the Eris situation, he upped the key and sang harmony. He called for all hands on deck and has the Supernatural Cases Division scouring the country for Nathaniel Wexford, the Sword of Souls, and anything else tied to the goddess of chaos' plan to bring down the Gauntlet. All of us are underfed, exhausted, and racking up immense overtime pay, but we're doing good work. The crackdown's netting more arrests, traces, and seizures in the last two weeks than in the last year combined. Every agent knows there's treachery afoot, thanks to Jack Alexander and me, and unlimited resources are at our disposal. It's a shame we're too bogged down with street-level crime to use them.

Careful what you wish for, eh, Riley?

Face still buried in the crook of my elbow, I transfer my phone from a pocket to the nearby end table with my free hand and set it to vibrate. I may be on call when I'm off duty, but I swear if this glorified beeper rings one more time, I'll be vacuuming it out of my rug. I just need a couple hours of peace and quiet to recharge—my energy, my magic, my patience—then they can call me back. I'll even frisk a slug monster. Although preferably not another ghoul victim. I'll never get those screams out of my head.

I leave my feet dangling over the arm of the couch and tuck myself up against the back cushions, snuggling them like a teddy bear. It'll leave corduroy lines on my cheeks, but I don't care. Gotta get comfortable as quick as I can so I can sleep. Four hours. That's all I need.

It's not that easy, though. In the space between wakefulness and dreams, my brain panics. All the sleep-sidestepping I did after moving back in with my folks made it hard to trust my unconscious. I don't dream anymore, post-underworld, but I do have a hell of a time getting to sleep.

This time, I think I can drift off without incident.

That lovely melting sensation trickles down my spine, my heartbeat slows to a lull, and my thoughts start to fuzz as I give my full weight to the cushions.

And then a clear thought: *They have a wizard.*

I moan like an exasperated toddler and roll back over to stare blearily at the ceiling, the promise of sleep vaporized. It's a key insight for my current case—a gang of brownies stealing jewelry through a box that I now realize has a portal in it—but, dammit. I was so close.

There was a time when I'd turn on the TV for comfort, particularly when I couldn't sleep. My drug of choice was crime dramas. You name it, I've been addicted to it. Probably written fanfiction for it. But these days, working at the SCD during a looming apocalypse, it hits too close to home. Especially the episodes where the main character has a breakdown because the work gets under his skin. I couldn't fathom that. Those guys had everything I wanted: purpose, authority, excitement, direction, respect. Plus, they were pretty sexy. What could possibly be so bad?

Now I get it.

The job gets to you. These last two weeks have stretched me so thin I'm afraid I'll disappear. Case after case out in the slushy Washington, DC winter, rarely speaking to another non-suspect soul, hypnotized by an endless sea of reports—it could drive a girl insane. Sure, I'm not tracking serial killers or examining mutilated bodies, but when you see the same thing all day, every day, it does something to you. I never thought living in a world where magic is real could be less than endlessly wondrous. I should be happy to be a full agent, thrilled I'm making headway in saving the entire world from being consumed by greedy supernaturals. Yet here I lay, wrung out by what amounts to another routine day at work, wondering if I'm on the verge of a breakdown myself.

I scrunch further into the couch and am about to try sleeping again when my phone buzzes. "Oh, thank God," I mutter, grateful for the interruption, even if it's another case. Anything to cut off this train of thought that tastes too much like depression.

I snatch up the phone before it rattles off the end table and squint at the caller ID. It says *Momma Bear*. I smile. Sofi and I haven't seen each other since coming back from Faerie. Ninety-Nine released her as my mentor immediately, and her bear senses and strength landed her on stakeout duty, while I'm using my interdimensional-door-finding powers and newly-acquired magic radar to track missing persons. We talk every day, though, and seeing her name on the screen is always a bright spot.

I pick up on the third ring. "Hey, Soph, Where are you?"

"On my way to the Fifth to drink away the smell of burnt yeti while I pretend I didn't see the new assignment HQ sent me an hour ago. You coming?"

I snort. "No, I'm sleeping."

"Dreaming about a certain tall, dark, and weird agent we both know?"

"Sofi!"

Jack's an open secret between us. The man literally asked me out on what could've been his deathbed if he wasn't some kind of werewolf-sidestepper hybrid. How could I not tell my best friend? But there's been no follow through. Which she also knows. I guess being a special snowflake doesn't mean he's different than any other guy who's scared of talking to girls.

It takes Sofi a good ten seconds to stop laughing. "You know I'm teasing. Seriously, though, come have a beer. At the rate they're handing out assignments, they're going to call you soon, anyway. Word is even One Hundred's on the beat."

I don't doubt it. But whether the director's working a case or not has no impact on my desire for z's. "An excellent reason for me to continue napping," I say. "If she's out there, they don't need me. Besides, it's not like I'm any more useful than a normal cop these days. The first thing Jack and I did was seal all the interdimensional doors in DC, and no one's reporting off-plane activity."

"Fine, be that way." There's a pause long enough for me to start to say I'll see her later, but then she says, "How are you holding up, Riley? Be honest. I know it's your first Christmas away from home, and the work's been friggin' brutal. You okay?"

Her directness catches me off guard. Our friendship was cemented after our trip to Faerie, and I'm used to Sofi's blunt approach, but after the dark line of thinking I'd been following before she called, it's eerie that she'd ask if I'm okay.

"Still there?"

"Yeah, sorry," I stammer. I'd prefer to brush this off, but when I'm this tired, filters are the first thing to go. The truth plops out. "Actually, I'm not doing so hot, Soph. I'm exhausted and confused and kinda bored, if that makes sense," I say, rolling to one side so the phone rests on my ear. "How do you do it? Go from being a muggle to being a supernatural action hero in six months?"

"Six months and two weeks for you, I believe," she quips back.

"You know what I mean." I pick at a rip in the couch with what's left of my thumbnail. "I spent my whole life wishing to be special, praying for an exciting, magical life, and then I got it. I'm living the dream." A pitiful sigh squeezes out. "It's kind of hard to believe this is it."

"Aw, sugarbean." The compassion in her voice is as good as a hug. Her momma bear powers must work through the phone. "I wish I had something profound to say. My story didn't go that way, you know? Superpowers sort of happened to me."

"I know. It's just.... It feels like there's a hole in me where the wishing was, and I don't know how to fill it."

"I bet Jack—" she starts.

"Dammit, Sofi," I sniff through a laugh. Why does fifth grade humor work on me? I'm thirty-one years old; you'd think I'd get over it.

"Sorry, honey. Couldn't help myself." I hear the texture of the air change on her end of the line from street to bar. "Tell you what, we'll talk it out next break, okay? It eats me up knowing you're having to put on a brave face all the time."

I wipe my eyes with the sleeve of my parka. "Thanks, Soph. You're one in a million."

"True fact," she says. "See you soon, spookybutt."

I hang up with a smile on my face, despite the awkwardness I vomited on her. Sometimes, you don't know what you think until you're asked. I'm glad she did.

I lay the phone back down and snuggle into the couch, feeling lighter for having unburdened myself, hopeful it'll help me get some shuteye before the inevitable call to action.

And then Sofi's words come back to me: *It's your first Christmas away from home.*

My eyes pop open. "Seriously, brain?" I whine. "Fine, you win. No sleep for me tonight."

I shoulder myself up to sitting, groping under the armrest for the TV remote. The screen flickers to life, and I flip around the channels. The first time I stop for *It's a Wonderful Life*. I watch Jimmy Stewart charmingly stammer through accepting the love of his family for ten seconds before I get choked up, then get annoyed at myself for being emotional. The next station's got *Rudolph*, Mom's favorite, and I settle back into the cushions. I always identified with Herbie, wanting something beyond what his circumstances dictated. I wonder how his dentistry practice turned out.

But not even Rankin and Bass can erase the reminder about me being alone on Christmas for the first time. I've been successfully ignoring that fact since the calendar hit December. Between the fight with Dad, the unending caseload, and my own existential weirdness, I'm borderline resenting the cheeriness of the season. Why did Sofi have to bring it up a mere three days away?

I wish *The Grinch* was on.

Yawning hugely, I stand up to stretch, and ditch the parka on the couch. I cross the floor of my studio apartment, ready to pry off my snow boots, but when I lean down to start unlacing them, I notice a spray of color next to the shoe rack. My eyes widen as I realize they're Christmas cards. Nosy Mr. Evans must've taken them off the communal mail table and shoved them under my door. I didn't notice them as I came in tonight; one has my muddy bootprint on the back.

I hurriedly kick off my shoes and snatch up the cards, shaking melted snow off them as I plop back onto the couch. There's a lonely flicker of holiday spirit as I turn them over one by one to see who thought of me at Christmas.

The first is from work, with a pre-printed label. Boring. I set it aside.

The second is from Sofi, covered in stickers. She already told me there's a Victoria's Secret gift card in there. I chuckle and set it aside, too.

The third makes me catch my breath. Under normal circumstances, I wouldn't be surprised to see a card from my parents. But Dad's flowing cursive script on the front is a sore reminder of our phone conversation after I returned from Faerie.

He wasn't the least bit sorry for lying to me about Queen Mab being my grandmother or for hiding the fact that I'm part faerie. He doubled down, said it was for my own good, to protect me. I called him so many names. The last thing I said was, "I'll never forgive you for this." I hung up as he started to cry. I didn't care. Holding this card in my hand, though, as drained and defenseless as I am, I'm ashamed of myself. I cast a glance at the phone, but I can't summon the courage to call. I lay the card on the end table next to the phone. Tomorrow.

I sigh and turn over the last card. *Hrm.* Its only distinguishing feature is my full name written on it in neat block letters. There's no address, no return, no postmark. My danger sense, well-honed by weeks on high alert, quietly comes online. I turn the mysterious red envelope over in my hands, scrutinizing it for clues. I don't recognize the handwriting. There's no scuffing or damage to the paper. And, thankfully, there isn't any powder or other suspicious grossness on the outside. Ordinarily, I'd be satisfied with that and open it. But now that I'm in the SCD, I'm more cautious. Things aren't always what they seem. There's one more test I can run.

It happens faster than the first time. My supernatural radar isn't experimental anymore; it's a vital part of how I do my job. When I discovered I could use the doorway-finding sensor circle from my sidestepping abilities to pick up magical signatures in Faerie, I'd thought it was a fluke. A temporary effect of using my faerie blood in its home territory. But it works in the real world, too, making me way more useful in the field. After a handful of hours practicing, I can locate magical objects and people in a crowd, plus differentiate power levels and occasionally type. Not bad for solo training. Still not sure how I'm able to do it—although after Jack's teleporting incident, I suspect it's more than coincidence—but I'm not complaining.

The sensor pops up with the speed and ease of flicking a light switch. It's a broad range, about ten yards, and I easily pick up the elderly banshee in the house next door. I narrow the focus to my personal space—I don't need Ana's energy interrupting me—but nothing pings when I sweep the envelope. I exhale and let the senor fall. Whatever this is, it's not magical.

I slide my least mangled fingernail into one of the corners and tear the perfect seal, pointing it away from my face, just in case. Nothing happens, so I pull out the white card inside. It's got a simple Christmas tree on the front, under which the gold lettering says, "Happy Holidays." I flip it open to read the inside, and a small sheet of paper slides out into my lap. Cautiously, I retrieve it with the thumb and forefinger of one hand to see the insert is a carbon copy of a receipt.

Roosevelt Center for Curious Cases
Temporary Permit
Level 5: Archives.
Issued to Agent 6, Cora Riley.
Mandatory chaperone.

Expires three (3) days from issue date.
Approval Code: 99.

It takes me a few seconds to parse what I'm seeing. When I finally do, my heart backflips in my chest, and I let out a squeak of excitement.

I get to see the Lorekeeper!

I bounce up from the couch for a celebration dance that'd be life-endingly mortifying should anyone else see it. I pump my fist and shake my butt as Rudolph and Herbie rejoice with me on the TV.

Finally, I can get answers about what Eris is planning and these weird prophecies going around and why my powers are changing. This is seriously the best present I could've asked for. Maybe this won't be the worst Christmas ever after all.

But, of course, my common sense won't let me stay this happy for long. *Where did this come from*? *I didn't put in any paperwork.*

The thought cuts my happy dance so short I lose my balance and tip over onto the couch again. Where indeed?

I pick up the accompanying card I'd dropped in my excitement and see there's writing inside in the same block lettering. I scan it fast, once, twice, not sure that I've read it right, then I squeak again, leap from the couch, and bolt to the bathroom for the fastest shower ever recorded. I throw on a fresh SCD-issue black suit and tie, shove my damp feet back in the snow boots, throw on my down parka with one hand, and lock the apartment door with the other. Pedestrians give me the side eye and veer out of my path as I sprint down the street, but I don't care.

I've got to be at the Roosevelt in twenty minutes. Jack kept his promise.

TWO

Dirty snow crunches under my feet as I hop off the bus at the edge of the national monument strip by the river. Arctic air seeps through the gaps in my protective layers, worming its way into my bones. We get blankets of snow and below zero temps back home, but the nearness of the ocean here makes the season exceptionally awful. Fortunately, my boots keep me dry as I hurry from the main street to the center of the Roosevelt Memorial where the Center for Curious Cases is housed underground. For the hundredth time, I wish I hadn't let Sofi convince me I didn't need a car. Never trust a bear to give you advice on dealing with winter.

It's not far, but the rush and anticipation make the walk feel like an eternity. I reach the statue of former president Roosevelt and his dog, Fala, at the heart of the exhibit and find I'm alone. I risk frostbitten fingers to check my phone for the time. Seven PM on the dot. I'm not sure if I'm disappointed or amused. It's not like Jack to be late; I swear that man's part atomic clock. I jam my hands back into my pockets with a huff and wait in one of the spotlights outlining the statues against the dark.

Sofi isn't the only person I've been missing these last two weeks, much as I hate to admit it. While he hasn't ghosted on me the way he did when I first arrived in the Capitol, Jack's been annoyingly busy with his responsibilities as Agent 97, going dark for high-level cases when he's not trapped in endless meetings. Or so I hear. This will be the first time that we've seen each other since Faerie, on or off duty, and I'm not sure what to expect. He could be cold and professional; he could be sappy and human. Hard to tell with him. But after the way he acted in med bay, I know which way I'm hoping for.

A plume of white steam billows into the air as I huff at myself. I should be glad I haven't had two seconds to worry about anything besides work. Keeps me from daydreaming about a romance I'm not sure exists.

I obsessively check my phone again. Just as the clock flips to four after, I hear the click of slick-soled shoes on wet cement coming towards me.

Jack Alexander, the SCD's most accomplished agent and general mystery to me, strides around the wall of engravings depicting wartime troubles, moving fast on his preposterously long legs and touching his earpiece to end a call. "Conference with the St. Louis office ran long," he says to me. "They're covering something up, but we can't pinpoint what yet." We meet in front of the president's statue. He half-moves like he's going to hug me but turns it into straightening his coat, and I pretend not to have butterflies at standing within arm's reach of him again. "I hope you weren't waiting too long," he says. Then he gives me a tight smile. "It's good to see you."

The sound of his voice puts an automatic smile on my face. I hadn't forgotten how smooth it is, like scotch mixed with honey, but the reminder is nice. "Nah, just got here," I say, more casual than I feel. I pat the stocking cap shoved over my copper hair. "Had to run, though—I didn't get your note until after I clocked out tonight."

His brow furrows. "I left it in your mailbox three days ago."

I flush, ashamed of the pity-party I've been throwing myself and for letting work stress get the better of me. There's a warning tug on my psyche, reminding me of how I retreated into work when I was bored with my life before, asking if I'm doing it again. I crush the thought before it can take root. I've done my time with depression. I have a new life, a new purpose; I refuse to let it leak out now. Particularly not in front of Jack. I doubt he'd understand.

"Yeah, sorry about that," I say. "I've been so busy lately I haven't had time to do much more than file reports and sleep. And sometimes not even that."

He nods sagely. Of course he knows. In the monument's dim light, I can see the dark circles under his brown eyes, the subtle ashen tones to his caramel-colored skin. I wonder how little sleep he's gotten in the last two weeks, what he's really been up to since 99 gave him free reign to tackle Eris and her cronies. A wave of empathy rises up in me, cresting in the urge to wrap my arms around him and tell him it's okay, he doesn't have to work so hard, he can rest—to take care of him where I know he won't take care of himself. But it passes. For all of our mutual adventures, I'm still not sure where we stand. Maybe he doesn't want me to take care of him. Maybe I don't actually want to, either.

There's no time for that conversation, though. We're running down the clock for us to see the Lorekeeper before my pass expires, and no confused titillation is more important than getting answers right now.

I turn my attention to the monument beside me. "Ready?" I ask.

"If you are."

I nod and move to the side. Jack tugs off a black leather glove and presses his hand to the frozen nose of the dog statue. The biometric lock reads his palm print with a green light, then beeps merrily as it accepts his qualifications. The stone foundation beneath the two statues swings aside to reveal a dim staircase that descends to a square room containing nothing but an elevator.

Jack pulls his glove back on. "After you," he says. I swear I see an amused sparkle in his eyes as he motions towards the stairs.

Is he laughing at me? He is. Crap. I'm more than excited to see the Roosevelt's archives, and I must be doing an awful job of hiding it if he notices. Normally, it'd bug me to be so easily read, but I ignore that old impulse and decide instead to be grateful that he's falling on the human side of the weirdo meter today.

I take the lead down the stairs, and he follows close behind, ducking as the stone slab reseals to hide the entrance. For a brief moment, before the fluorescents come on in the claustrophobic waiting room, we're alone in soft shadows. The smell of him so close, the scent of cinnamon and sage, warms me all over. I look up at his eyes, made darker and deeper by the half-light, and try to remember how to breathe. My hand fumbles for the call button behind me, pressing it on the third try. Then the lights come on full, and I swallow the sandpaper in my throat as I turn to wait for the elevator, sucking down cold air to douse burning memories of having less between us than three inches of space and flimsy clothing.

I've been in the Roosevelt once, escorting the newly-awakened King Tut, but I'm dying to see the rest. To hear other agents tell it, the building is sort of a combination of warehouse and jail. The upper four levels are straightforward: administration, library, minor holding, supermax. The fifth level, the final and deepest one, is a mystery. It's called the Archives, but it's more than a holding facility for records and documents; it's also where the SCD stores its magical artifacts. Fake holy grails, the mast from the Argo, Merlin's grimoire—stuff like that. Access is restricted to Agent 70 and up, and even then only with special clearance. The potential for theft or magical abuse of the objects and knowledge contained there is too high to let in the riffraff.

Unless you're me. And you're being escorted by Agent 97.

After eighty million years of descent, the elevator doors slide apart to reveal the Archives. A wall of dense, musty air collapses over us, and I cough to clear my lungs of dust and mildew as we step out. The doors close silently behind us and Jack starts walking, but I'm rooted to the spot, head on a swivel, my brain scrambling to take in everything I'm seeing.

Where I'd expected a stately museum-style storage facility, what I see is row upon row of floor-to-ceiling wire racks arranged in parallel lines in every direction. Crates, boxes, papers, statues, clothing, instruments—a dizzying array of items that'd make a pawnshop owner weep. From where I stand, I can see bins of dragon's teeth, a dozen dead man's hands on a string like chili peppers, a glass case of gold jewelry, and enough mithril to outfit an elvish legion. Not a single inch of storage space is unoccupied, labels with varying degrees of legibility mark the contents, and it goes on forever. A thrill rolls up my spine. I could spend the rest of my life in here spelunking for magical objects and learning their secrets. I'd never be bored again.

"Whoa," I whisper. "It's like I died and went to

hoarder heaven."

At the sound of my voice, Jack reappears at the first junction next to a sign that says "circulation" with an arrow pointing left. I wonder at what point he noticed I wasn't with him.

"You're not far off," he says as he comes back to me. "The agency's collected so many artifacts and 'objects of interest' over the last century that no one's a hundred percent sure what's down here. Any time they try to catalog it, the lists are different." He glances at the yawning corridors of stuff. "We've lost a couple of interns in here, too."

"No way. How do you lose human beings in an underground warehouse with triple security?"

He shrugs and says, "You'd have to ask them," then heads off again.

This time I follow. We have to walk single file since the corridors are barely wide enough for me to pass without whanging into something. From this position, the stacks aren't the only thing that get my attention, though. I notice there's an easy, relaxed quality to Jack's stride where his usual step is clipped and urgent. It occurs to me that he was as nervous to meet up as I was. Maybe more so. Thankfully, now that we're moving and talking and working, neither of us is anxious anymore. This is where we understand each other and know who we are. Business as usual.

Left, left, right, straight, straight, right....

"Are we there yet?" I ask. "I didn't think the building was this big."

"Almost. When you get this much magical

material together in one place, it distorts time and space on a minor scale. We're not entirely sure how it works, although Cid's got a theory. It mostly involves saying, 'It's magic,' as far as I can tell."

I chuckle. "Of course it does." The SCD's quartermaster has a *Star Trek* knack for simple explanations for complicated phenomena. "But seriously," I say, "how do you find anything in here?"

"You don't!" screeches a voice from down one of the left-hand pathways. Its shrillness dies off fast, like it's being pushed through a tin can.

I shoot Jack a questioning look. With a muted sigh, he turns and walks towards the sound. I follow along, straining to pinpoint the location of the third person, but all I can pick up is our footsteps. Azrael blowing out my eardrum in the underworld made my life a lot quieter, which isn't necessarily a good thing in law enforcement.

After two more turns in the creaking maze, we find a wide-open space nestled among the shelves. It's small, about eight by eight, and contains an old-fashioned teacher's desk that occupies it with the authority of a 300-pound bouncer named Tiny. It's oddly neat, a stark contrast to the groaning mass of things around it, and illuminated by a single lamp with a green shade.

As we get nearer, I see the desk isn't totally empty. There's a thimble-sized silver bell underneath the lamp at the front right corner. Jack takes the bell delicately between two fingers and gives it a ring. The sound is high and clear as it echoes off the concrete floor but is quickly absorbed by the reams of parchment and clutches of scrolls that are this section's specialty.

Jack replaces the bell. Seconds pass. Nothing happens. Whoever snarked at us a minute ago doesn't care that we're ringing for assistance.

I'm about to ask what's happening when the biggest, ugliest, scaliest locust I've ever seen plummets from out of nowhere and divebombs the desk. It lands with an angry buzz, rolling around gracelessly to get itself upright.

I hate bugs. I can do mice, spiders, maggots, snakes, and dead bodies. But not bugs.

I'm halfway through an open-hand slam to squash the nasty thing when Jack catches my wrist. I turn to rebuke him, but I notice he's actively trying not to laugh. This does nothing for my annoyance.

I snatch my hand back. "What the—" I start.

Jack motions at the massive bug. "Agent 6, allow me to introduce our Lorekeeper."

My mouth falls open. "What?" I manage.

"Close your trap, girl, or a bug'll fly in it." The high-pitched squeak again. I realize it's coming from the desk. Or, more accurately, from the thing sitting on it.

Past my shock, a helpful tidbit of story is tossed out by my mythological memory. I take in the scaled shell, the light creating bronze diamonds in the cracks and pooling in the fine membrane of the wings. That's when I get it.

Feeling incredibly stupid, I address the critter on

the desk. "Tithonus, right? The guy Eos granted immortality but not eternal youth?"

"That's right, rub it in," he squeaks. I didn't know bugs could be sarcastic, but he manages. The tin-can voice we heard is definitely his, though I'm not sure how I'm hearing it. "How many centuries have you lived, eh? Tell me that, you snotty ginger whippersnapper."

I'm not about to take that kind of shit from someone I can kill with a newspaper, no matter how many thousands of years old he is. I open my mouth to fire back, but Jack slides into the conversational gap.

"Tithonus, this is Agent 6," he says, stepping closer to the desk. "She's new, but she's got information to share that you'll find highly engaging."

The locust rubs his wings together, which I take as him thinking it over. When he doesn't respond, Jack pulls out the official paperwork that's allowed us to be here and slides it to him. Tithonus skitters directly onto it and, I assume, reads it.

"This is all in order," he says. He uses a wispy leg to push the paper ineffectively back towards Jack. It's like he thinks he still has a human body, even after millennia without one. Anthropomorphization in full swing. I repress a giggle. On second thought, he's sort of cute in a disgusting, buggy way.

Jack tucks the papers back into his pocket, saying, "Did Ninety-Nine tell you why we're visiting?"

The locust snorts, an ear-wax melting sound that

makes me wonder if it's what people hear before they have a stroke. "That curry-muncher doesn't tell me anything. Thinks he's so mysterious and wise." Another snort. "What a moron."

I shoot a horrified look at Jack, whose expression doesn't change at the balls-out racist comment. I'm suddenly painfully aware of being the lone white person in the room and have no idea what to do. Too many years in a backwater town made these situations deeply uncomfortable for me. Conflicted, I opt for silence. My awkwardness aside, this could be our one chance to find out what Eris is up to, and I won't be the one that blows it. The angel on my shoulder kicks me hard enough to leave a bruise, though.

"Good," is all Jack says. "This will be quicker and easier if you're not comparing stories." He looks to me. "Would you like to do the honors?"

Hell yes, I would.

Stepping up next to Jack at the desk's edge, I position myself directly in front of the Lorekeeper and deliver what we know. "Essentially, Agent 97 and I have heard two different but related prophecies. The first came from Lady Hel, who was captured and tortured until we were able to rescue her. She revealed that Eris intends to bring down the Gauntlet and unite the worlds." I'm rewarded with a startled chirp. While it's not great that this is news to him after the agency-wide memo, it's a good sign that he's upset by it. It means he's on our side. I think. "We've had contact with several of Eris' allies already," I continue, "and the consistent story is that the Otherworld is too unstable to survive much longer. She believes that uniting the worlds will save what remains of the magical races since the mortals will have no choice but to believe in what they see, effectively sustaining supers permanently."

"And the second prophecy?" Tithonus says. "I'm hoping you have something more than the word of a lonely widow and an interworld ecology theory."

I shift my weight from one foot to the other. I hate to throw Arachne under the bus for her drunk-weaving episode, but this is too important to hide. "There was a possession incident that resulted in Arachne weaving a symbolic tapestry. It was crude, but the images were clear enough. A tall figure in the center, wearing a crown and wielding a huge sword, standing in front of a shiny wall. There were other figures on both sides, some behind the main person and dozens on the opposite side. All contained in what could be the outline of an apple." I fish out my phone and show Tithonus the pictures I took of the tapestry before I had Arachne destroy it. He makes the bug version of a *hrm* noise. I finish by saying, "We reported everything to Ninety-Nine, along with the evidence about Queen Mab allying with her and the Sword of Souls being brought over here from Faerie, but he hasn't been terribly helpful, even after greenlighting the investigation. That's why we're here: We figured if anyone knows what these prophecies mean, it's you."

To this, Tithonus is silent. No sass, no chirps, no rubbing of wings. After all his bluster earlier, it's disconcerting. I raise an eyebrow at Jack, who gives a brief shrug, and I get the impression I should wait.

It takes ages. In the warehouse, these many stories underground, there's no sound. The overhead lights don't even buzz. Minutes crawl past. I become keenly aware of the sheer volume of earth over and around us and imagine what it's like to be buried alive.

But before I can say anything to relieve the pressure, there's an abrupt series of squeaks from the desk, and the fist-sized locust leaps right at me. I scream and swat at the air to protect myself, completely losing my cool. A buzzing breeze passes within inches of my face as the Lorekeeper flies easily out of range of my flailing hands, over my head, and plunges into the towering pile of scrolls behind me.

Flushed and embarrassed, I look down at my feet and straighten my clothes to avoid Jack. I can feel his eyes on my back, but thankfully, he doesn't say anything.

Half a minute passes and Tithonus returns, flying much lower this time, his wispy legs gripping a leather thong wrapped around a scroll. I can hear tiny swearing as he flits between Jack and me, then he flumps his cargo and himself back onto the open desk. There's a busy couple of seconds as he disentangles himself from the carrier.

"Well, go on," he huffs once he's free. "Open it." Jack reaches for the scroll but an angry buzz stops his hand halfway. "Not you, genius, the girl."

I give Jack an apologetic smile, then take the scroll and unroll it. The parchment's brittle, crackling and browned, and smells dustier than the rest of the archives. I hear Jack inhale deeply and wonder what else he can tell about the paper through his werewolf senses. But there's surprisingly little written on it. I figured if you took the trouble to write a scroll, you'd have the decency to fill it. Then I remember all the notebooks I've bought and how few lines made it in each one and have more empathy for the ancient scribe. Maybe he had blank book addiction, too.

I peer at the scrawl—ten lines in fading brown ink, the origins of which I'm not keen to ponder. It's English, in a third-cousin-twice-removed sort of way. Thank the gods I took advanced literature in high school.

"There's something about a sacrifice?" I try out loud. "Cutting the bonds and merging sides? And a summoning?"

"Keep going," Tithonus says.

I squint and hold the delicate paper up to the light, trying to find the edges of the lettering for better clarity. "Here's one I can actually read: 'The new world reflects the old world. The new king is the old king.'" I lower the scroll in frustration. "Sir, this is more obscure than what we already have. What are you trying to show me?"

He makes a disgusted noise. "Think about it for five seconds, would you? I hear you're quite the mythological marvel." Jack starts to ask a question, but Tithonus cuts him off. "Yeah, I hear things down here, towel-head. Just because you're a boss doesn't mean you know everything."

A chill rolls off Jack so hard it gives me a shiver. His face goes stony, a curl in his lip all that reveals his anger. But he doesn't cut back. I have to admit I'm impressed at his restraint. I also kind of want to barf.

"I, uh...," I stammer, making noise to fill the bitter silence. "If I had to guess, judging by what I can make out, I'd say these are instructions for a ritual to bring down the Gauntlet."

The giant locust hops excitedly, turning his striped eyes to me. "Excellent! What else?"

"Well, considering you dug it up based on Arachne's prophecy, I'd say it connects the elements of the ritual to the tapestry." I scan the paper again, willing the words to make sense. "Assuming Eris is the crowned figure in the center, that's the 'new king,' and the sword she's holding must be the Sword of Souls. Mab claimed it could cut through anything, so that'd do it for severing the bonds between worlds. But the rest of it doesn't make sense."

Tithonus bounces on his bitty bug legs with a pleased chirp and plops onto the floor at the other side of the desk. There's scuffling as a drawer is pulled out, and I resist the urge to crane over the desk to see how he's doing it. A single piece of white paper and an ink pad are tossed onto the desktop, and he follows shortly after. Flipping open the ink, the Lorekeeper squishes a single delicate leg into it, then begins to draw. I lean over, intensely curious;

Jack does the same. Quick black strokes accompanied by adorable squeaking begin to form an image in front of our eyes. He does a fairly good job of recreating Arachne's tapestry, but this time there are labels to identify the components.

When he's finished, and his bronze shell mottled with black ink, he steps off the paper and says, "There," with pride so big I'm amazed he doesn't explode.

Jack picks up the paper and turns it right-side up, careful not to smudge the wet ink. I inch closer to him to see, despite the mild distraction of Old Spice. I read it over hungrily. Then I read it again. I frown.

"This doesn't say anything different," I say.

Tithonus flicks his wings indignantly. "Like hell it doesn't. Don't you see the labels?"

"They just say 'mirror' and 'apple'. Hardly helpful."

"Actually, they are," Jack says. "If I understand correctly, these are types of magical artifacts."

"S'right," he sniffs.

Jack peers at the paper, and I try again to see what he sees. But despite my extensive mythological education, I simply don't have his vast databases of information or perfect recall. While it irks me not to have the answers, I'll have to be satisfied with committing the drawing to memory.

Eventually, Jack says, "I see. The sword cuts a hole in the Gauntlet into which the mirror is inserted, reflecting the worlds into one another, and the apple is what summons Eris out from the

Otherworld."

"Got it in one, smartypants," Tithonus says begrudgingly.

Jack lowers the paper, his eyes wide. On anyone else, I'd easily pin the reaction as fear, but the label slips off him like butter in a hot pan. Jack's not afraid of anything.

Is he?

"A simultaneous apparent horizon," he says, staring hard at nothing. "But that's going to cause—"

"—systematic instability with cataclysmic potential," the Lorekeeper finishes.

The words echo around us. And make absolutely zero sense to me.

"Uh, one of you fonts of wisdom want to explain to the layman here exactly what that means?" I ask.

Jack blinks hard against whatever horrors he's seeing in his mind's eye and looks at me with a furrowed brow. "It means that if Eris executes this ritual, the two worlds will exist in the same space for a fraction of a second. It can't be stopped once it starts, but the resulting probability is split. The overlap could find purchase and all the beings from the Otherworld and their habitats will be successfully translated to this side. Or...," he trails off.

"Or everything could be destroyed right down to quarks," Tithonus says.

"Holy shit," I murmur, the weight of the idea sinking in. But I shake myself free. We need answers. "Eris already has the sword on this side," I say to Tithonus. "What mirror does she need and what apple? If she needs all three, we should be able to stop her by grabbing the other two objects first."

"No idea," admits the Lorekeeper. "I've read every scrap of paper in these archives, but the records don't include anything more on this insanity. That scroll's everything I've got."

"Mr. All-Knowing-Bug doesn't have any suggestions? It's pretty obvious that the golden apple of chaos from Eris' own legend would be the one we're looking for."

He buzzes his wings testily and snips, "It's the background magic fluctuations. From what I heard about the sword, this mirror could be an obscure relic or it could be an abomination, combining several different ones. Same with the apple. It might be a whole different fruit by now, mixed up with Persephone's pomegranate or Hina's coconut. There's too much up in the air to say for certain."

I groan as my brain starts assembling a list mythological food. It's longer than you'd think.

"Look at the bright side, Red," Tithonus chirps. "You know what she's up to and what she needs next. All you have to do is find it."

There's a faint buzz in the silence that follows. I pat my jacket for my phone, but it's not me. I raise an eyebrow at Jack, but he's a hundred miles away.

"Do you have any other information for us?" he says.

"She's got a major head start. You may not be able to stop her in time. But, there are artifacts that might help you get a leg up. Diogenes' Lantern springs to mind. Could help you ferret out any avatars or moles in the ranks."

Another buzz.

"Where is it?"

"Damned if I know," Tithonus says. "We had it after the Bush/Gore election, but when the CIA tried to check it out to use on Obama, it was gone." He does the locust equivalent of a shrug. "Like I said, the flux makes everything unpredictable. We lose half our inventory on a weekly basis, only to find it again right where we left it."

Another buzz.

"You going to get that?" Tithonus snips.

Jack exhales sharply, then answers his phone without bothering to walk away. I raise my eyebrows. How does he get service down here? Smart money's on Cid.

There's a string of, "yes, sir"s and "right away, sir"s. The call takes seconds. Then he hangs up, turns to me and says, "Ninety-Nine wants us in his office as soon as possible. Some sensitive assignments have come up." He turns back to the Lorekeeper, folding up the labeled tapestry map and tucking it inside his jacket. "You've been very helpful, sir."

I give a respectful bow to the locust, what with the lack of hands to shake, and say, "Thanks, Tithonus. You're a lifesaver."

"Yeah, yeah," the locust says. "Get out of here. Go save the world and leave this extremely old man to his papers."

We turn to leave, Jack striding out fast and me

jogging to keep up, but as we reach the first turn back into the stacks, Tithonus calls after us. "Hey, Red! Don't you want to know how you got bonded to Aladdin there? Or what he did to your powers?"

I stop dead in my tracks. In the excitement of ferretting out Eris' plan, I'd forgotten the other purpose for my visit. A hundred questions flood my mind. I've been over the single, handwritten volume on sidestepping a thousand times, but there's nothing about changing powers or bonding. What does the Lorekeeper know about my secrets? And how?

I get two steps towards the desk before Jack puts his hand on my shoulder, gentle but insistent. It's the first time we've touched since I dragged him out of Faerie. A blue warmth runs through me, derailing my urgent thoughts, and I glance over my shoulder to see him shake his head. I start to protest, but he shakes his head again.

"We need to go, Cora. He's baiting you." With a meaningful look, he adds, "I already know."

I stare at him dumbly for a full three seconds as I catch up with the exchange. Then he squeezes my shoulder and walks into the stacks, fully expecting me to follow. I hustle to keep up, not wanting to meet the same fate as past interns but unable to do more than trail him out as I imagine what he knows—and what he's not telling me.

THREE

The ride between the Roosevelt and headquarters in Jack's SUV is too short for conversation. At least, for the kind I'm dying to have right now. I file everything the Lorekeeper said—and didn't get a chance to say—into a massive mental folder for later. If Jack knows how we developed these extra powers or about this bonding thing that keeps getting thrown around, he's going to tell me. After we meet with 99, anyway.

Agents shuffle out the revolving door past us as we go inside. No one's remotely curious about Jack and I coming into the building when everyone's heading out, either home or to the Fifth, between the office closing and being on call for the night. It's par for the course these days. All one hundred SCD agents are working around the clock with extra pressure on the thirty housed here. Exhaustion is plain on everyone's face. I have a pang of guilt for being so self-absorbed earlier; I'm not the only one suffering as we deal with Eris and her cronies.

Jack and I ride up to the top level offices in silence. There's no small talk with him. I've watched him change dramatically over the six months that we've known each other, but no matter how casual he tries to be or how many bad jokes he painfully inserts into conversation, idle chatter hasn't worked its way into the programming yet. It used to make me uncomfortable, letting dead air hang between us. For the moment, though, it's oddly soothing, a welcome change from the loud haze of the field.

The silver elevator doors slide open at the third floor where Jack's own office shares space with those of Agents 98 and 99. I peer at the tinted glass of 98's unfamiliar office with curiosity. Sofi told me it's been empty for years, the agent drowned in suspicious circumstances during a cannibal mermaid case. When I'd asked why no one took his place, she shrugged. Above her pay grade, she'd said. I cast a sneaky glance at Jack as we pass the dark office, but his eyes are straight ahead, pointedly not looking at 98's door. It occurs to me for the first time that he might have ambitions beyond the next assignment. What a slap in the face. How many times was he passed over for promotion?

As we close the distance from the elevator, I see that Agent 99's door is ajar. Odd, considering how private he is. It's a quick walk down the hall, and soon I hear voices from inside. With a delight that erases my curiosity, I recognize all of them. This meeting might be okay.

But as I reach out to push open the door, Jack taps me on the shoulder. I raise an eyebrow, and he whispers, "Be careful. Tithonus has his flaws, but if he's suspicious of moles, we should be on our guard. Until we find the lantern, we've got to rely our instincts to root out Eris's eyes and ears."

I recall the Lorekeeper insinuating that Patel isn't a great guy, and the bug was pretty insistent about keeping things close to the vest. Everything I know about stories says this is exactly the right time for an ally to turn. But I have a hard time imagining that anyone in the room we're about to enter is on Eris' side. We're the Supernatural Cases Division. We're the good guys.

Right?

Jack nods at the door to indicate he's finished. A little less sure now, I push it open and plaster a professional smile on my face. Everyone stops talking and turns to watch us come in.

Sofi Strella, Agent 21, waves despite being directly in front of 99. When she was my mentor, I had to work to avoid her; it's strange to see her after weeks apart, and I miss her terribly. I notice her perpetual tan's faded in the DC winter, but she's still a ball of sunshine in a black suit and blond ponytail. I wave back at her, keeping it as hidden as I can.

Assistant Director Samir Patel is seated behind his impeccably neat desk, unmoved by our late arrival. He blinks at us slowly but says nothing. I note with amusement that he's wearing a red and green Christmas tie. An appropriately festive touch for someone who looks like an Indian Santa Claus. He waves Jack and me forward to stand next to Sofi.

Once we reach the desk, I can see the owner of the third voice. Ninety-Nine's computer monitor is filled with the shaggy head and smiling face of Immanuel "Call Me Manny" Boxer, Agent 42, whom Sofi and I worked with on the creed case that led us to Faerie. Unlike the rest of us, he's not wearing his standard-issue black suit and tie. From what I can tell, he's in his pajamas. The ratty collar of a grey t-shirt pokes up above the video frame, and his long brown hair is pulled back in a ponytail. No wonder 99's in such a pissy mood; it's hard to have a serious meeting when Manny's involved.

I step in between my friends at the desk, put my hands behind my back, train my eyes on a point slightly over Patel's head, and wait for Jack to start. While I've been given a massive dose of responsibility and deference since being proven right about the interworld apocalypse, I'm lowly Agent 6. No matter how crazy that makes my overachieving side, it's how things are. Better to let the boss take the wheel and see where we go. I can always argue later.

Jack addresses 99 directly. "My apologies, sir. Agent 6 and I were speaking with the Lorekeeper, as per our clearance, and it took longer than anticipated."

Patel waves away the niceties. "You're here now, Ninety-Seven, and that's what counts." He nods to me, then says, "I'm glad you could make it, Six. I appreciate that this method of handing out assignments is unusual in our current situation, but what Agent Forty-Two has brought to my attention is urgent." He looks to Manny on the screen and his mouth draws tight. "If you would, please, agent."

There's a flash of huge white teeth, and Manny says, "Sure thing, bossman." He waves. "Hey, Cora! Nice to see you. Although the circumstances sort of suck." I smile but don't provoke 99's wrath by doing more. Manny grins again and clears his throat. "Okay, so, basically there's been a rash of spontaneous combustions here in New York City. We've found six bodies—well, piles—in the last week. Forensics is working on the ashes."

"Are there any leads?" Jack asks.

"Not yet. I'm trying to get in touch with some of my contacts, but everyone's being super sketchy about it. Especially the vamps."

Jack's forehead scrunches as he mulls this over. Spontaneous combustion isn't normal, even in the supernatural world, and it must be worse for vampires. He turns to 99. "I assume you're assigning us to assist Agent 42?"

"You, yes," Patel says. Pointing to Sofi and me, he says, "Them, no."

Now it's my turn to scrunch my forehead. "Then why are we here?" I say. Sofi elbows me in the ribs, but it's too late.

Agent 99 doesn't miss a beat, though, "Because there are other assignments that require your particular talents. I simply found it more expedient to address you all at once. If you can be patient for a moment, your turn will come." Fire blooms along my ears at the chastisement, but I deserved it. "Agent Ninety-Seven," he continues, "I'm sending you to New York City to assist Agent 42 in his inquiries. I have reason to believe that this could be the work of Eris or her allies, and you'll be invaluable in the event that she is encountered."

Jack nods in acceptance. On the screen, Manny is beaming with pride.

"However," Patel adds, "because we are severely overbooked for cases, I am giving you an additional assignment." He raises his bushy white eyebrows with a hint of a smile. "Might as well kill two birds with one stone, eh?"

"Certainly, sir," Jack says stiffly. His eyes are fixed over Patel's head, too. Man, he must be pissed.

But the assistant director doesn't care. He pushes a manila envelope in front of Jack. *Escort/International/NYC.* "The Japanese ambassador is arriving in New York tomorrow, accompanying a large shipment of art and historical artifacts on loan to the Met. Minamoto Akiko is a supernatural in her own right, descended from some deity or another, and thus will require a supernatural chaperone for the duration of her visit."

Now I'm pissed on Jack's behalf. They're sending a sidestepper, one of the most rare and powerful metahumans in the world, to babysit a stuffed-shirt politico while she gladhands with high society? The arctic rage pools out around him, giving me goosebumps by proxy. I inch towards Sofi to escape it.

But Jack says nothing. He simply picks up the folder and tucks it under his arm, nodding again to show his understanding. I can't believe how calm he's being about this whole thing. If I were him, I'd be screaming, "Don't you know who I am?" at the top of my lungs. He must have a lot of practice swallowing bureaucratic bullshit to take this so well.

Manny chimes in, breaking the tension. "Awesome, dude! I can't wait to see you. We could sure use that nose of yours, too. I bet you'll figure this out with one sniff."

"Ninety-Seven's duties to the ambassador will come first, Forty-Two. He will assist you when time and duty allows," Patel says. Then, in a moment of candor, he pinches the bridge of his nose and says, "And please stop calling people 'dude.' You're making us look bad."

The smile slips from Manny's face. I can't imagine this is the first time he's been told that, but his wounded expression is heartbreaking. Like a puppy being told to stop licking your face. "Yes, sir," he says. Patel taps a button on his computer, and the program closes, taking Manny with it.

Having been given his shitty assignment, Jack steps back from the desk, making Sofi and me the center of Patel's attention. I find myself nervous in anticipation of what he'll hand down. If he suspects Eris in the combustion cases, and he's called us here to give out work himself, there must be something huge on the table for us.

He starts with Sofi. "Agent Twenty-One, you have been invaluable in the numerous local cases you've worked on. Your stakeout record is the best the agency has ever seen." A proud smile builds on her face as Patel continues, "That is why I'm handing the Nathaniel Wexford case over to you. You leave first thing in the morning."

The pronouncement sucks all the oxygen out of the room. He wants Sofi to track Wex and the Sword of Souls? By herself?

Sofi's eyes grow to the size of saucers. "You what?" she gasps.

"As of today, you are the lead investigator on the Wexford case," he says slowly. "Agent Seventy has produced no results from his efforts, despite two weeks and six states' worth of searching. I believe your supernatural talent for tracking will succeed where he has failed. Seventy will hand over his documentation when you arrive in Phoenix." He pushes the second manila envelope to her. *Person of interest/Wexford, Nathaniel/Eris*. "I'm trusting you to find our missing man and the relic he's carrying before it's too late."

Her hands are shaking as she takes hold of the papers and clutches them to her chest. I can't tell if she's excited or terrified. Could be both. "Yes, sir. Thank you, sir," she says, taking a step back.

And then I'm alone in front of the desk. First Jack gets assigned to New York, then Sofi's assigned to Arizona. What Eris-related awfulness did he save for me?

Agent 99 pushes the final manila envelope to me at the edge of the desk. I pick it up cautiously and read: *Avatars/Santa/DCA*.

I raise my eyes from the envelope to 99, who's looking like a cat that's proud of eating my hamster. I get the distinct impression that he's screwing with us, but I can't put my finger on how or why. There's something about his eyes that makes me feel like I'm being hypnotized. Empaths do that, I hear.

"Sir...," I begin.

He holds up a hand. "I assure you that this is an essential task, Six. We have a team of agents who normally work this beat, but they're all tied up in monitoring other Holiday Conflict issues. All rookies do at least one Santa shift. Besides, with your magic-detecting radar, you're the ideal person to cover it. It's a simple job, and it should leave you free for further investigations into Eris activity here in the Capitol, should it arise."

I open my mouth to argue, but Jack's speaking my mind before I can. He moves beside me, using his free hand to punctuate his sentences. "Sir, this is ludicrous. You're taking two sidesteppers and putting them on menial duties. I know that interworld activity has dropped practically to zero, but that in itself is suspicious, even with the doorways sealed. Surely there's a better use for Agent Six and myself given the...," he hesitates for the briefest of seconds, "developments in our paired abilities."

Behind me, I hear Sofi cough. It's wet, like she choked on her own spit. I feel bad for not telling her that my ability to pick up magical signatures is permanent and that it might come from a psychic link to Jack. But when did we have time? Besides, she's given me enough crap for admitting I have a crush on the guy; I can't imagine what she's thinking now. I coax my posture a little straighter, pretending I didn't hear it, and trying to believe I'm as important as Jack's insisting I am.

Jack's outrage doesn't have the desired effect, though. "Agent Ninety-Seven, are you questioning your orders?" Patel says smoothly. "Because if you are, I think you know where that sort of behavior lands you, particularly during a state of heightened observation such as we're in currently."

But there's no hesitation. Jack doubles down. "Yes, sir, I am. I understand that the agency is stretched to the breaking point, but that should mean we use each agent to their full potential, not scrape together whomever happens to be free at the moment." He takes a deep breath and straightens to his rather intimidating roughly-seven-feet height. "Six and I should be operating in the Otherworld, gathering intel to support our investigation. We could be contacting supporters on the other side of the Gauntlet, disrupting fortifications or alliances— anything. The information we received from the Lorekeeper this evening—"

"—is not relevant at this time," Patel interjects. The simple statement is like a slap across Jack's face. Shock isn't the word for it.

Slowly and purposefully, Agent 99 pushes his chair away from the desk and stands. His paunch presses against the strained buttons of his black suit as he pulls it closed. He rests his fingertips on the desk, leaning forward and meeting Jack's steely gaze with one of his own. There's a ripple in the air, but whether it's powers being used or the psychic fallout from their wills clashing, I'm not sure. "You have your orders, agents," the assistant director says. "I expect you to report to your posts promptly tomorrow morning without complaint. I refuse to see this agency embarrassed and to see our world fall because you think you're too good to do as you're told."

There's a beat, the tension of which could tune a violin string, and then Jack steps back beside Sofi. I quickly follow suit, not wanting to be the lone target. The three of us, once a team but now disbanded for different assignments, all in one line.

Patel tucks himself back into his desk and sweeps his eyes over us with satisfaction. "You are dismissed, agents," he says with a curt smile. "Good hunting."

We nod with a chorus of "yes, sir" and file out the door one at a time, manila envelopes under our arms. We walk down the hall in silence and share the elevator down to the garage level the same way, each wrapped up in our own thoughts.

For my part, I'm brimming with resentment. Why do we need to watch Santa Claus, for fuck's sake? I'm being forced to stay here on the frigid Eastern Seaboard writing up misdemeanors and trailing mall elves when I could be hot on Wex's trail or twirling in a ball gown at a New York City gala and solving a real case. The more I think about it, the angrier I am. What a huge waste of resources. I'm a fully-trained FBI agent who's also a sidestepper with magical radar, godsdammit, not some rent-a-cop with plastic handcuffs and a metal detector.

It's not until Sofi tries to split off without saying goodbye that I snap out of my funk.

"Hey, wait," I call after her. "Where are you going?"

She stops and half turns, her face serious but neutral. "Home. I have to pack," she says in clipped syllables.

I turn from her to Jack, who's stopped patiently nearby and throw him a look that I hope says, "Give me a minute?" Thankfully, he picks up on it. He gives me a short nod, then one to Sofi, then heads off towards his parking space.

"Soph, what's wrong?" I say, closing the distance between us. As if I wasn't feeling the same thing she is.

She sighs loudly and wraps her arms across her chest, over the manila envelope containing her orders. "He's splitting up the team, you know? I mean, we've had separate cases to tackle since we got back from Faerie, but it always felt like we'd be fighting crime side by side again soon." She shuffles a bit. "I thought you and me'd be saving the world together."

"Yeah." I look at my own envelope with disdain. "I guess there's too much going on. Gotta take what we get."

There's an awkward pause as we both search for something to say. All I can think about is how lonely I'm going to be without my best friends. Just knowing they're around has helped keep me sane. Given my histrionics at home, I'm not sure how I'll handle it when they're gone.

Sofi's better at this than I am, though. "There is one upside," she says with a sly grin.

I give her the side-eye. "Oh yeah, what's that?"

"This'll get you away from Captain Grimpants long enough for you to realize your hugemongous crush on him is ludicrous."

"Sofi!" I scoff, color rising up my neck and into my face.

She laughs. "What? Seriously, you guys are the worst. Dancing around, pretending no one can tell you're stupid about each other. You all but stuck a flag in him back in Faerie. I thought Limerence was going to literally explode, she hates you so hard for stealing her man."

My entire head is on fire. Damn girl emotions. I squeeze my eyes shut and rub them with my free hand. The icy fingers do wonders for bringing down my shame temperature, although Sofi's chuckling isn't helping.

"Ugh, I so wish I had a comeback for that," I say, dropping my hand in resignation. "Things with him are...." I trail off, the memory an afterlife I could've stayed in too real for me to speak. Sofi snaps her fingers in my face impatiently, bringing me back to the moment. "Complicated," I finish lamely.

"Clearly," she snorts.

I expect more digs, but she lets it drop, stepping forward to wrap her arms around me. There's no resisting her hugs. I relax into the embrace, letting her momma bear vibes soothe both our nerves. Times like this, I forget she's ten years younger than I am. Times like this, she's the one watching out for me.

She pulls away too soon, leaving me feeling the frosty burn of the garage more sharply than before. She holds me out at arm's length, inspecting me critically. I smile with more confidence than I have.

"Be good," she says.

"Don't die," I reply.

Sofi grunts good-naturedly. "I'll do my best." She starts to walk away, then calls back over her shoulder. "And don't do anything I wouldn't do. Or anyone!"

"Sofi!" I shout after her. But she's laughing too loudly at her own joke to hear.

I watch her walk away, blond ponytail bobbing into the distance, and I feel a little emptier. We joke about "be good, don't die" constantly, but this time I know it's serious. She's off to chase Wex, a deranged sourcerer wielding a blade that can cut the soul right out of you. With his powers, he could be anyone, do anything, go anywhere. And who knows what evil beings and gods he's calling together to pull off this Gauntlet-destroying ritual on Eris' behalf? Part of me doesn't want her to find him. I don't know what'll happen if she does.

I watch her fade into the shadows of the garage, then remember that Jack's waiting for me and go to join him, shivering from more than the winter air.

FOUR

When Jack asked me to go for a drink two weeks ago, I assumed his brain was addled from intense pain and Doc Sandow's drugs. Reasonable, given the canyon Wex carved up his spine with Excalibur. There was so much blood. I also assumed it wouldn't happen. Between the ludicrous workload post-Faerie and the man's painful shyness, I'd felt justified in writing it off. I convinced myself I didn't care, that I needed to focus on work, that I was being silly for hoping. Besides, he's broken promises to me before.

So finding myself sitting across from him in a secluded booth at the back of the Fifth Amendment with a hot toddy in my hand came as a bit of a shock by the time I realized it was actually happening.

I'd met Jack at his car, fighting tears at losing Sofi to her case. But instead of offering me a lift home in his decrepit red Alfa Romeo, he'd suggested we walk over to the supernatural bar. To wash down the bitter pill we'd been made to swallow, he said. I was so eaten up with worry about my friend, and my own selfish needs, that I'd agreed and shuffled the four blocks in the snow without a second thought.

Smooth bastard.

An hour later and the bartender is picking up the detritus of our second round as she sets down the third. Blessedly, Darynda doesn't say anything about us being here together, but she does give me a saucy wink. Jack never comes in here, and I'm sure the entire bar is buzzing with gossip, which undoubtedly includes who he's here with.

I wrap my fingers around the ceramic mug filled with rum goodness as warmth seeps into my bones. I'm no lightweight—years of slinging drinks at a redneck dive gives you a decent tolerance—it's something to do with the atmosphere. The Fifth is mellow and warm, decorated with holly and pine, and classic carols float through the stereo. A drop of holiday spirit trickles through me, helping to defrost both my skin and my heart after the freezing they've endured tonight.

What brings a smile to my lips isn't the cheeriness of the bar, though. It's Jack. No one would ever believe me, but he hasn't stopped talking since we sat down. He's gesturing as he tells me about his own time on Santa Watch, laughing with his eyes shining, suit jacket laid aside and shirt sleeves rolled to the elbow. The scent of peppermint and chocolate wafts towards me as he speaks. I had to swear not to tell Sofi about his penchant for barely-alcoholic girly drinks.

"I had to tackle the guy from behind, in his full suit, in front of a dozen kids," Jack is saying, shaking his head. "Every single one of them started screaming and crying as I put cuffs on him." He smiles and takes another pull on his drink. "His beard flew off and everything. Never did find it."

"Wait, so he wasn't an avatar?" I say incredulously. "You tackled and cuffed a legit mall Santa for saying he could eat up a two year old blonde girl? My mom says that all the time, and no one's so much as hip checked her for it."

He shrugs his thin shoulders. "We all do stupid things as rookies. I certainly did my share." He points around the bar at the other agents he sees. "And his share, and his share, and her share."

"I find that hard to believe."

"Everyone does unless they knew me back then," he says with a wry smile. "I suspect I hold an agency record for reckless self-endangerment. Why do you think there are so many regulations for new agents?"

I chuckle into my drink without saying what springs to mind. The other thing I can't believe is how different he is now than in the summer. I've never seen him so...normal. It's like a switch flipped inside. When I met him, he was a stern, arrogant, guardian angel type, who was dead set on the job and didn't quite get contractions. To see him almost happy and telling funny stories while getting shitfaced in public is highly entertaining, to say the least. I wonder if anyone else has seen this side of him.

I roll my cup between my palms in the conversational lull. There's something nagging at me, keeping me from getting swept away in the golden moment. I'm trying to drown it in brown sugar and rum, but it refuses to die. Stupid brain. Can't give me one measly night.

My eyes are on the table, but I soon feel Jack's on me. "Everything okay?" he asks. "You've hardly said anything since we got here."

Ugh. The downside of him learning empathy— it's hard to hide in plain sight anymore.

I look up to see him smiling uncertainly. The best I can manage is rueful amusement. Without knowing a better way to phrase it, I simply ask, "Why didn't you let me go back when Tithonus mentioned us being bonded?"

His relaxed, easy posture goes rigid as his guard visibly comes back up. I wince. Dammit, we were having a legitimately good time, and I ruined it. But he said he already knew what the Lorekeeper was dangling in front of me, and I'm tired of everyone knowing more about me than I do.

Jack drains his drink and sets the glass at the edge of the table. He runs a hand over his dark hair, putting both elbows on the table. The longer he waits to speak, the more it's starting to freak me out. I'm no empath, but the vibe he's sending out is so strong it's probably messing with other people in the bar.

When he does start talking, it's in a low, strained voice. The kind doctors use to tell distressed relatives there's nothing more they can do. "I haven't been entirely upfront with you," he begins.

I snort. I've come to expect lies of omission from him, sad as that is. But my sarcasm makes him flinch, and I'm instantly sorry. He's obviously struggling, and that was bitchy of me. I take a quick pull on my drink and scoot forward in the bench seat to show I'm listening.

He winds up and starts again. "I went to see Tithonus before I applied for your permit. As soon as I got out of med bay. I wanted to know about Wex's involvement with Eris, certainly, but what bothered me more was the change in our powers. The idea of sidesteppers bonding the way only psychics have...," he trails off. "I've never heard of it before. So I had to know."

I bite down on the urge to reprimand him for going to the Lorekeeper without me, especially about something this personal. But I remind myself that he did make good on his promise to take me. Just not the way I'd expected.

"What did he say?" I ask, matching his low tone.

A heavy breath. "The history of sidesteppers is scant, to say the least, but what he did find is unsettling." He spreads his thin hands over the pockmarked wooden table, but he doesn't look away. "This digs down into microprobability. To begin with, we estimate that one percent of metahumans who are a quarter pure will be sidesteppers." I nod. I learned that the hard way after finding out that Queen Mab is my grandmother, though I haven't asked Jack about his lineage. I file it away for later as he continues.

"Then, pair bonding—individuals whose resonance syncs up to the point they can act as a single magic source and alter their abilities—occurs in approximately ten percent of metas. Every documented case involves psychics. And they're all same-gender pairs."

He pauses, but I'm hungry for the rest. "How does it happen?" I ask.

"We aren't positive, mostly because we don't know how to test it. But we do know it's individuals who are...," he hesitates and his eyes flick away.

Even in the murky lighting of the Fifth, I can see a blush creep into his dusky cheeks. A reciprocal blush rises in mine as it dawns on me what he's dancing around.

"Emotionally tied?" I offer.

A relieved exhale. "Yes."

I lean back against the bench seat, fingers wrapped around my mug as if it's all that anchors me to the earth. Emotionally tied? After a torrid night between the sheets when we first met, him taking two separate stabbings for me, and my rescuing him from Faerie ownership, you better believe it. And the blue sparks that literally fly between us at high-intensity moments are basically a magical flare. Then there's the new developments in our powers. It adds up, though there is one discrepancy.

"We're the only male-female pairing on record?" I say. I choke on the words, trying not to think about other words that begin with *R*. Like "romance" and "relationship."

All he does is nod. His ears are practically purple with blushing. I smile in spite of the awkwardness of the moment. This is the strongest emotion I've seen him show outside of anger, and I can't help but find it endearing. After years of being treated as a weird, delicate flower whose sole use was for making babies or extra income, I realize might be talking to a man who cares about me because I'm me. Someone who sees me for who I am and believes I'm strong and capable. How long have I wanted that and not known I did?

Maybe it's the rum making me bold. Maybe it's the tug on my heartstrings. Whatever the case, I reach out and lay my hand on his, curling my fingers into his palm, and give it a squeeze. Sure enough, a blue spark pops from between our hands and skitters across the table. The mark of our bond, of our magic being so tightly entwined it's changing the fabric of our beings. I give his hand another squeeze as my throat tightens.

He watches the blue spark roll onto the floor and wink out, then his brow furrows. Doubt cuts through me like lightning. I'm afraid he'll pull away, that I've been a foolish, sappy girl. But instead, he folds my hand inside both of his and bends down to rest his forehead on them. I can feel the heat radiating from his skin but cooling fast. There's the odd sensation of unravelling tension around us. Like the moment in a fight where you realize it's over, that everything's okay.

Over Jack's bent shoulders, I see Darynda sweeping over to check on our drinks. I make wide eyes and head gestures to tell her to go away. She makes an O with her mouth and takes the hint, but winks salaciously before heading back towards the bar. I swear that woman's magic, regardless of what she says.

Jack sits back up as Darynda leaves. His dark eyes are shining, although I can't tell what from. Surely not tears. I doubt the man knows how to cry. He lets go of my hands with a sheepish smile. "That was so much harder than I thought it would be," he says, running a hand over his face. "You have no idea how many scenarios I came up with where this ended in me covered in beer."

"I can order one, if it'll make you feel better."

We both laugh. It's the sort of gallows laugh you hear when people are nervous and don't want to be. The unspoken end of the conversation passes us by, carried away with the joke. The implications of how we feel about each other don't need to be said. Not yet. Not now. We've known since the underworld house, anyway. The magic there made what happened easy to dismiss. But the real world didn't dissolve how we felt. We had no idea that the attraction we've tried to ignore would take matters into its own hands.

Jack peers into his empty glass. "Given the situation, I think we've moved beyond Darynda's talents to alleviate our problems. It might be time to head out." His face falls abruptly. "I've got a long drive ahead of me, after all."

Every drop of alcohol I've had in the last hour hits me at once. The room blurs a bit and my head swirls. I'd totally forgotten that he's leaving in the morning, off to New York to wait on the Japanese ambassador. It's cosmically unfair for us to finally come to grips with our feelings and magical connection with mere hours between realization and separation. Will this woman swoop in to claim him the way Limerence did? Does the bond work when we're so far apart? What if he runs into Eris? What if he dies? Questions turn the butterflies in my stomach to lead.

He must notice the shift in my mood because he slides out of the booth, pulling on his coat, and says, "Would you do me the honor of walking me home? I'm fairly certain I'm past the driving stage, and I believe my building is on your way."

I eye him suspiciously. There's no way Mister Werewolf Blood is anywhere near the legal limit. He raises both his eyebrows expectantly. Then I realize he's making an excuse for us to spend a few more minutes together.

"I think I can be that kind of friend for you," I say with a grin as I lever myself out of the booth. "But you need to know that I'm onto you, buddy."

The look he gives me is all innocence. "I have no idea what you're talking about."

Good lord, I can't tell if he's serious or making a joke. Maybe I need to revise my approach. Operating on the more-machine-than-man template isn't working anymore. He's getting good at being human.

Flurries dance around us as we walk down the brightly-lit street. It's closing in on eleven on a weeknight, so no one else is out. You'd have to be nuts to stroll around DC in this weather, anyway. Or slightly tipsy. Which we are.

There's not a lot said. I wish there were. It's odd to be walking arm in arm with the guy who's basically my magical soulmate and to not say anything. But on the other hand, there's something comforting in the silence. If we did talk, it'd either be awkward fumbling about emotions or avoiding that by talking about work. Knowing we can be together and say nothing and have that be okay is sort of awesome.

It doesn't take long to reach Jack's building. Of course his house is within easy walking distance of SCD headquarters. The grey row house is divided into three floors, each with their own mailbox, a setup not unlike my own five blocks away. The apartments are dark, but the porch light casts creamy shadows over us as we climb the stone steps to the porch.

Jack digs in his pocket in front of the door, and all of the sudden I'm sixteen again. Standing on the front porch, filled with sticky-hot adrenaline and covered in goosebumps, breath catching in my chest, waiting for what comes next. The jingle of keys as he turns to face me is all that's keeping me from floating away.

"Thanks for the company, Cora," he says with a smile. "Never know what could happen out here."

Oh gods, he's so pretty, I think.

"Anytime," I say.

There's an awkward pause. Both of us are thinking it. It's just a matter of who's going to move first.

He takes a half step towards me, leaving less than an inch between us. I forget how tall he is until we're this close; I have to lean back to meet his eyes. The heady scent of warm spices puffs out from his coat and swirls around my head, making my heart beat faster. I'm giddy, lost in time.

Don't make me wait.

His lips part to speak, but he doesn't get the chance. Without thinking, I take hold of his coat and pull him forward, closing the gap. The sound of our coats brushing together fills the air as I press myself to his chest. I feel him inhale before I hear it, a gentle tug on every blue-tinged nerve in my body. His arms wrap around my shoulders, and we meet in the middle.

No sparks fly this time, and the urgent insistence of our first kiss is missing. But that only sends my heart to greater heights. It means that this isn't just magic. We're not being coerced by a greedy afterlife house or drawn together by unknown forces. This is us, two mortals stepping into deeper waters, propelled by something real.

For precious seconds, there's nothing but us and the kiss.

And then my mind floods with horrific images, some real, some imagined.

Jack sprawled on Hel's throne room floor, his dark blood pooling around his lifeless body. Jack weak and fighting for air after being nearly split in half, trembling in my arms. Jack tortured by unspeakable creatures draining him of magic and life for information he refuses to give. Jack forced to turn against humanity as Eris's pawn, sacrificing himself to protect one person.

Because of me. Because of our bond.

I gasp, buckling down on a sob, breaking the kiss and pushing him away. It warps the flow of energy between us with a dose of vertigo. Jack reaches out, his face filled with confusion and concern, but I twist away.

"I'm sorry," I murmur, forcing words around the rocks in my throat. "I can't.... We can't...."

He steps towards me anyway, and this time I let him pull me in. I lay my head against his chest, his cheek pressed to my hair. I listen to his steady breathing, hear his speeding heartbeat betray his calm. Does he know my fears without me speaking them?

After long seconds of silence, he whispers, "Why not?"

I don't know what to say. All I can see is his broken body splayed out, murdered by Eris in the course of our mission because he cares more about me than he does about himself. Stories are true. Everything we've been through proves we're the heroes of this epic tale, stronger together than apart, a powerhouse for good. And yet, if I let this happen before we've finished the dangerous work we've started, if I give in to what my heart so dearly wants—what magic has decreed is right and perfect—he could die and take the world and everyone in it down with him.

No love is worth that. Not even this one. I can't be so selfish.

I mutely shake my head and disentangle myself from his arms. The tears are coming now, and I can't stop them. They leave frosted tracks on my cheeks. He reaches out to brush them away, and I want so badly to let him, but I gently pull his hand down. I want to look anywhere but at the hurt in his eyes, but I can't be a coward. The least I can do is look him in the face.

"We have a job to do," I manage. My voice is creaking, but I say as much as I can, the best I can. "Eris is still out there, and we might be the only people in the world who can stop her. If we're...." I stop to clear my throat. I'm getting a taste of his anxiety from back at the Fifth. This is so hard. "If we're together, she can use it against us. We'd be a liability to each other and every other being in our world." I sniff. "There's too much at stake."

I don't know why I expect him to say something romantic, like out of a movie. That's not who he is. Which is why what he does say surprises me.

"I know what's at stake." He reaches out to touch my face again, and this time I let him. "But I also know how I feel. That I *am* feeling. You didn't see who I was, the machine, but you've watched me change in our short time knowing each other. You've helped me get free." I tremble as I remember Limerence's faerie brand, a mark of a love he couldn't escape, finally gone. "We're stronger than chaos." He smirks lopsidedly. "We're the good guys, Cora. One of the things you've taught me in the last six months is that what separates good from evil is love."

In this moment, I wish I wasn't so stubborn. Because he's right. Without love, it's too easy to lose sight of what's right and wrong. Every story says so. But no matter how much his words ring true and melt my heart, they don't wash away the blood in my mind's eye. His blood. The blood of millions. I can't be responsible for that.

I take his hand from my face, holding it as I lower it back to his side. "I know. But if you die because Eris used me against you...." I trail off, unable to finish the thought, much less the sentence. "I'm sorry, Jack. I am. But there's no safe space for an 'us' until this is over."

There's a soft squeeze on my hand, then a rush of air as he moves away. I look up through blurred vision, the lead butterflies in my stomach turning into molten guilt as I watch his face, so open and warm just now, close and harden. The glint in his eyes is like the edge of a knife, rejection visibly resecuring the armor he'd loosened to let me in.

More tears stream down my face. I wipe at them with the back of my glove and step back until I'm at ground level. His eyes are on me every inch of the way. When I reach the bottom of the stairs, I turn around to look at him one last time. But I don't see Jack there anymore. All I see is Agent 97, my superior officer, impatiently waiting for a dismissed agent to leave his presence.

There's no goodbye, nothing I could say or do. The cut's been made. The damage is done.

I nod to him. He nods back. I turn and start down the sidewalk towards my own house. I manage to keep it together until I hear the door click shut. Then I start to run, sobbing like a deranged widow in the snowy DC night.

I did the right thing, I repeat to myself, desperate to believe it. *But what have I done?*

PART II
CHILDREN OF
THE NIGHT

FIVE

As if he'd called her over by thinking her name, Agent 12 appears at his side. She kneels down and casts a discriminating glance over the only clue they've found in the entire room. But it's no use. Her powers are plant-based; she's here because everyone else is either balls-deep in their own cases or too exhausted for duty. *Or dead*, he remembers with a wince. *Poor 26.*

"Whaddya think, boss?" she asks. "Same as the others, right?"

He nods. "No blood, no footprints, no nothing. Just a pile of some poor bastard's ashes." He peers around the anonymous motel room with its outdated décor and beige walls. "At least this one had the decency to explode indoors. I was getting super freaking tired of scooping up snow to see if we'd missed any body-part flakes."

"This is what, number six?"

"Seven. Third in the last week." He drops his

gaze back to the remains. "They're speeding up."

Jimenez shakes her head, making her tightly curled hair bounce. "Jesus," she whispers.

"Pretty sure he's not responsible," Manny quips back, standing up and brushing his pants to remove any John/Jane Doe stuck to them. "We haven't heard from that guy in years, and the Council refuses to admit he's missing."

Twelve huffs, "You know what I meant."

He grins at her, then turns his attention to his pocket notebook. There isn't much written in there; if anyone saw the contents, they'd either be impressed at his memory or report him for dereliction of duty. It's supposed to contain his clues, facts, and theories, but three quarters of it is filled with what he knows is terrible poetry. An anxiety-fighting method recommended by the SCD shrink when he wanted off the anxiety meds. Dude probably didn't mean for him to write on the job, but it's gotten him to half dosage. Can't argue with results.

Besides, it's not like anything on this case has been new or interesting since the first body. What would he write down? Seven incidents, all with the same hallmarks, and the coldest trail of evidence since the frost giant sighting after *Thor* premiered. Not even his astounding supernatural luck is helping. He's tried the focusing technique 99 taught him to bend it to his will, but it's hit or miss. Any breaks he gets are pure serendipity, utterly at the whim of Lady Luck. Evidently, she's not interested in this case.

After noting assorted details of the room, Manny looks up to see Agent 12 staring out the window with bloodshot eyes, her SCD shades tucked into the collar of her shirt. He moves to join her. The view is hazy between the heavy iron bars on the inside and snow-thickened night outside. Neon Christmas lights cover the wet pane with green and red glitter.

Manny watches his partner in his peripheral vision as they stand there. She's his first mentoring gig for the agency, together two months and a good fit. They've got a tight good cop/bad cop dynamic that works because she knows how to push when Manny's too nice and he knows how to slow her roll when she gets too excited. Still treats him like a supervisor, though, which tends to cramp his laid-back style.

"Everything okay?" he ventures. They rarely stop talking for this long.

She shakes her head, eyes forward. "What are we doing here, boss? We know this is vampires, even if we can't prove it yet. Nothing else leaves pure ash when it dies. Does anyone really give a shit if fangbangers wax each other? They're parasites who feed on mortals, then run to us for protection when the fuzzies play too rough." She casts a glance at the pile of ashes. "They're bad guys. Always have been. What the hell are we doing taking care of them like they're not?"

The smallest possible flare goes up in Manny's gut. A temper buried but not deceased. He closes his eyes against it, dousing the spark with practiced calm, and walks himself through it. She's not wrong. It's a common complaint for rookie agents. It's his job to explain it quietly and calmly, not to let frustration run his life.

"We're mediators, Jimenez," he says, watching cars pass on the street below. "Our job isn't to punish or even to bring justice to the supernatural world. It's to supervise the balance between the magical and mundane. To act when things go sideways. And that often means caring for folks who don't deserve it." He turns towards her. "The dude we're picking out of this rug was somebody's friend, somebody's kid. We're not a hundred percent sure he was a vamp. Maybe he was. Maybe he was a bad dude. But maybe he wasn't. We don't get to decide who's worthy of help. It's our job to give it if we can."

She turns away from the window with a wry smile. "Damn good speech, boss," she says.

Any other time and he'd press the issue, but it's late. He returns her smile with extra warmth and says, "Alright, dude, you can head home. No reason for you to stick around. I'll finish up here."

"You sure?"

"Yeah, get outta here. Not like it's going to take long to scoop."

She dips her head in acceptance. "Awesome, thanks. I'll see you in the morning, Forty-Two." She heads out, grabbing her overcoat off the back of the open door, then half-turns. "Hey, you know any good Italian places close by? Could stand to get a calzone in me before heading home."

Inwardly, Manny groans. The number of times he's been asked for ethnic restaurant recommendations. It's not that he doesn't know where to eat in this town—he does—it's that they always get it wrong.

"Go to Tony and Tina's on Arthur," he says with a grin. "Tell them I sent you. They'll hook you up."

Jimenez salutes smartly and heads off. He waits until he hears the elevator ding before muttering to himself, "Greek. I'm Greek. Can't you people see the nose?" He huffs self-centeredly, but it's gone as quickly as it came. No point holding onto it.

Alone in the room with the pile of ashes, Manny turns his attention to cleaning up the space. If there's one bright spot in this whole frustrating investigation, it's that spontaneous combustion is easy to clean up. He grabs a double-sized evidence bag from his crime scene kit, along with latex gloves and a fingerprint brush, then kneels down and begins the tedious task of sweeping up the luckless bastard. If only he could use a dustbuster.

It's weird to think that this handful of fluff used to be a person. A metahuman like him, technically. He tries not to linger on that. Being raised in a family where everyone's a paragon or supernal twists your concept of death. For twenty-odd years, he'd believed these magical people, the ones who took him in after his mother abandoned him, would never leave. It wasn't until he was grown that his aunt and uncle explained how his immortal relatives were killed by declining human belief, how he was immune to that fate as a meta but had to be careful with his fragile life. Hard lessons to learn right before he signed on with the SCD. It's why he doesn't take homicide if he can help it. The reminders are too sharp. But they needed him for this case—he always gets the tricky ones—and with the increased workload, he couldn't refuse. Doesn't mean he likes it, though.

About halfway through the sweep-up job, there's a clicking noise that brings Manny back. He turns toward the door saying, "Jimenez, it's not hard to find. You go—" but by the time he sees who's standing there, it's too late.

There's a crowded second where Manny realizes it's not his partner, the intruder realizes there's a cop in the room, and they both lunge towards each other at the exact same time. Ashes fly as Manny leaps to his feet, abandoning his delicate work, and reaches for his gun. The man at the door swirls his black trench coat as a distraction with one hand and uses the other to slam the door behind him, trapping them in the room together. Manny frees his sidearm as the intruder starts to advance.

"FBI! Hands up!" Manny orders, gun leveled at the guy's forehead.

The man obeys, his pale face creased in a threatening grimace. They stand locked that way for a tense moment as grey specks float down onto their clothes. Manny tries not to think about the massive mistake he's made with the evidence. The guy standing in front of him has moved way up the list of things that are important for the time being.

"Who are you?" Manny demands.

The man lowers his arms slowly to his sides but doesn't step forward. "None of your damn business, spook," he spits. The thick New York accent tells Manny he's local. Could be from Queens, although not originally.

He ignores the bad attitude. "What're you doing here?"

"None of your damn business, like I said." The man grins horribly, then his incisors slowly extend, dropping an inch.

The dramatic display doesn't get the reaction the guy was going for, though. Vampires are nothing new to Manny. After an incident involving a bloodthirsty purse-snatcher, a foot chase, and an early sunrise, he'd made it a point to get friendly with each of the five New York clans, connecting with one member in each burrough. He figured if they knew each other, the future would be less full of ash and awkward reports. The contacts' names are highly classified, but it's made him the resident vampire expert. When a New York agent has a question about the clans, they come to him. He can't help being proud of that.

Manny squints at the intruder, trying to identify him. The guy's good looking but not magazine-cover pretty, so he's not a Founder, and the battered trenchcoat means he's not an Aristocrat. Add in the Queens accent and the Bluetooth earpiece he's wearing, and Manny's confident he's dealing with a member of the Tech clan. This vamp's in the wrong territory.

"You're in Bruiser country, Techie dude," Manny

says. "What're you doing on Nexus' turf?

"Fuck you." He flexes his hands and yellow fingernails pop out, longer than the trademark teeth. Tech vamps may prefer Apple over assault, but they'll mess you up if they get a chance. And Manny gets the distinct feeling that him being here's interrupted something rather important.

There's another standoff as the two men continue to size each other up. Manny's weapon doesn't waver despite knowing there's no chance he'll get away clean if the vamp decides to rush him. Normal bullets don't do anything but piss them off. He crosses his mental fingers and hopes the chatty nature of this clan sees him through. Best to keep him talking.

"I'm going to ask you one more time. What are you doing here? You got anything to do with this?" With his eyes, he indicates the ashes scattered over the beige carpet.

But as the vampire opens his mouth to spout more insults, a name finally comes to him. Manny's tilts his head to the side. "Wait. You're Gabriel Morris, aren't you? Zackary's sire?"

The guy looks shocked. "How did you know that?"

"Lucky guess?"

Gabriel's shoulders slump defeatedly. "Dammit." His incisors and talons retract, and the vampire throws himself into a creaky chair by the door. "I am going to be in so much trouble, they find out I fucked this up."

Manny cautiously lowers and holsters his gun. A

familiar tingle under his ribs tells him he's about to get very lucky indeed. "Fucked what up?" he asks.

Gabriel waves a hand at the grey mist. "This. It's already gone. Plus, you're here, which means the feds are looking for it, too." He smacks his head against the wall behind him. "Fuck."

"Hey, no need for that." He crosses the room and puts his hand on Gabriel's shoulder. A risky move, but he's pretty sure they've passed the point of real danger. This guy's a minion, not a boss or even mid-boss. Some mercy's in order. "Tell you what. Tell me why you came, and I'll pretend I never saw you. Won't even put it in my report."

Gabriel's dead eyes widen. "You can't do that. Feds don't lie."

"I've been known to bend the rules from time to time," Manny smiles. He has zero intention of forgetting what Gabriel tells him, though he'll have to fudge the paperwork. There's potential for a contact here that he doesn't want to burn.

The vampire squirms in the chair, but it's obvious he's interested. Manny backs away to sit at the edge of the hotel bed and waits. Gabriel's eyes roam around the room, taking in the ashes and doing mental calculations, likely scanning for clues of whatever he's been sent to find. Eventually, he makes his decision.

"Everybody's looking for this box, right?" he says. "And before you ask, no, I don't know what's in it. But the Draculas are hot as hell to get it, so it's got to be amazing. Trouble is that even when someone finds it, no one can keep it." He shifts uncomfortably, then points at the remnants of the ash pile. "They all end up that way. Robbed and dusted."

"You're saying vampires are dying because of whatever's in this secret box?"

Gabriel nods.

Manny's brow furrows. The vampire ruling body, a council composed of the five clan heads, each touting the honorific of "Dracula," hasn't been friendly in the last hundred years. But if the elders are willing to sacrifice their dwindling children to get a box, it spells much bigger trouble than the SCD has bargained for.

"You think these are murders and robberies?" he says after a moment. "We're pretty sure they're spontaneous combustion. I mean, the victims being vamps does explain the super compact, dry ash, but that still leaves a lot of question marks. We haven't found any evidence of foul play or foreign objects."

"You're tracking victims, we're tracking the box, but they're related."

Manny leans over with his elbows on his knees, chin cradled in his hands, thinking. What could be in the box that would make vampires kill and steal from one another? It's worrying. While the clans have zero love for one another, there are no recorded cases of vamp-on-vamp murder. They much prefer to kill outsiders and manipulate each other instead.

"Is there a reward?" Manny asks.

"Yeah, from Kincaid."

Manny's eyebrows go up at the mention of the

Founder's Dracula, the oldest vampire on record in the States. Manny's never met him personally, but word gets around. He's over five hundred, from Roman-ruled Ireland. His standard wardrobe includes a battle kilt and chain mail. He owns the largest collection of historical and magical artifacts outside the Roosevelt. He once killed a werewolf who broke into his haven by snapping its neck and draining it dry. His blood can't be consumed by other vampires or they go insane.

Not only is Seanan Kincaid from Don't Fuck Around Town, he's the mayor.

"Shit," Manny whispers.

Gabriel seems pleased with that reaction. "He wants it bad. Opened the search up to all five clans," he continues, "which pissed off the rest of the council like whoa. A bunch of people reported they've found it or seen it. Nobody's come to the Belvedere haven with it, though." Gabriel gazes mournfully at ash pile. "Poor Sian."

Manny files away the name of the victim for later. Right now, the excitement of cracking this case is dancing in his brain, making it difficult to focus on anything else. The trail is hot again, which means he's got work to do.

He stands and goes to shake Gabriel's hand. The vampire is mildly stunned but lets his arm be pumped like he's greeting a politician.

"I appreciate your help, Mr. Morris," Manny says cheerfully. "Don't worry about a thing." Then curiosity gets the better of him. Still holding the other man's hand, he adds, "Can I ask you a quick question before you go?"

The Tech raises an eyebrow. "Sure," he says slowly.

"Why'd you stop when I pulled my gun? You could've run right over me, easy."

"Just because I don't die when I get shot doesn't mean I like it," Gabriel scoffs. "You try walking around with the wind blowing through a hole in your forehead for a night, see how much fun you have."

Manny chuckles. "Okay, you got me there." He shakes Gabriel's hand a second time and says, "Thanks again for your assistance. You have no idea how useful your information has been."

Gabriel stands, wresting himself from Manny's grip, and says uncertainly, "Uh, you're welcome? Just don't tell anyone I told you anything, okay? Last thing I need is my boss finding out I talked to you."

"No worries, dude." He grins broadly. "Your boss won't hear about it unless you tell her. I protect my sources."

Gabriel grimaces and opens the door. "Find out who did this, okay? We're already low on numbers these days, and I'm tired of seeing my friends getting dusted for no reason." He steps into the empty hallway, heading for the elevator. "Figure it out. Or next time I won't let you talk me out of killing you."

The words echo against the flimsy walls, and Manny winces. How many people heard that? Then again, given the kind of motel this is, the number of people who care is approaching zero. Asympathetic anonymity is both a pro and a con in New York.

Once Gabriel's gone, Manny eases the door closed, making sure the electronic lock secures this time, then turns back to the room, now coated with a fine dusting of Sian. He runs a hand over his eyes as he imagines the bawling out he's going to get when he reports this. Maybe his luck will hold out there, at least.

He retrieves the plastic bag and brush from where he dropped them and kneels down beside the largest remaining deposit of ashes. It irks him that he knows this victim's identity but not the others'. It's also super bizarre that the vamps are out en masse to track down a mystery box without knowing what it contains. What's inside? Why is it so valuable? Why does Kincaid care so much? He decides to call Finn as soon as he gets a chance. His tie to the Founder clan in Manhattan has been with him the longest and is tight with the boss, what with being his sole remaining child and all. He should be able to fill the gaps in Gabriel's story.

As Manny works to finish sweeping up the last of the evidence, he wonders how differently this entire incident would've gone if Agent 97 had arrived tonight instead of tomorrow.

SIX

When Jack wakes up, it's dark out. He hits the alarm with practiced precision and rolls off his stomach to stare at the ceiling. The few hours of sleep he managed to get were filled with white-hot, shameful dreams. Not quite nightmares, but scenes tormenting enough that he's not rested. She was in every one.

The room glows from streetlights through the curtains, and the ceiling spins gently in his vision. It takes him several breaths to steady it. Deprived of other company last night, Jack invited an old friend to share his troubles. Johnnie Walker's green calling card lies empty and accusing on the pillow beside him. He'd resisted at first, brain not addled enough by low-percentage cocktails or fresh heartbreak to open that door again. Their last commiseration, after the Z. Carter case, started an internal avalanche he couldn't stop; liquor dissolved his grief and guilt, but stole his memories and dignity. When he resurfaced from that haze six months later, it was for an AA meeting he didn't attend. He'd stood outside the church doors and, instead of humiliating himself, resolved never to touch hard alcohol again. He left without a twinge of regret or a backslide since, barring the rare indulgence under Darynda's watchful eye. But last night, when he'd emptied his pockets to find Tithonus' diagram and a receipt for her visit to the Archives, his hands started to shake, and he knew no other way to stop the tremors. The single bottle he'd kept as a reminder of his weakness was too easy to find after that.

Self-loathing wells up in his chest as he remembers what he can from the rest of the night, and his hand darts across the bed, flinging the empty bottle to the floor. It makes a disappointing *thunk* instead of shattering. He winces and drapes his arm over his face with a muffled groan. The lycan healing factor that requires him to drink near-fatal quantities to feel the effects and precludes the alcohol poisoning he surely deserves does let the hangovers linger.

There's a nudge at his knee that keeps him from closing his eyes again. He's scheduled to pick up the Japanese ambassador at JFK International at one, and driving in New York lunch rush demands all the patience and concentration he can scrape together. He needs to sleep off the rest of the hangover, but the nudge is more insistent this time, and he can't ignore it. He shifts on his sweat-soaked pillow to glare at the hairy, basketball-sized creature sitting on his mattress.

Popular belief in tribbles made them a hell of a problem back in the Seventies, but the SCD managed to contain their population with simple spaying and neutering. Most were returned to the wild, but a modest cuddle—the group term coined by a sentimental agent—is maintained for SCD agents as pets. Jack, who refused to keep animals after his first dog died, acquired Bitsy against his will. When he'd applied for psych leave last year, Agent 100 gave him a warm box instead of a handshake. "It'll be good for you to have something else to care about," she'd said with a matronly smile. Dammit if she wasn't right. Even in the most inebriated, least conscious moments of his breakdown, he always remembered to care for Bitsy. She kept him grounded and present when he easily could've left it all behind. Here on the other side of that darkness, he's grateful for the hairy freeloader. Although he'd never admit it to Dora.

"You do know it's six in the morning," Jack says as he motions for the critter to come to him. "I should be sleeping off a hangover."

Bitsy responds by shimmying up the covers to his shoulder and purring loudly in his ear, which she hasn't done since the worst of his depression. Perhaps she can sense what he's trying hard to ignore right now. He turns on his side and draws her in, to her great purring delight. The silky softness of her black and white fur is reassuring as he pets her, but it's not enough to allay the growing disquiet as his mind comes fully online.

He hates that he's feeling this way. Hates that he's feeling anything. The old, familiar voice of Agent 97, the machine-man who wiped out Jack's humanity and ruled him for too many years, is begging to be let back in. He promises to quell the hurt, to take it all away, to return him to his former efficient, clockwork glory. But Jack grits his teeth and reinforces the door against him. He's worked too hard, suffered too much to regain control of himself to let something as common as a rejected advance take him out again. Even if it did come from the woman his soul is bonded to.

Bitsy squeaks unhappily and nips his fingers. Must've been petting her too hard while he thought. He rubs the sting out of his hand. "Sorry, girl. I was somewhere else."

Jack sits up, swinging his legs over the edge of his bed. He hisses as his feet touch the chilly wooden floor, but it doesn't stop him. If he lays in bed too much longer, the memories of last night will keep replaying, and the emotions he's still learning to cope with will suck him into their undertow. Better to keep moving, to stay focused on the day ahead. It's going to be a hell of a long one.

He shuffles to the bathroom and turns on the steaming water in the shower. He avoids looking at himself before the mirror clouds over. The Lorekeeper's mention of one being used in Eris' plot left him uneasy. He's seen the power mirrors can wield, and he'd prefer to avoid anyone traveling through the other side. He's also not eager to see what he knows is a drawn, heavy-lidded caricature of himself reflected there. He doesn't want to see her aftermath.

Dressing and packing prove difficult. The studio apartment is narrow and spare, an echo of his office with the addition of a wall of crammed bookshelves, which ordinarily makes navigation easy, but Bitsy refuses to leave him alone. The tribble trails him from dresser to suitcase to bathroom and back with the attention of a tuxedo-colored shadow, making distressed noises the entire time. At one point, he nearly squashes her underfoot and is forced to bend down and collect her. He rotates the thick sphere of her body, inspecting it for a face to talk to. "What's the matter with you, Bit?" he asks. He gets a coo and nudge in return that tugs a little at his heart. He sighs and sets her down, unsure whether to be concerned for her or for himself.

A glance at the analog clock over the front door tells him he's running on time, despite the tribble's attentions. He adjusts his black tie, pulls on his heavy coat, then tosses the last items into his bag and slings it over one shoulder. Double checking Bitsy's food and water dishes, he grabs his SUV keys from their hook by the door, and sets his official SCD shades on top of his head.

"No wild parties, okay, girl?" he says to the furball at his feet. Bitsy whines in reply. "Don't worry, I'll be back soon." He reaches down and ruffles her fur, getting a brief purr in return.

Then he strides out into the first streaks of morning, scarcely noticing the ache in his chest when he passes the spot where she told him she didn't want him. The memory doesn't haunt him as he makes his way down the sidewalk, past the Fifth Amendment, into the SCD garage. And he certainly isn't thinking about red hair and the scent of cotton and leather as he turns north onto the interstate, case files in the passenger seat.

No one drives in New York. There's too much traffic.

Jack exhales testily as the dashboard clock ticks over the hour. He's getting dangerously close to being late to pick up the Japanese ambassador at the airport. He's moved two miles in the last thirty minutes, his full-sized vehicle ponderous and bloated on narrow Manhattan streets crammed with SmartCars. Minutes tick past like hours, taking his blood pressure higher. His fingers and arms ache from clenching the steering wheel.

As much as he wants to blame the city or the other drivers, this is his own fault. This snarl could've been avoided if he hadn't let his mind wander. The GPS did warn him about the backed-up traffic and the wrong turn he made, but his thoughts were two hundred miles and a day away.

By the time the fourth car muscles into the queue ahead of him, Jack's contemplating an escape plan. He hasn't attempted to teleport since accidentally discovering he could in Faerie, primarily because none of his assignments since have required travel more urgent than a police siren provides. But it's also because he's hesitant to use a power he doesn't fully understand. While Cora's magical radar is reliable and safe, teleporting is essentially sidestepping at will, without doorways. It's unnatural, and he can think of a eleven ways for it to go wrong. There's also the question of whether or not he can do it at all since the bond has been damaged. He's not ready to test that. Not yet.

With a small sigh, Jack straightens in his seat and rolls his stiff shoulders, willing his thoughts back in line. Teleporting isn't an option. Even if it worked perfectly, he'd be abandoning government property in the middle of a freeway, plus he'd have no way to transport the ambassador. Better to stick with the vehicle and ride out the traffic. There has to be a shortcut.

As he reaches over to punch new instructions into the GPS, the dashboard screen replaces the city map with a ringing phone. The shrill noise grates against his eardrums after driving in silence the entire way from DC.

Agent 42, the display says helpfully.

Recomposing his annoyed expression, Jack accepts the call. "Yes, Manny?"

"Hey, Ninety-Seven! Wasn't sure if you'd pick up. You got the ambassador yet?"

"No, I'm still on my way. Caught in traffic by NYU."

"Oh, snap. Take Second to Queens Plaza to Astoria, dude. It'll bypass that mess and get you to the airport faster."

Jack shakes his head and redirects the GPS to surface streets. Of course Manny knows. He should've called the second he hit the city limits. "Thanks," he says, cranking the wheel to head down a side street. It's clearer already.

"No problem. Hey, I was calling to see if you were going to make it into the office today." There's a second's hesitation that gets Jack's full attention. Manny's usual chatter is non-stop confidence. For him to pause at all means he's off. "I found something you're going to want to see," he continues. "I'd tell you over the phone, but you know. People could be listening."

Jack doesn't argue. Living in New York makes people paranoid, but he has to admit it's possible that Eris' allies have high enough connections to eavesdrop on them. "Give me the summary?"

"We got another combustion incident last night, but this time a vamp showed up at the scene. I know who's involved. And you're not going to like it."

Jack attempts to fill in the gaps, but there are too many things he doesn't like to make a deduction. "Anyone we know?" he asks.

"Yeah, a couple."

Damn. "I need to make sure the ambassador is received and settled in her hotel first. Can it wait until morning?"

Another nanosecond's hesitation. It must be bad. "Yeah, sure. I got calls to make, anyway. Should have a file for you when you get here."

"Sounds good, Forty-Two."

"Later, dude."

Jack hangs up as the black SUV trundles toward

the airport and shakes his head. Three years with the agency should've polished professionalism into Manny. The lack of it has certainly gotten him in enough trouble; Jack's personally written him up twice. But there's sharpness under the surfer-hippie attitude, an intuition that sees into the heart of a situation, that reminds Jack not to underestimate the young agent. Manny playing it close to the vest trips an alarm in Jack's mind. What has he discovered that's worrying enough to avoid sharing on the phone but can wait another day? He's tempted to call back and ask but thinks better of it. He's here to advise Manny's case, not take it over.

By the time Jack arrives at JFK, he's made up an hour lost to traffic, but he's still ten minutes behind schedule. The ambassador's plane has already landed and he's not in position to collect her. He parks the SUV with its government plates in the fire lane, throws on the four-ways, and darts into the terminal.

He makes it five feet inside.

A stocky, blonde man in a grey airport uniform steps directly in Jack's path as he bolts to the international arrivals gate. The two nearly collide as Jack screeches to a halt, stopping within inches.

The man holds up a callused hand and says, "Sir, I'm going to have to ask you to please step to the side and wait for a TSA agent to arrive. I don't want to have to call security."

Jack flexes his jaw to keep from shouting. He does not have time for this today. "You don't need to do that, Mister...," he glances at the man's nametag, "Harrington, but I do need you to let me pass." He draws himself up to his full height, fishes out his badge, and flips it open, peering at the security officer over his dark glasses. "I'm a federal agent here to meet and escort a foreign dignitary. You're interfering in government affairs."

Harrington takes the leather square out of Jack's hand and squints hard at the brass shield, turning it over several times to inspect it. Then he looks up and says, "You got any other identification?"

Jacks blinks. In ten years at this job, he's never been asked that. Everyone's simply acquiesced to his authority. The badge has always been enough. Dumbfounded, he slides his driver's license out of his wallet and hands it over, too, mind seething.

The man's thick moustache twists as he makes a thinking noise and shoves the ID back into Jack's hand. "These are the fakest names I've ever heard, 'Jack Robert Gregory Alexander' from the 'Supernatural Cases Division'," he says with air quotes. "I'll be a horses ass if you ain't got a gun or a bomb or anthrax on you right now. You aren't going anywhere." He reaches for his walkie-talkie.

Tactical options speed through Jack's mind. He could snatch the com out of Harrington's hand. He could start walking towards the terminal. He could comply with the search. Every one of them is wrong. This isn't the first time he's been stopped in an airport, but it is the first when someone important is waiting for him.

As much as he wants to tear a strip off this self-important ass, Jack grudgingly elects for compliance. That behavior serves no one in the end. He takes off his shades and tucks them into the front pocket of his black suit jacket, then steps to the side, out of view of the crowd that's starting to gather. Not every day you see a clean-shaven guy in expensive clothes getting hassled by security.

Harrington looks smug as his walkie crackles to life. "This is Officer Harrington here, Command. I've got a Muslim male, about six foot seven, hundred and eighty pounds, approximately forty years old, saying he's a fed. I'm waiting for Baker to get here for processing."

"I'm not Muslim," Jack growls. He knows it's the wrong tone, but after Tithonus' barbs yesterday, the attitude is getting under his skin.

"Fine, Islamic."

"That's the same thing."

Harrington takes his finger off the talk button. "Okay, what are you, then, Mr. Politically Correct?"

"I am Agent 97 of the Supernatural Cases Division of the FBI, and you're impeding me in the execution of my duties."

"Wrong answer, buddy," he says under his scruffy mustache. He holds the talk button again. "He's giving me sass, Command, want me to bring him up there?"

"Ten-four, Harrington."

The security guard smirks at Jack with the satisfaction of a fat kid descending on a chocolate cake. "You heard the man, Mister Alexander—or whatever your real name is. Step quick." He points Jack towards a steel door on the far end of the lobby.

A fine red mist tints the edges of Jack's mind. This sanctimonious prick thinks he's caught a terrorist; he has no idea who he's talking to. Fortunately for Harrington, years of Jack denying his emotions includes sublimating the predatory rage lurking below the werewolf scars on his chest. It's anger that doesn't belong to him, but he can control it. Mostly. He breathes deeply, in and out of his nose, forcing down the beast in his blood, reminding himself that people like Harrington are simpletons that buy whatever the TV's selling. The supernatural world needs them to keep itself afloat with their easy, quick, junk-food belief. It sustains more than a few magical beings these days. Thor is certainly grateful.

They're halfway to the security office when a sharp, commanding voice cuts through the background buzz of humanity in the terminal.

"Agent Ninety-Seven! Where are you going?"

The words echo against marble and tile as every soul in the vicinity falls instantly silent. Harrington and his captive stop dead in their tracks. Jack slowly turns to see who's called his name.

An Asian woman wrapped in a snowy white peacoat with gold trim is striding towards the two men, high heels clicking on the tile floor. Her glossy black hair is pinned severely back from her round face in a heavy bun with lacquered sticks. Eyes like inkwells are wide in indignation as she closes the distance, stopping inches away from Harrington. She jabs a perfectly-manicured finger in the guard's face.

"Where are you taking my escort?" she demands. Up close, Jack can hear traces of an accent, but her English is polished.

That's when it dawns on him who he's looking at: Minamoto Akiko herself.

"Madam Ambassador," Jack says, switching to professional mode. "This is Officer Harrington with airport security." He gives the rent-a-cop a look just this side of dirty. "We were having a discussion about your safety, in fact. He's been most helpful." He puts a thin hand on the man's meaty shoulder.

To Harrington, she says, "Officer or not, you will release this man. I am a visiting diplomat and require his services. Your government has assigned him to me. You will not delay him further."

Harrington shrugs off Jack's hand and does his best to look dignified. "With all due respect," he says without respect, "I need to see your identification, ma'am. You could be a plant in league with Al-Qaeda sent here to help this guy blow himself up."

The ambassador's eyes flash, but she merely scowls and reaches into a deep coat pocket, retrieving a piece of paper tied with yellow ribbon. She hands it to Harrington. He takes it uncertainly, then unrolls the fine parchment, reads it, mutters "oh, shit," rolls it up, and hands it back. He looks from the woman in front of him to the man he's been hassling. "Sorry, agent," he mutters. It's half sincere but good enough.

In the airport lobby, the tension breaks.

Everyone starts breathing again and resumes flight-related activities with mild disappointment. Show's over.

Jack puts his hand back on Harrington's shoulder, a bit more friendly this time, and the man deflates. He knows he's been beat. "Thank you for your cooperation, officer," Jack says. "Your dedication to the security of your country is admirable. I'll be sure to inform your superiors of your conduct."

Harrington's eyes widen and beads of sweat stand out on his forehead. Jack's face stays stony, but he's inwardly pleased at the reaction. Let him agonize over what that report will say. While it rankles Jack that it took the ambassador's intervention to rescue him from what would've been a department nightmare, it amuses him to see petty men get their comeuppance. With any luck, Harrington will be more prudent about whom he stops for being brown in the future.

Jack releases the security guard's shoulder and lets him scuttle away before turning his attention to his charge. The outrage in her face has downgraded to irritation, although she's probably furious if anything's showing through her groomed manners. He's committed several social offenses already, beginning with not meeting her on the tarmac, so he can't blame her. This is a terrible start to their acquaintance.

He attempts to smooth over the bumps by bowing. "My apologies, Madam Ambassador. As you can see, I was detained. Thank you for intervening."

"You are welcome," she says, giving a curt bow in return. "I thank you for your assistance, as well."

As he scans the crowd in the lobby behind her, a disturbing thought arises. "Madam, are you alone?"

"Of course. Is this a problem?"

"Not at all. However, I had expected you to be accompanied during the flight. I wasn't informed that I would be your only security during your stay in New York."

"I requested the best, Agent Ninety-Seven, and you are who they sent." For the first time, she smiles. It's a subtle politician's grin that instantly makes Jack suspicious, though he's not sure about what. "I am afraid it is you and me. I trust this is acceptable to you."

Jack's mind overflows with reasons why it's absolutely not. The list gets very long, very fast, and it includes Manny needing his help, the potential dangers of having one man on watch, uncertainty about whether or not she's flirting with him, and the definite impression that she's hiding something. None of those things are acceptable. But he's been given orders, and he won't allow Agent 99 the satisfaction of berating him for not following through.

"Of course, Madam Ambassador," he says with a professional smile.

It's half a lie, but she smiles back anyway, deepening his sense of unease.

As he leads her out to the waiting car, his suspicious mind already generating theories, the dark thoughts turn bright: Perhaps this case will be more interesting than he'd thought.

SEVEN

The dossier Agent 99 gave Cora states that the Santa Problem dates back to the 1890s when department stores became a regular attraction. When reports started popping up of Santa impersonators becoming full-blown avatars of Kringle himself, the SCD didn't take it seriously because, aside from the Tooth Fairy and Easter Bunny, supers don't manifest minions. It took the first kid going missing for them to pay attention.

It's not that Santa's evil, per se. The trouble is that belief in him is hyper-concentrated for six weeks out of the year and zero for the rest. In the supernatural economy, that means he's practically dead before Easter. The only way for him to stay alive until Thanksgiving, when he can gorge on belief to grow fat and happy again, is to consume the energy of lesser beings. Elves were a cheap and easy fix; the ranks automatically replenished when the holidays hit. But as Christmas became more commercial and Black Friday gained clout, Santa's magic wasn't enough to meet the world's demands. Thus, the avatars. Mundanes dressing up for a bit of holiday cash magically found themselves with real beards, a hefty paunch, and an undeniable hunger. Like the best multi-level marketing, Santa receives a portion of the belief his flunkies generate, but because avatars use magic, too, they're driven to feed. Naturally, elves being scarce on this side of the Gauntlet, they have to find other sustenance, and there's no greater generator of magical belief than a human child. The SCD got involved when consumption escalated from basking in a kid's laugh to hollow bodies in mall dumpsters.

Cora shudders as she watches her latest Santa hoist a snot-nosed toddler onto his lap. It's her sixth stop of the day, and she's got four more to go. While she's grateful that there are only ten confirmed avatars out of the crop of a hundred suits this year, it's literally an entire day's work to visit them all. It's easy, but tedious. Show up at the location, hang around for an hour, check for signs of magic and/or potential kidnapping, remind them she'll be back tomorrow. Repeat until December 26.

The black-haired kid in the Santa's lap yanks on his bushy white beard, making him wince. It's real. Or is now, anyway. Joshua Matthews didn't have one when he started two weeks ago. He chuckles at the brat's behavior, saying, "Aren't you a strong lad?" then dips into the comically oversized bag at his side and gives the boy a model race car. Cora narrows her eyes. Her radar tells her it's not store-bought; the guy's manifesting toys. She notes that development as Matthews hands the kid back to his mother, who's about to cry herself.

The line moves forward. Another tyke in the red velvet lap. Cora yawns and checks the clock. She's timed her arrivals and departures by a meticulous set of schedules, and it's close to the end of Matthews' shift. She makes sure to have her briefing with the Santa when he goes on break to avoid prying eyes and to preserve the kids' belief. Cora's always been told children are precious, but it hadn't hit home until she learned how much of the supernatural is powered by them. In an increasingly secular world, they're all that keeps some species alive.

Or at least they were until Eris started mucking around with the magic.

She latches on to the thought like a life preserver in a sea of boredom. She's been mulling over the visit to the Lorekeeper, carefully editing out Jack's involvement to maintain her professional demeanor. The comment Tithonus made about Diogenes' Lantern being useful stuck with her. It makes total sense that if Eris needs specific artifacts to execute the Gauntlet-crashing ritual, then the SCD could use different ones to fight back. That should be great news, but the range of options is so broad that it's deflating. How are they supposed to identify the artifacts they need, even with her vast mythological knowledge? And how will they find them when the guy in charge of inventory keeps losing it?

Always more questions, never enough answers.

"Ho, ho, ho! Time for Santa to go feed his reindeer."

The Santa ruffles the hair of the child at the front of the line and lays a finger beside his nose with a wink. The girl screams louder, but he's unfazed as he strolls leisurely from his gold throne to the break room behind the North Pole backdrop. Cora follows at a discreet distance and slips in the door after him. The security guards give her a nod of acknowledgment as she passes. Generally, uniforms are on a need-to-know basis with the SCD and most people don't need to know. Agents are supposed to protect people from interacting with the supernatural, after all. But this is a special circumstance, and Cora's grateful for the backup; Santa Watch has the potential to get ugly. She nods back and closes the door behind her.

Matthews makes a beeline for the catering table, whistling a Christmas carol to himself. He stacks a paper plate with sugar cookies and pours himself a steaming styrofoam cup of hot chocolate before sitting in a folding chair that creaks under him. He doesn't seem to notice he's fifty pounds heavier than when he took this gig. That's one nice thing about becoming a Santa avatar—you don't mind the weight gain.

Cora stands in front of him as he tucks into his treats. She pulls out her SCD badge and says, "Mr. Matthews, do you know who I am?"

"You're from the agency, right?" he says without looking up.

"That's right, sir. Do you know why I'm here?"

He takes a noisy sip from his cup. "Can't say that I do."

She'd forgotten that this is his first year. Poor guy. He must've been ripe for the magic when he signed on. Most guys don't go full-blown Kringle until their fifth or sixth year in the suit.

She flips up her badge to identify herself. "I'm Agent Six from the Supernatural Cases Division. I've been assigned to you for the remainder of the season. The previous agent was called away on other business." He nods his bushy white head. He's got the Santa bad—the file lists Matthews as having short brown hair. "I've concluded today's observations," Cora continues, "and it's my opinion that you've safely executed your duties. I do need to warn you to be judicious with toy manifesting, though. It draws on a lot of resources, which means you could be approaching dangerously low magic levels. I'll be back tomorrow to check in on you, and I would hate for that visit to be an unpleasant one."

Matthews peers at her through his round wire spectacles. There's a twinkle in his eye. Of course. "Thank you, agent. You're doing a good job of getting yourself off the naughty list this year."

She bites back the urge to ask what the hell he's talking about. Any other case, she'd write it off as weirdo talk, but knowing he's plugged into the real Santa makes the statement downright sinister. It prickles at the back of her neck. "Sir?" she says.

"Oh, Cora," he says with an indulgent chuckle. "You always tried so hard to stay on the good list.

But it was tricky for you, wasn't it?" He slips another cookie under his mustache, then says around the crumbs, "Making up for lost time."

Her entire body erupts in goosebumps. How could he know that? Memories race back of letters to Santa demanding proof of his existence—reindeer hoofprints, photographs, anything. All so she could know whether or not it was "worth it" to be a good girl. Grownup Cora is ashamed as little kid Cora stomps her foot. She can also think of a dozen things that would land her on the naughty list this year alone.

Matthews laughs again and sets the empty plate and cup on the service table, then pats his velvet-clad leg. "Why don't you sit on Santa's lap and tell him about it?" He smiles, bunching his red cheeks into apples.

Cora's eyebrows go up as she notices the magic at work around her. She doesn't need her radar to pick it up; it's not hiding. The decorated sugar cookies, the cider and hot chocolate, the gold decorations, the spare bags of toys lined against the wall, the pine tree in the corner, the Santa eager to hear her wishes—all of it working sweetly together, urging her to do what he asks. It presses against her heart, already sore from being away from home at Christmas and the self-inflicted wounds of rejecting Jack. It's followed by a nudge at her mind that puts the sweet taste of gingerbread in her mouth. She brushes it away, but finds herself smiling.

It can't hurt, right? she reasons. *I've done the right thing and taken the high road for ages. I'm allowed a minute of rebellious fun. Besides, I've withstood attacks from High Fae and angry goddesses. There's nothing a dimestore Santa can do that's worse than that.*

Matthews' smile shines brighter as Cora removes and pockets her sunglasses. His arms open wider, and she sits on the edge of his lap, aware of the chair's dangerous creaking under her added weight. She holds her legs and back taut, ready to bolt, just in case.

"Now, little girl," the Santa says, "what would you like for Christmas?"

Up close, the rich aroma of eggnog and peppermint clinging to Matthews' suit turns texture of the world soft and twinkly. Nostalgic images of presents never delivered float across her mind's eye. The clichéd pony, of course. The Raggedy Ann doll. The electric typewriter. They rise up in red and green bubbles and pop like soda fizz on the end of her nose, making her giggle. But none of them are quite right. There's something else, something important, that she's been wanting recently. What is it again?

"Well?" Santa prompts.

"I don't know," she says. There's an odd, dreamy echo in her voice. It doesn't concern her, though. She's trying so hard to remember the name of the thing she wants.

"That's okay. Santa knows. Let me reach into my bag and see what we've got, hrm?"

Through the sugarplum haze, Cora's dimly aware of movement, but her thoughts are drifting through

Christmases past with her family, her friends, and Jeremy. Each one is so perfect with their puffy snowflakes and thoughtful presents and sparkling lights and people she loves. Why couldn't this year be like that?

Because you have a job to do.

The answer slices through her like a hot iron in the snow. Cora gasps as the delicious fuzz vaporizes, and she bolts to her feet as razor-sharp fangs whiff through the air where her neck used to be. Matthews, unbalanced by the force of his attack, tumbles out of the folding chair and hits the concrete floor with a meaty *thud*. Fortunately, Cora's agent training kicks in before she can process that she's narrowly avoided being eaten by Santa Claus. She throws herself down and plants her right knee firmly in the small of his back. He snarls as she pins him with her full weight, his pointed monster teeth bared. She has to turn her face away as she puts the cuffs on him; the juxtaposition of fat cherub and cannibalistic fiend is too much.

The mall security guards burst through the door as Cora's getting to her feet, hands on their guns. She knows how red her face is, but she's confident they'll write it off as exertion rather than embarrassment.

"You okay, ma'am?" asks the short one.

She nods. "Not a problem, officers. But you should let the parents know that Santa's done for the day. I'll notify the service and have them send you a new guy first thing tomorrow." She nudges

Matthews with her foot. Thankfully, he's normal-looking again. "This jolly old elf won't be heading back to the North Pole."

The officers look at one another uncertainly but let it drop.

Cora waits until the door's closed to release the breath she's been holding. She can't believe she fell for this asshole's magical trap. She knew it was happening and convinced herself to walk right in. Does she want a good Christmas that badly? Or is her subconscious trying to put her in a situation where she'd need Jack to rescue her? Neither thought brings any comfort.

Matthews squirms on the floor nearby, and Cora puts a foot on his generous backside to stop him from getting too far. She takes a second to appraise the situation. He's way too big for her to safely escort to headquarters. She's going to need backup.

"Stay, you cookie-munching jerk, or I'll punt you into next Christmas and bust you again," she says as she fishes her phone out of her pocket. He grumbles but stops wriggling. "Good move."

She steps away for a modicum of privacy, but as she starts to dial the SCD switchboard, her foot catches on something metallic. She shoots an annoyed glare at the ground that instantly evaporates when she sees what she's stepped on. Kneeling, she draws the rest of the object from the toy sack Matthews had been digging in and holds it up. It's an old-fashioned brass lantern, square with glass panes and a slot for a single fat candle inside. Her mouth falls open in disbelief. It's the thing she was trying so hard to remember in her sugarplum haze, the one thing she wanted.

"Diogenes' Lantern," she whispers to herself.

Keeping the lantern aloft in one hand, she dials the switchboard. But instead of asking for Agent 11's desk to get the backup she needs, she first asks to be transferred to Agent 100 directly. The director is going to want to hear about this one.

By the third time Cora tries getting through to Agent 100, she's officially worried. While they haven't met face to face, she knows from workplace gossip that Dora Boxer is meticulous in her habits, virtually lives in her office, and always makes time for agents. Which is why it's troubling that she isn't picking up her phone, regardless of whether or not she's working the beat.

Having passed the vicious Santa impersonator off to booking with 11's help, Cora finds herself sitting in the bullpen facing an awkward choice. If 100 isn't answering, what does she do with Diogenes' Lantern? She can't take it to Tithonus because her permit's expired. She'd rather swallow hot coals than try to explain to 99 what happened at the mall. Sofi doesn't have Roosevelt clearance. And Jack isn't an option. For now, it'll have to stay stashed in the locked drawer of her desk.

She fires up her computer to start her report on Matthews. Then a lightbulb comes on in her mind. What if Dora's here but on "do not disturb" or passed out after too many hours poring over reports? Gods know they're piling up these days. Given the oddly archaic security tech in the building, elevator access is unrestricted; there's nothing to stop her from taking the lantern directly to 100's office herself.

Grinning at her own cleverness, Cora snatches the lantern from its drawer, then heads towards the central elevators. *See, I can do this,* she says to herself. *All I have to do is keep my head clear.*

When the doors open on the top floor, Cora steps out with a low whistle. Where Agent 99's office is impressive with its heavy wood furniture and leather books, this entire level is dedicated to one office with a lobby that'd make Martha Stewart cream her shorts. It's nicer than any house Cora's ever lived in—more like a salon. Grecian urns adorn decorative tables, thick tapestries line the walls, and large, welcoming chairs face each other in natural conversation circles. Motion-sensitive lighting switches on and plush white carpet dampens Cora's footfalls as she crosses to the single wooden door on the far side of the waiting room.

There's no answer to her first knock, and she waits a second or two before knocking again. If Dora's sleeping, she feels bad for waking her, but only a little. Any annoyance on the bosslady's part has to be mitigated by the magnitude of the find.

Another knock. Still no answer.

There's a prickle at the back of Cora's neck that tells her something's not right. She gives the opulent lobby another survey, this time using her investigator's eyes. Right away, she notices the flowers in vases—dead. Not just wilted but dried up. She sniffs the air and notices mildew and dust. Like boxes of clothes opened after spending the winter in storage. How long has it been since anyone's been up here?

Danger sense clanging louder and louder, she tries the door handle. Locked.

Cora casts a furtive look around, then sits the wrapped lantern in the corner and reaches into her back pocket. She may be bitter about her relationship with Jeremy, but she's grateful for some things he did—like teach her how to pick a lock when she forgets her keys. The solitary credit card in her wallet is thin enough that it should do the job. She inserts it into the slit between door and jam, sensing the mechanism through the plastic. It catches, and she quickly bends the card and gives it a twist. There's a gut-wrenching second where the plastic threatens to give out, turning white in a line down the center, but she holds firm and is rewarded with a soft *click*. She shakes her head as she pockets the card. You'd think the director of a government agency would have high-tech locks on their door. Looks like the rumors of Dora being too archaic for her own good are true.

Micromillimeters at a time, Cora presses down on the hooked door handle. It gives easily, swinging the door inward on silent hinges. The scent of old paper and musty carpet breeze past in its wake. Light from the hall spills into the darkened office, illuminating everything she'd feared.

A fine coating of dust hangs in the stale air,

disturbed by the opening door. Paperwork litters the floor, the stately executive desk is in disarray, the leather visitor's chairs are overturned. Broken glass from a shattered lamp glitters on the carpet. All the signs of a robbery. One that happened quite a while ago.

Police instincts sharpened by two weeks of nonstop cases tell her to go carefully as she steps into the office. This is a crime scene, she's sure of it. She tries the light switch, but none come on. Her eyes rove around the darkened room, desperate for signs of what happened.

Another two steps inside tell her more than she wanted to know: There are dark spots on the carpet in front of the desk. With trembling fingers, she kneels and brushes them with her fingertips. They're crusted and brown. She doesn't need a lab test to tell her what that is: old blood. She chokes down a cough, less from the blood and more from the implications of it. This must've happened weeks ago, and no one reported anything. Not a break in, not an attack—nothing. Whoever did this had the power to cover it up, to make it look as if Dora never left.

Which means someone in the agency is responsible.

Cora covers her mouth to stifle a gasp. The adrenaline pumping through her veins aches for her to flee. She wants to. It'd be so much easier to go home pretending she didn't see anything or to run straight to the bullpen and tell the first person she sees. Whatever she can do to get the burden off her shoulders. But she doesn't. She stays. There's work to do.

Pushing herself back up to her feet, she retrieves her phone and methodically begins taking pictures of the room using the flash to guide her progress. She may not understand everything she sees here, but she knows people who will.

Flash. Scattered papers covered in angular script.

Flash. Blood in the carpet, on the desk chair.

Flash. A large footprint—a men's 10.

Flash, flash, flash.

After she's taken as many evidenciary photos as her phone can hold, she backs out of the office, resets the lock, and pulls the door closed, rubbing out her footprints in the carpet and wiping her fingerprints off the handle. Then she does the same through the waiting room and elevator, picking up the lantern on her way out. Whoever did this can't know they've been discovered. Not until she finds out what happened. And why.

EIGHT

Jack's trip from JFK to the ambassador's hotel in Manhattan is far less stressful than his trip in. Traffic's eased up post-lunch-rush, and although he'd never admit it, he enjoys having another person in the car. Less time alone with his thoughts. And with his remaining inhabitant voice.

Ishtar's scarce lately, though. Even as the ambassador—Akiko, she said to call her Akiko—explains the details of the art shipment she's here to present, Jack's wondering where the warrior goddess has been. Since he was forced to swear allegiance to her in the underworld, she's drifted in and out, usually turning up in stressful moments to hint that there's purpose to his suffering. But she stayed silent when he stood alone on his front porch last night. If that wasn't enough stress to get her attention, he's vaguely concerned about what's yet to come that she deems more deserving of her attention.

"Agent 97, are you listening to me?"

Jack blinks hard as Akiko's voice cuts through his wandering thoughts. "No, ma'am," he admits.

The ambassador narrows her eyes at him, but she doesn't press the issue. Instead, she repeats the information, which turns out to be details not in the dossier.

"I was saying that the artifacts I am accompanying will arrive at the Metropolitan Museum this evening. I am scheduled to meet with a contact there to authenticate the materials before they are prepared for the exhibition soiree tomorrow night. I must ensure that they are not damaged or forgeries made in transit."

The meeting is new, but Jack can handle a scheduling change; what snags him is in a different part of her explanation. "Soiree?" he repeats.

Out of the corner of his eye, he sees faintest smile on Akiko's face. "Yes, agent. You are to be my escort. Did your agency not inform you of this?"

The air in the SUV is suddenly stifling. He makes a mental note to have the heat checked when he gets back to DC and turns it off to avoid breaking out in a sweat.

"You do have proper attire," she says. It's not a question.

"No, ma'am. I wasn't informed of the event."

The ambassador makes a tutting noise. "That is a shame, agent. You will need to acquire proper clothing. I cannot go unattended nor can I be accompanied by unsuitable security."

That stings, but it's true. The people they'll be

meeting will know the difference between a tuxedo and his usual SCD suit, regardless of its quality, and he needs to blend in. As Akiko's escort and lone bodyguard, his presence must be as invisible as possible for maximum effectiveness. The trick will be finding a tuxedo that fits his unusually tall, thin frame on short notice.

That hurdle doesn't irk Jack as much as the idea of attending a high society party itself, though. Guard duty is one thing—standing for hours on end doesn't bother him—but pretending to enjoy caviar and fumble through small talk with the art set is another. He's already bored thinking about it. He'd much rather be tracking down vampire assassins in the dirty slush of the city, and he wonders if he can convince Manny to trade places that evening. With his gregarious nature, 42 will be better company if he can rein in the surfer talk for a few hours. Jack makes a note to discuss it with Akiko once she's settled in.

The New Yorker Hotel looms into view as the SUV rounds the corner of 34th Street, then swallows them up as Jack guides the bulky vehicle into the underground parking garage. The New Yorker has been the SCD's hotel of choice for decades due to its high concentration of ghosts and its association with Nikola Tesla, a friend to the agency in his time, and the staff are used to hosting agents. The valet keeps his distance until they pull into a marked spot at the back of the lot, then quick-steps over to retrieve their bags. Jack comes around to the passenger side and opens the door for

Akiko, who's waiting patiently. She steps down lightly and takes Jack's arm as they make their way to her suite on the fortieth floor.

It's not until the room's been swept and cleared and the door locked that either of them speaks again. Akiko shrugs off her winter coat immediately, fanning flush skin and muttering to herself. Underneath, she's wearing a cream-colored silk kimono, shortened to modern tastes with a gold obi around her waist. The hem lifts dangerously high as she bends to unlace her boots, and Jack moves quickly past with her suitcase, eyes forward.

"What time is your meeting tonight?" he asks over his shoulder, situating her belongings on luggage racks in the bedroom.

"Eight."

"And what will you be doing in the meantime?"

"Sleeping."

Her voice is closer, and he turns sharply. The ambassador is staring at him from the opposite side of the king-sized bed. He didn't hear her come in, despite the stiff silk of her robes. They stand that way for several seconds before the impropriety of him being in her bedroom dawns on him.

"I'll take my post in the hallway," he says, dipping his head and moving towards the door. "You can—"

"You will stay within line of sight."

Jack looks back at her, confused and close to annoyed. He's worked a number of protection missions, but no one has made a demand like that. "Ma'am?"

Instead of replying, Akiko turns to the huge picture windows behind her and throws open the heavy curtains. Watery winter sunlight flows into the room like a dam breaking, touching the room's brass decorations and making them gleam. The table lamp Jack had turned on pales in embarrassment; he has pity on it and turns it off. The ambassador steps into the broad sunbeam and smiles with her eyes closed. Takes a deep breath. Lets it out slowly. And then she loosens the obi, shrugs off her kimono, and lets it fall to the ground, revealing smooth skin and nothing else.

Jack nearly gives himself whiplash turning away so fast. He stares pointedly out the bedroom door with such intensity that the couch might burst into flames. "Madam Ambassador," he says, "those windows aren't tinted. Everyone can see you."

She laughs. It's a schoolgirl giggle, but it fits her. The first peek through the political facade. "Let them look," she says. "I have nothing to be ashamed of."

There's a shift in the air behind him. Jack's entire body tenses as he senses that she's moved directly behind him. Not touching him, thank the gods, but standing incredibly close—naked. Heat radiates from her skin, forcing a steady blush up his neck.

"You will stay within line of sight," she repeats, lips next to his ear. "That will ensure no time is lost between my cry for help and your response, should villains make their way inside."

"Yes, ma'am."

"And Agent 97?"

"No peeking."

Jack coughs hard as she puts a single finger into his back and pushes him firmly into the living room. Keeping his eyes glued to the carpet, he takes a seat on the emerald green couch while the covers rustle in the other room. He waits until there's silence before cautiously lifting his gaze to survey the area. Through the open door between rooms, he can see the soft curves of the ambassador curled up in the center of the bed. He shakes his head. There has to be a reason why every woman he's come in contact with has hit on him since he returned to work in July. Except Sofi. Small miracle. He shrugs off the thought as he settles into the couch. As much as he'd like to distract himself from Akiko's odd behavior, the last thing he wants to think about is failed romances.

Her odd behavior. Of course he's thorough in all his cases, but this awkward exchange, added to the suspicions he had earlier, gives him pause. He pulls out his phone to check his notes. The paper dossiers that the director insists upon are too old-fashioned even for his tastes, and he's taken to copying them into his personal digital records. But the file containing Minamoto Akiko's dossier is remarkably thin—on everything. Scrolling through the document tells him the barest minimum of information. She's a paragon, centuries older than she appears, deeply involved with... there's an empty space. His near-eidetic memory supplies snapshots of the originals. Perhaps thirty percent of the content is redacted with thick black lines, including her magical abilities and list of previous SCD consultations. How did this escape his notice?

Because your mind is on her even when you try to forget.

Jack lets his head fall back onto the high cushions of the couch. The rusty voice of his own conscience is new to him yet, and he's not used to its forthrightness. The ceiling leers back at him with swirls of cream-colored plaster. Spirals that remind him of Faerie—or rather, what Fae are now. What her people are now. He sighs. Everything is linked to her. Why he let it happen, he doesn't know, but it's too late for him. Although her reasoning is sound, his heart is set. Dozens of scenarios run through his mind, taunting him with what ifs and possibilities. Maybe if he'd done things differently, hadn't been so distant or tried harder to stay away. Something. He hates not knowing.

The phone in his hand buzzes to life, earning him a goblin swearword for letting his mind wander. He reads the display. His forehead creases. His heartbeat doubles. But he doesn't answer. With every silent ring, he finds himself tensing, bitterness and resentment pooling in the cracks of his heart. Eventually, it stops.

Jack gives a measured sigh and positions himself to stare into the bedroom where his charge is sleeping in the fading sunlight. He wills his attention to stay there despite starting to feel drowsy himself. He's got a job to do like every other agent. Everyone's got to stand on their own. There's only the slightest twinge of regret as he tucks the phone back into his pocket, pretending he didn't see the notification.

Missed Call: Cora Riley.

It's dark when Jack bolts awake. Soft and sticky dreams are blasted apart by fresh adrenaline pounding in his veins, an unconscious alarm jolting him directly into wakefulness, sharpening his vision in the darkened room. But he doesn't need to see to know that Akiko is gone. He can sense her absence in the texture of the air.

He curses in a filthy goblin language he picked up expressly for the purpose and bolts to his feet. How he managed to doze off and not come to when the ambassador left is a mystery that'll have to wait for later. Right now, he needs to track down his charge and find out why the hell she's sneaking out into the city alone.

Outrage and pride have the magic moving before his conscious mind catches up. His energy snakes through his veins into his core and spools into a tightly-wound mass, welding years of sidestepping experience to the memory of a single interrupted experiment two weeks ago in Faerie. His fists clench at his sides, fingernails biting into his palms. Power strains his skin and gives him in an eerie cerulean aura in the beige hotel room. He braces for the jump, corralling the uncertainty that he can duplicate the trick without Cora's assistance across the dimming bond. Carefully, he tucks her into a quiet space in his injured heart. There's no room for doubt or distraction in teleportation; he has to be confident or he'll be dead. Refocusing, he bends his will to draining his magical reserves into primary usage. Some of the feeling goes out of his legs, but he's quickly filled to capacity, anxious to leap through space in pursuit of a quarry that has no idea who they're up against. He takes a slow breath and closes his eyes, ready for the release, drawing the image of his destination in his mind.

But nothing comes—he has no idea where he's going.

His eyes snap open and his breath catches. The magic stutters, wobbles, fails. Vertigo takes over as the unused magic floods back into his reserves, and he lets himself fall back onto the couch to get his bearings. It takes several minutes for the room to stop spinning and for him to understand why he failed. While it's comforting to know he can use this new ability under his own power, teleportation is useless without knowing the ending location. He rubs a thin hand over his face in frustration. Looks like he'll have to track down Akiko the old-fashioned way.

Jack levers himself off the couch and checks the bedroom for additional clues. The suitcase is open and has been rifled through, but since he didn't know the contents beforehand, it's no help. He can assume she's in street clothes at this point; going around in Japanese robes would garner too much attention, even in this town. Her purse is on the end table, but the phone is locked and the paperwork he finds is in Japanese. Despite his excellent language skills, this isn't one he reads. Another disgusting goblin swearword.

Fortunately, he does have a special edge to his detective skills. The lycan streak in his blood rises to the surface at his command, bolstering his naturally fine sense of smell to supernatural levels. He snatches a pillow from the bed, presses it to his face, and inhales deeply. Her scent is strong and sharp: cut grass, polished wood, and sunshine. He couldn't have asked for an easier signature to follow through the polluted winter streets of New York City; he could find the smell of summer anywhere.

Well, then, ambassador, he thinks, *the game is afoot*.

Jack Alexander steps out of the New Yorker Hotel into the snowy Manhattan night and sniffs the sharp air. A dangerous smile curls his lips as he starts jogging up Park Avenue towards Central Park, the thrill of the hunt already singing in his bones.

NINE

Cora's flight from the horrors of Agent 100's office back to the safety of her apartment is cut short at the SCD's front door by a quiet thought. A simple, yet terrifying plan crystallizes around what should've been obvious. She stares at Diogenes' Lantern with new eyes. If she's got it, she should use it, right?

Before she can change her mind, she's up the elevator and striding through the aisles of the agent bullpen. The floor is mostly empty—everyone's on assignment or stealing an hour for food or phone calls—but the guy Cora's hunting for is rarely doing any of those things.

Nerves shorten her patience for the search. "Scott? You here?" she calls out across the floor.

A round head pokes up above the flimsy dividers two aisles away, followed by a pair of black glasses. Agent 19 glowers at her, then ducks back down.

Cora rolls her eyes and crosses the floor. As a

deadspeaker, Scott Kim's role in the agency is feast or famine. When the zombie outbreak happened at Halloween, you couldn't find the guy because he worked 48 hours straight. Now, without much activity in the way of reanimated or recently deceased bodies, you can't find him because he's hiding. Cora's certain he's the last agent not working overtime in the hunt to dismantle Eris' plans, which is vaguely suspicious. It's also why she's looking for him.

"What're you doing?" she says as she stands in the opening to his cubicle.

Scott huffs and extricates himself from a fairly impressive nest of blankets in the cubby underneath his desk. His black suit is rumpled, his hair is a mess, and he's glaring at Cora like she's interrupted a sweet dream. "What's it look like?"

Cora ignores the snark. She needs to do this fast. "Can I ask you for a favor?"

He squints at her. "Depends on what it is." Then he notices the lantern in her hand. "What's that?"

"The favor." He raises a questioning eyebrow, but she waves it off. "All I want to do is shine the light on you for a second. I promise it won't hurt." She doesn't actually know that, but it's a reasonable assumption. There's nothing in the legend about it, anyway.

"I guess," he says slowly.

It's then that Cora realizes she has no idea how to use the damn thing; the story is all about the effects. Muttering to herself, she gropes around all its sides, then opens the little door to peek inside.

Candle.

"You got a light?" she asks.

Scott huffs melodramatically but fishes in his pocket and retrieves a lighter from inside a pack of Marlboro Lights. The flame sputters and spits when the wick is lit, then finally grabs hold. The instant the glass door is locked, thin yellow light streams out, not in a diffused halo, but pointed at Scott's face like a spotlight. It grows in intensity the longer Cora keeps it trained on him. The light wraps around his short, round body outlining him against the background of the bullpen, as if he's more real than his surroundings.

Scott holds up a hand against the bright light. "Hey, what gives?" he complains.

"Sorry!" Cora says. She hurriedly snuffs the candle. The light goes out immediately, and the magical outline fades. "It works," she murmurs with a semi-hopeful smile.

"What works?"

She hoists the lantern. "This will prove it."

"Prove what?" Scott huffs.

But Cora's in a different world. She walks away from the deadspeaker, completely distracted by the next step in her plan.

The thing works. Legend claims that the philosopher Diogenes ran around with a lantern, using its light to search for an honest man—a magical lie detector that reads the hearts of mortals. He meant it as a metaphor, but the story survived over centuries, withstanding the test of time and garnering belief, which turned its imagery into real power. When Tithonus mentioned it might be useful in the Eris investigation, though, Cora was skeptical. She could see it surviving as a historical object, but she was convinced it was too obscure in the modern age to give the lantern any clout. She's thrilled to be wrong; having a way to tell friend from foe, no matter how clunky and obvious, will be a huge advantage in their fight.

But that pride is severely mitigated by the next stage of her plan. In fact, she's so caught up in building her nerve that she collides with the janitor as she's getting into the elevator. They crash into each other, neither looking where they're going. His cart spews bottles and bags across the floor, and Cora automatically stoops to help him retrieve them.

"Oh my god, I'm so sorry," she says. The next apology dies on her lips. She pauses with a bottle of Windex halfway back in the cart and tilts her head to the side. "Tut?"

The former god-king of Egypt, whom Cora personally processed three weeks ago, glares back at her with liquid brown eyes. The last time she saw him, he was half-mummified, but now he's entirely in human form: a handsome teenage boy with dark features that strike a familiar chord in Cora's heart.

She puts down the bottle of cleaner harder than she means to and stands up. "What're you doing on cleanup duty? Last I'd heard, you'd volunteered to join the staff and were slated for a cushy assignment at the New Mexico office."

Tut puts the rest of the items into the cart and

stands, too, but he refuses to meet her eyes. "I heard no such thing. I stayed seven days in the Roosevelt, and then a man arrived and informed me that I would be a servant in this place."

Cora takes in his grey uniform, wobbly cart, grimy rags, and stooped shoulders and has an overwhelming wave of sympathy for him. This is no job for a king, former or otherwise. She reaches out and gently touches his elbow. "Who was it?"

The boy yanks his arm away with a snarl. "He did not tell me his name, only that he is the master here," he says. "A fat man with dark skin and white hair."

An icicle floats through Cora's heart: the same person she's on her way to see. More evidence she's on the right trail, though she wishes she weren't.

"I'll talk to him," she says as he pushes the cart onto the floor. "This isn't right. You deserve better."

Tut nods perfunctorily and rolls past her, his eyes forward and jaw set. She watches him go, then calls the elevator back and punches the button that'll take her to 99's office.

Knock, knock.

Pause.

Knock, knock.

Nothing.

Cora's resolve wavers as she raises her hand for a third knock. This part of her plan requires a level of deceit she's never attempted before. There's a yawning gulf of difference between lying to your parents about going to a booze-soaked party in high school and testing one of the world's most prodigious empaths for chaos-goddess contamination without him knowing.

Though her knees are turning watery, the combination of iron will and quiet dignity inherited from her Southern mother have made Cora the best kind of stubborn; she can't run from a fight that matters. She knocks again.

"Come in."

Cora isn't sure if she's relieved or disappointed, but she swallows her doubt and pushes open the door anyway. The office is the same as always, though it now feels claustrophobic, as if her plan is taking up the entire room. She steps in front of the desk and draws her energy tightly around her like armor. Showtime.

Patel peers at Cora over the top of his half-moon reading glasses and lays aside the papers he's holding, face down. "Can I help you, Agent Six?" he asks.

Cora keeps her eyes trained on a blank spot on the wall above his right shoulder. "Sir, I thought you might want to know I've recovered one of the artifacts that's gone missing from the Roosevelt."

His furry white eyebrows arch up as she sits the lantern on his desk. "Diogenes' Lantern, I presume."

"Yes, sir."

"We've had several agents on the lookout for that artifact for weeks. How did you manage to locate it?"

She hesitates. Telling him about her Santa mishap could land her in more trouble than she's bargaining for. But the truth now will pave the way for trust if this goes the way she's predicting it will.

"It fell out of Santa Matthews' toy bag, sir."

Patel lifts his chin and makes a thoughtful noise. Cora suddenly feels extremely exposed. He stares at her for a moment, then, as if on cue, there's the sensation of a stone skipped over the pond of Cora's mind. She knows 99's an empath, of course, and she's here to test him for treason, but using powers against other agents is against regulations; having the rules-enforcer break them is disturbing. Thankfully, the foresight to channel her energy into guarding her mind pays off. The intrusion bounces harmlessly off her shield, protecting everything but her surface thoughts, which are currently of sitting on Santa's lap with fangs coming at her. Patel's brow furrows for a microsecond, then clears as if nothing happened. Cora's not sure if she's won or lost ground by resisting.

The senior agent doesn't address it, though. "I trust the full explanation will be in your report, Agent Six."

"Yes, sir. What should I do with the lantern, sir?"

He considers this for a moment. "Is it operational?"

"I don't know, sir. If you have a light, I'm sure we can test it, however."

To his credit, Patel doesn't hesitate. He reaches into a desk drawer and hands Cora a matchbook. She smiles politely, lights the candle inside, returns the matches, and closes the glass door. The glow from the flame builds inside, and for a moment, Cora can't breathe. Then the wick sputters, sparks, and extinguishes itself.

Exactly as she expected.

But the confirmation brings her no joy. How can she relish being right when it means the man organizing the mortal world's resistance to the magical apocalypse is corrupt? How much damage has he done by twisting the trust of his agents? Her heart shrinks and tries to drop into her stomach, but she rallies by remembering the blood on Agent 100's office floor. Outing Patel isn't enough; the information needs to be used. That brings her to the hard part—escaping without being found out.

"Huh," she says, tapping on the glass. "Is that normal?"

Patel shrugs and puts away the matches. "The Lorekeeper has complained about the more unusual legends—including his own—dying out recently. The change in background magic levels rewards the popular and punishes the obscure." He peers at the lantern critically. "I suppose Diogenes' time has come. A pity." Then he waves a dismissive hand. "Speak to Wesley in HR for a temporary permit to the archives. Tithonus will be thrilled to have it back, even if it's no longer magical."

It takes all of Cora's willpower not to run out of the room at full speed. The plan worked. If she can make a clean exit, then she can have a nervous breakdown at home. "Yes, sir. Thank you, sir," she says with a partial bow.

She's pulling the door closed behind her when Patel adds, "By the way, Agent Six." She peeks back inside to see him staring intently at her. "You're still new to the supernatural, so I understand the eagerness of your investigations, but I advise caution in the future. Under Eris' promise of a united world, there are beings that will fight for their existence to the bitter end, regardless of the cost. There are forces at work you cannot possibly fathom. Be sure you understand with whom and with what you are dealing."

There's an intense pause the length of a heartbeat, but to Cora it takes years. The primal part of her senses a threat, the logical part agrees, yet she isn't sure what he means. Did he see through her trick? Does he know that she knows? What will he do? Dread paralyses her as she waits for the hammer to fall.

Then the moment breaks, and he says with a lighthearted smile, "Such as evil Santas luring naive young women onto their lap at Christmas in order to eat them."

She almost collapses with relief. "Understood, sir. Thank you," she says.

Patel nods at her by way of dismissal, and she gently pulls his office door closed behind her before sprinting to the elevator.

She's still shaking by the time she locks the deadbolt in her apartment. Between the encounter with 99, dodging other agents on her way out the door, and conveniently not stopping to talk to HR as instructed, she's ready to pass out from adrenaline overload. If this is what it's like to be a real secret agent, all lies and stress and potential bodily harm at every turn, she's not convinced that this is the right life for her. No wonder there's no Agent 007 in the SCD—the sheer weight of pop culture belief would crush their head in seconds.

Cora sinks into the couch, bundled in her winter gear with the lantern beside her, and stares blankly at ceiling. It takes ten minutes and half as many short pulls on a bottle of rum she fishes out of the cushions before she's calm enough to process what she's discovered.

Recovering Diogenes' Lantern, while admirable, pales in comparison to the insight that Samir Patel is a traitor. Not an honest man, according to the criteria of the lamp's wielder—Cora—who's so fixated on Eris's sedition that it's her sole guideline for good and bad these days. And if he's on Eris' side, it's an easy leap to say he's responsible for Agent 100's kidnapping and possible murder.

It's all so huge Cora can't take it in, and she closes her eyes against frustrated tears. Crying when stressed is her least useful quality, particularly as a federal agent. She colors at the memory of having to leave halfway through interrogating an shoplifting sphinx who wouldn't stop repeating her questions. She wipes angrily at her eyes and shoves the bottle back into its hiding place in the couch.

"Dry it up, Riley," she mutters to herself. The

imitation of Sofi's tough-love encouragement lifts her spirits somewhat. She considers calling her former mentor for advice, then decides against it. The last thing a tracker needs is a ringing phone to blow their cover.

Another five silent minutes roll past as Cora starts to construct a plan for how to use the tools and information she's gathered. She could storm 99's office and demand he confess everything. She could use the lantern to ferret out loyal agents, starting her own resistance inside the agency until they can take down 99 and get to Eris. She could search for Agent 100 herself, staging a rescue if possible.

Each new idea feels more fruitless than the last. While she's no helpless damsel by any stretch of the imagination, she's also not foolhardy enough to think a situation of this magnitude can be tackled by a solitary person, no matter how cool they are. Even Gilgamesh and Achilles put their faith in their friends when shit got too real. But who can she call for help? Sofi's out tracking, Manny's dustbusting, and Scott's unreliable.

You're leaving out the most obvious choice.

Cora lets out a soft groan as the thought cuts through her. She knows she should've reached out the second the lantern came into her possession, but the mere idea gave her nervous barfs. There's no avoiding it now, though. Not if she wants to keep saving the world.

Shaking her head at the histrionics, she digs her phone out of the inner pocket of her suit jacket. It takes two false starts, but eventually the phone rings. And rings. And rings.

"You've reached the voicemail of Agent 97. Leave the relevant information after the tone and I'll return your call as soon as possible."

Cora's heart dives into a pool of acid in her stomach. Jack's not picking up. Something tells her that he won't, no matter how many times she calls. The one person she's positive that she can trust, who might know what to do next, and he isn't available. Not to her. Not anymore.

TEN

Manny brushes fat snowflakes from his shoulders as he steps under the overhang at the employee entrance of the Metropolitan Museum of Art. As much as he loves New York City, he can't get the hang of winter. He wistfully recalls a trip to Mexico with his mom before she sent him away. He might have been a toddler, but the memory of hot beaches and hotter food is so real it warms him just thinking about it. The chill returns with a vengeance when he wonders what she's doing; she hasn't called in weeks.

"Pull yourself together, M," he mutters as he blows hot air into his gloved hands. No sense in dwelling on the past when there's such an interesting future ahead inside the museum.

He raises a fist to pound on the metal door, but it pops open before he can connect. He stops inches short of punching Finnegan Kincaid right in his pointed nose. Which, as he's learned from experience, could've made for a much more interesting future than he'd bargained for.

"Hey, dude," Manny chirps. "Thanks for meeting on such short notice. I know things have gotten pretty wild for you guys."

The lanky man sniffs disdainfully, rubbing a hand over his bald head. "You have no idea," he says sadly. But then he smiles and swings the door open wide. "Come on in, you'll catch your death out there."

Manny steps through, pulling off his gloves and hat. The loading area of the Met is no warmer than the outside, and it's filled with wooden crates of myriad sizes. He follows Finn across the floor, marveling at the potential treasures hidden inside each one. He's heard stories about the Roosevelt back at headquarters, crammed with magical objects long forgotten, and he wonders if it's anything like this. He also feels a stab of sadness. While art and artifacts certainly belong in a museum, these are trapped in lonely boxes. He sort of pities them as he passes by.

Finn appears to have no such compassion, though. He heads directly for the main doors without a glance at the crates. Not surprising, really, since he's from the Founder clan. They're the original North American vampire family, the largest, most powerful, and least changed. They're what most mundanes believe the race to be: sexy and smart, classy and cruel. Academic hedonists and staunch traditionalists. Classic Anne Rice. And Finn is no exception. His sire—the elder vampire who turned him—is the clan leader, Seanan Kincaid, which literally makes him the prince of princes with access to political and supernatural power that other vamps envy. Anything he wants, he can have. And yet, he's held down a "day job" as a night watchman at the Met for years. Busting a fellow Founder absconding with a Faberge egg one night is how he ended up meeting Manny. It turned out to be a prank, but Manny's investment in vampire affairs impressed him enough that he agreed to become an SCD contact.

However, Finn's been withholding at least one piece of information. As he walks under one of the pendulous overhead lamps, Manny notices a faint sparkle in the vampire's pale skin. Like he wiped his face on a club girl's cleavage.

"Finn...?"

"Don't ask about the glitter," he says without looking around. "*Twilight,*" is all he offers and keeps walking through the swinging double doors.

Manny frowns behind Finn's back. The virus created by the insane popularity of Meyers' franchise isn't new—*éclat mort* has been on the SCD radar for years—but the data says it only hits vamps less than five years turned, starting with a sparkle to their skin and ending with intense romanticism that makes them useless in their cutthroat society. Last Manny heard, the clan elders had ordered a stop to new turnings, but the Founders, the closest to real-life Cullens, are still being infected. Finn's case is the first time he's seen an older vampire with *éclat*, though, and it sours his stomach. If a middle-aged vamp can contract it, it's possible elders can, too, which leads nowhere good. Forget the dangers of newbies going emo—what happens when the wisest and strongest turn soft? Between the lack of fresh kin, the alarming rate of ashings, and the potential dissolution of leadership, if things don't change soon, the vampire race will die out. Another victim of the modern era's junkfood belief.

And another potential ally for Eris' plan, Manny reminds himself.

The thought chills him deeper than the bitter cold outside. The day's research turned up little more than what Gabriel had divulged and the suspicion he might be on to something bigger than a series of body bags. He needs Finn's particular insight to clarify a few things. Assuming he knows. It'd be embarrassing to meet up with Jack in the morning with empty hands.

"So," he says as they move into the marble corridor of the food court, "what do you know about this mystery box that people are ashing themselves for?"

The moment the words leave his mouth, he knows he's been too blunt. Finn stops dead in his tracks and slowly turns around. For a second, the Founder looks every day of his seventy-four years. Manny's struck by the mad glint in his green eyes that reflects the moonlight through the narrow windows—a hint of the temper he inherited from his sire.

"They were friends of mine," he hisses.

But Manny doesn't let this intimidate him. At least, not on the outside. If he's learned one thing in his tenuous association with vampires, it's to hold your ground. The instant they think they can manipulate you, you've lost. So far, he's been lucky enough to avoid losing any ground, and he's not about to start tonight.

Being strong isn't the same as being a douchebag, though.

"Hey, I'm sorry, Finn. I didn't mean that." He holds up a hand with three fingers. "Scout's honor."

The right angles in the vampire's posture soften, and he looks twenty again. He runs a hand over his face and gives a tired exhale. Not that he needs to, but it's a good human expression. It's also helpful for Manny. Between that and the fierce outburst, he can tell Finn's *éclat* hasn't progressed beyond the superficial glitter stage. He's still himself. For now.

"I know you didn't," Finn says. He sounds exhausted. "But they were. And my sire is having a shit fit about it. Half the ashed were ours."

Manny nods. "But Cade getting it was okay, yeah?" He tests a smirk and is rewarded with one in return. The goon from the Bruiser clan hadn't made any friends in the Founders by kidnapping a promising girl last year and draining her dry. Big no-no in the vamp community. Finn tangled with him several times, once so badly they both ended up in SCD lockdown overnight. Manny knew he'd win points with that dig.

Sore patch successfully glossed over, the two men resume walking, this time side by side. Manny can see from the signage that they're heading for the sculpture garden in the vestibule to the American wing. It's good lookout spot that happens to be his favorite section of the entire museum.

"Kincaid tell you what's in the box?" he asks.

Finn shrugs his bony shoulders. "No. We had a meeting the night after the ice storm, just the Founders, and he said it contained a precious vampiric artifact that he needed for study, but that's it. We were told to spread the word about the reward and open it to everyone. He said it'll change everything for us."

"That fits our timeline. The first combustion case turned up a week after that." Manny absentmindedly tightens his ponytail as he thinks. "No details about the artifact, huh? You'd think if it was worth killing other immortals for that he'd at least give you a hint."

"You'd think. Whatever it is, the Draculas have their knickers in a twist. They're sending more guys, exhausting their resources trying to track it down."

"I'm sure losing people over it isn't helping. They're probably getting more pissed by the night."

"You'd better believe it." Finn gives Manny a probing look. "Your people really don't know anything at all?"

The agent huffs. He hates revealing SCD weaknesses, particularly to vampires. The race isn't exactly known for its peaceful and tolerant worldview, and they're consistently on the shitlist for supernatural crimes. Agent 12's harsh assessment of "fangbangers" lacked sensitivity but not fact. He knows the price for Finn's help, though. Besides, he's not revealing secrets per se. More explaining pertinent details of the case. Helping Finn help him.

"Forensics got the identities of four of the seven bodies, but we haven't figured out exactly how they died. None of the ashes contain any silver or wood, so the spontaneous combustion theory is still on the table. It's ridiculous, but it's all we've got so far. That's why I came to see you. I'd sort of hoped you knew what was in the box so I could pick up another trail."

As they round the corner into the spacious indoor courtyard dotted with marble and bronze sculptures, a figure stands to greet them. Manny's hand automatically goes to his sidearm, but Finn waves him down. The shadows separate, and the figure steps into a wide strip of moonlight in the center of the courtyard, revealing it to be a short Asian woman in jeans and a heavy peacoat, her glossy black hair pinned to the back of her head. Manny looks from her to the vampire with a questioning eyebrow.

"Agent Forty-Two, this is Minamoto Akiko," Finn says with a faint smile. "She's here to tell me what's in the box."

While he's supremely annoyed that Finn neglected to tell him he had another appointment tonight, Manny can't help chuckling softly to himself. Arriving on the same night as the person with the information he needs most? Quite the lucky break. He refastens the strap across his weapon and follows Finn across the courtyard.

Minamoto bows politely to Finn, then reaches out and shakes Manny's hand. She must see the surprise on his face, because she smiles vaguely and says, "When in Rome, agent," and turns expectantly to Finn.

The vampire doesn't waste any time. "This agent is investigating the box, as well. He's been following the trail of ashes it's leaving in its wake. I thought you two should meet so we could form a complete picture of the situation." He lowers his eyes respectfully. "I apologize for the deception, *hogosha*."

She nods and Finn lifts his head. Manny notes the exchange with interest. For a powerful vampire to show deference to this way says there's more to this woman than she's letting on. Which could be good or bad at this point.

"So...," Manny says. "You want to tell me what's going on here, dude?"

Finn seems moderately embarrassed at the casualness of the address but lets it slide. He ushers his two guests to a high marble bench next to a statue of a grieving woman in delicate robes. No one sits.

"Minamoto is here as a representative of her government," Finn begins. Manny's eyebrows shoot up. "Trust me, the diplomacy side is taken care of. But her real purpose here is the secure the box and its contents." He looks to Minamoto. "Although it's not going well."

The woman nods, face neutral. "At home, my role is not dissimilar to yours, Agent Forty-Two. I oversee the local vampire population and ensure that they do not overstep their boundaries with the mundane world. When the object in question was stolen, havoc broke loose in the provinces. It took some time to discover the artifact had been shipped to America, delaying my involvement and arrival. Your Agent Ninety-Nine also took his time approving my paperwork." She dips her head to Manny. "I apologize for any inconvenience this has caused you and your agency."

Before Manny can ask how Finn got involved, the Founder picks up the thread. "I have a distant cousin in Japan who turned recently and put Minamoto in touch with me after the theft. She knew our clan's proclivity for collecting and thought we might be able to help." He narrows his eyes. "I don't think she knows how far Kincaid has fallen."

Minamoto nods, her folded black bun bobbing. "The artifact did not behave as we anticipated when it arrived on these shores. This is both helpful and regrettable. It has caused much sorrow here." To Finn, she says, "Your sire's ambition requires discipline."

The vampire's jaw tightens. "He is not well."

"I have heard. Both his body and his mind suffer." She gives him a meaningful look. "He is not alone."

"I'm aware."

Manny listens to the exchange, mystified, his gaze bouncing between the two as they speak. The last time he checked on Kincaid—on any of the Draculas—they were fine. As arrogant and frustrating as ever, but not dangerously so. The way Minamoto's talking, it sounds like he should be worried. But as many questions as he has, he doesn't break in. He gets the feeling they've forgotten he's here. If his luck holds, they'll drop more information before they remember.

"What will you do?" she asks Finn.

He lifts his chin proudly. "Should my sire fall, I will become Dracula Founder."

A tight smile plays across Minamoto's face. "You will do things differently."

"I will. My sire is the best of our kind. But archaic ideas and secrecy are killing us—literally. All vampires deserve to know the trials and hopes of their race."

That one, Manny understood. Despite their differences, the clans have a few things in common. One of them is the leaders' habit of keeping their people in the dark. Whether it's good or bad—a werewolf attack or an advance in synthetic plasma—it's kept to the Dracula Council until long after its relevance. To keep peace, they say. But the younger vamps are accepting it less. Unrest was already stirring before the ashings began. With Eris' plans in motion, the clans are ripe for civil war. He wasn't aware that Finn fell on the progressive side of the fence, though. Good to know.

The silence that follows is colder and deeper in the stillness of the sculpture garden. It's so quiet, Manny can hear his own blood pumping. He shudders a bit when he remembers that Finn can hear it, too.

Then there's a soft noise made loud by the intense quiet: footsteps. The three of them turn in different directions to search for the source. Manny and Finn put their backs together, and Minamoto drops into a low crouch, but the marble echoes the susurrus across floors and walls, making it impossible to pin down.

"Who else is here, Finn?" Manny whispers.

"There are three other guards on watch tonight, but I'm the one assigned to this area," he replies.

A woman's rough voice comes to them from the eastern corridor. "Dammit, Kincaid, what the hell are you doing?"

Two people step out of the dimly-lit hall, one of average height and weight, one extremely tall and thin. They aren't more than silhouettes, but Manny instantly recognizes the second figure. He groans. Maybe he's not as lucky as he thought.

Agent 97 strides into the sunken courtyard, his face expressionless but his eyes blazing. "I don't know what's going on here, but you two," he says, pointing to Manny and Minamoto, "are coming with me. Right. Now."

ELEVEN

No one speaks on the way to Manny's SUV parked behind the Met. Jack knows he's radiating emotions, none of them good, and he couldn't care less. The audacity of the Japanese ambassador leaving the hotel without him. The shock of seeing Manny consorting with a vampire. The danger he put himself in by coming to Central Park. The exhaustion from running under lycan power. The self-directed fury at literally falling asleep on the job. It's all seething out of his pores, making both his agent and his charge visibly uncomfortable. And he's fine with that.

What he's not fine with is leaving the museum by the back entrance that opens out into Central Park. He knows who and what is out there. He managed to stick to city streets as he tracked Akiko's scent on foot, but they need to return to the hotel as quickly as possible, which means they need a vehicle. There's nothing to be done for it. His pace doesn't slow as they cross the loading dock and he braces himself for the possibility of an encounter.

Of course, Manny tries to break the tension. "So, uh, Ninety-Seven. It's good to see you, dude, but, you know, you could've called if you wanted to meet up."

Jack doesn't turn around. "It wasn't you I was after."

Silence. Good.

When they reach the rear door, Jack hauls on the handle, easily swinging aside the heavy steel, and a blast of icy wind sweeps over them, making Akiko gasp. The snow is falling faster than when he'd arrived, pellets of ice interspersed in the drifts forming against the building. He sniffs the air. It brings him the scent of a bigger storm to come. And of them. He shrugs off his disquiet again and pushes the door aside, motioning for the other two to exit. He watches both their passage and what lies ahead. It could be nothing. It could be any minute. Hackles he doesn't have raise painfully, instincts sharpening to razor's edge. They have to hurry.

The door eases shut as he descends the short staircase to the parking lot, his eyes scanning the street-light dotted park. The others are already at the car. The unease in Jack's bones must be more contagious than he'd thought; Manny's fumbling with his keys in the pool of light by the driver's door.

Three steps—long ones, given his height—puts him within arm's reach of Akiko at the passenger side. But three steps is as far as he gets.

The growl is low, virtually subconscious. It strums a primal chord deep in Jack's psyche, making him shiver with the urge to respond. To howl out his ownership of these people and this vehicle, to make sure the other knows not to come any closer. But he clamps down on it. He knew this might happen. He prepared for this. In the hours spent alone on the drive from DC to NYC, he tamed it, soothed it, reassured it. He hasn't come this far, in miles or in himself, to let the lycan taint in his blood rule him. It's not who he is. Not entirely.

The growl continues, increasing in volume until both Manny and Akiko turn in alarm. It creeps to the edge of the narrow parking lot between streetlamp puddles. Jack lifts his chin, inhaling the scent on the wind with closed eyes. Tar, permafrost, moldering leaves. And wet dog. They always smell like wet dog in the winter. He breathes in again, deeper this time. The owner of the scent is unfamiliar to him, but there's only one signature: a scout.

"Ninety-Seven...?" Manny's barely whispering. He smells like fear.

Jack waves his hand for them to get into the car. Doors unlock, open, close. Each sound is a bomb detonating in his extra-sensitive hearing, but he doesn't flinch. The scout is watching. Waiting.

Jack crosses to the far side of the pavement, mindful not to step onto the snow-covered lawn and staying beneath a light that can be seen from Manny's rear view mirror. While he's not certain how this encounter is going to play out, he knows that if it goes south, he wants the luckiest man alive within shooting range.

He takes another taste of frigid air to discern the last pieces of information. Not the alpha or the beta. A new change. Higher on the hierarchy than he is, though, by default. Best to show proper respect. Holding his hands out to the side, Jack folds himself down to kneeling, head lowered, eyes on the ground.

It's only then that the scout approaches. A slow change in air pressure indicates his nearness, followed by hot breath and the end of a growl. There's a thick, wet crack. Blood droplets pat into the snowy grass inches from Jack's face. A partial shift.

"Greetings, whelp," the scout says. His voice is raw and heavily accented, not used to human speech.

"Greetings," Jack replies. He lowers his hands and raises his head but avoids the scout's eyes. All he can see is the matted grey-brown fur of an enormous wolf with a bloody human mouth.

"Why are you here?"

"I am simply passing through, brother. I do not intend to trespass on your territory."

"Your intentions are of no consequence. The Alpha instructed us to watch for you. And now you are here."

Alarms blare in Jack's mind at the mention of the Alpha. He's had no contact with the Central Park Pack since they tried to kill him five years ago. Steps have been taken to keep him hidden from them. How did they know he was coming? What does the Alpha want? But asking the scout is pointless; he needs to get Akiko and Manny to safety, which means continuing to play the submissive.

"I am no threat," Jack says.

The scout gives a rasping, humorless laugh. "You speak the truth, outcast." He lowers his head until Jack is forced to meet his eyes, yellow and glowing pale. "But the Alpha bids you brought to him. You must face justice for your betrayal of the Pack."

Jack looks away again, trying to maintain proper respect, but he's quickly growing tired of the game. "I betrayed no one. He allowed me to leave."

A cruel grin shows bloody, pointed teeth. "He has changed his mind."

The bitter cold swirling around them slices into Jack, freezing every thought so fast his mind creaks with the effort of not shattering. Extensive practice in detachment is all that prevents him from screaming in panic. The memory is five years old but as fresh as if it were happening now. The attack that mutilated him, his desperate fight to stay alive and stay human, the partial success that cursed his blood. He can't go back. He's been punished enough.

The scout laughs at the scent of Jack's anxiety. "You will come with me."

Faster than his fear can react, a hot, dry voice rushes through him. A voice that is not his. *This is your moment, Jack Alexander. Begin the service I require in exchange for my protection. This is the price. It will not be without reward.*

There she is. Ishtar materializing at the worst possible moment. Again. But this time is different. Until now, she's asked nothing in return for his oath to her in the underworld. If only she'd stop speaking in riddles. Jack reaches within himself to take hold of her, to make her stay and answer his questions, but she's gone, leaving nothing but echoes of her demand.

Jack straightens at the waist but stays on his knees. He knows he's bound to Ishtar's bidding, but putting himself at the questionable mercy of the Pack is not something he's prepared to do without full comprehension of the consequences. He raises his chin and stares fully into the scout's eyes. With an unwavering voice, he says, "Tell Rhand that I will present myself to him to discuss his changed mind, but I will come in my own time and without duress. I have other loyalties and packmates; I must care for them first."

The scout snarls with a ferocity that manages to startle Jack even though he'd expected the angry response. The human mouth splits violently, teeth falling down the bloody throat, jawbones cracking and elongating into a muzzle filled with yellowed fangs. Fully wolf now, the scout rears up on his hind legs and unleashes a howl that echoes against the museum behind Jack and reverberates with supernatural chords across Central Park. The warcry.

In the decrescendo, car doors fly open and feet hit the pavement. Jack braces for what's coming.

They won't be fast enough.

The blow lands in the center of his chest, talons ripping through his coat and clothing directly into his flesh, tracing the old scars, and it sends him hurtling backwards. He hits hard, landing flat on his back halfway across the parking lot. The air rushes from his lungs, the edges of his vision grey, and warmth oozes across his front. It's several seconds before he can draw a breath again, and when he does, it's a shallow, painful thing that tells him he's broken a rib.

The howl goes up again as the scout stands victorious at the borderline between concrete and grass. One by one, other voices join in, starting nearby and stretching far into the distance. Every member of the pack now knows that Jack Alexander has returned to New York and defied the Alpha. The werewolf gazes at the metahuman sprawled on the ground and snorts derisively. It doesn't need to be spoken for the message to be clear: *You screwed up, whelp. You're so low you're not worth killing.* Then the scout drops back to all fours, turns, and melts into the snowy park.

Manny gets to him first. His shaggy hair trails in his aghast face as he surveys the damage. "Holy shit, dude. What did you say to that guy?" He starts to help Jack up without waiting for an answer.

Jack lets himself be lifted to his feet, then shrugs off the younger man. He knows the scout is watching how he reacts to the punishment, eager to report back and collect his reward. Jack refuses to give him the satisfaction of seeing him truly hurt.

He steadies himself, willing away the scent information brought to him on the wind and forcing his human side to the front. He breathes through the pain and crosses to the SUV, taking sure steps that communicate that he's fine.

It's not until they've pulled out onto Fifth Avenue that he lets his muscles relax. The blood flows stronger, breaking the delicate membrane already knitting around the wounds and leaking into his heavy coat.

"You gonna live, dude?" Manny asks. "Do I need to take you to a hospital?"

Jack shakes his head. Both the break and the gashes will be virtually gone by the time they reach the hotel, thanks to his accelerated healing, but they'll need to dodge mundanes until he can get into another set of clothes.

In the rear view mirror, Jack notices that Akiko is staring at him. There's no trace of concern in her face. Instead, she seems intrigued, as if she's weighing him in her mind. It rekindles his earlier suspicions that she's hiding something, and he finds himself wondering which side she's on. It wouldn't be the first time he's been played, but he's determined not to let it happen again.

He switches his attention to looking out the window, watching Christmas lights and decorations flick past as they drive on. Just as he's shutting his eyes to catch a few minutes' rest, Manny's phone vibrates in the cup holder and triggers an errant thought that makes him wince harder than any of his wounds.

I wonder if Cora's okay.

Fortunately, there's minimal hotel staff by the time they get back to the New Yorker and most of the clientele is out taking in the city's pleasures for the night. The odd trio makes its way to the fortieth floor without incident.

Until they're within eyesight of Akiko's room.

They're walking slowly, no one commenting on Jack's pace, when he stops and signals for the others to do the same. Manny furrows his brow, but all Jack does is point at the open door. It's ajar half an inch, and there's light shining through the crack. Jack can't remember if he touched the switch or closed the door before he tore off after the ambassador. Sloppy.

The two men exchange a glance and free their weapons. Jack winces as his tender flesh complains, but he ignores it. He's had worse. A pulverized femur and mangled thigh during a foot chase with a Chinese demon comes readily to mind. This is much easier to work through. He lifts his gun and slides to the right side of the door frame. Manny takes up the left, motioning Akiko to stand behind him.

From next to the door, the sound of the television is clear. There's definitely someone in there, although if they're an assassin, they're doing a terrible job of hiding. Jack presses his ear to the wall, trusting his heightened senses to pick up signs of life inside. But whoever it is isn't moving; all he hears is an ad for a new season of the "hottest crime drama on network TV." Manny doesn't see anything helpful through the opening in the door, either. He nods his head to Jack as an invitation, offering him the honor of surprising the intruder. An invitation he gladly accepts.

In one fluid movement, Jack kicks open the door and steps into the living room of the suite. He darts automatically to the right, Manny to the left, both training their sights around the room, seeking out the threat.

"FBI!" Manny shouts. Jack winces; too many crime dramas.

A beat passes. No one moves. A commercial ends on the TV. Then a red head peeks up in front of them.

The bottom drops out of Jack's stomach as Cora appears, perched backwards on the couch cushions, her face a picture of amused guilt. Behind her, a poorly-timed laugh track mocks their awkward situation.

It's enough to break the tension. Both agents lower their guns with matching expressions of disbelief. Manny grins as he slots his gun back in its holster and crosses the room, but Jack is paralyzed. He wasn't ready. He didn't expect to see her for at least two more days, back within the comfortable parameters of the DC office, after he'd had time to wrap himself in protective layers of detachment. The blow of encountering her without warning rips open the safe in his heart where he'd stored his feelings for her mere hours ago, bleeding messy emotion into his adrenaline-worn mind. But underneath the hurt, there's a blue-tinted hum as the bond between them tightens. He wonders if she notices, searches for something to say. The moment goes on forever.

A thousand miles away, right next to him, Akiko clears her throat, bringing him politely back to the here and now. He pretends not to hear Manny's chuckle from the kitchenette as he regains his composure and holsters his sidearm.

Cora's eyebrows go up when Jack peels off his winter coat. His wounds are healed, but the bloody remains of his suit jacket and shirt are undoubtedly alarming. She takes in the sight, then purses her lips thoughtfully and says, "I was going to say I've got some big news, but I think maybe you should go first."

TWELVE

Ten minutes and a round of introductions later has everyone settled into the compact living room while Manny passes out minibar drinks. Cora takes hers— a mix of tiny rum and tiny Sprite—with a grateful smile, despite Jack glowering at her from the wingback armchair on the opposite side of the room. But she's ignoring him. She'd suggested they could all use a stiff drink after the way they'd greeted each other, and everyone else had heartily agreed. Except Jack. He's the only one with an empty hand. While she didn't expect him to break down in tears when she arrived, she had hoped for a modicum of warmth. No such luck. But if this is how he wants to act, fine. He's a big boy, he can do what he wants.

Done playing bartender, Manny takes the other armchair, leaving the couch for the women. Cora notices that the four of them are sitting in the four corners of the living room at equal distances. It makes her uncomfortable, like it's a metaphor for something bigger. She pushes the uncomfortable thought away and turns her attention to the job.

"So, what happened to you guys?" she asks.

Manny looks to Jack, but gets no response. "Near as I can tell," he says uncertainly, "Jack got in a fight with a werewolf in Central Park."

She snorts. "Sounds like a bad movie."

"Right?"

"What were you guys doing there at this time of night, anyway?"

Manny glances at Akiko. She nods. "Meeting with a contact on this vampire case. Turns out the ambassador and I know a few of the same people." He indicates Jack with his head. "This guy turned up on his own. He was pretty pissed that Akiko had run off alone."

Cora smirks. She'd assumed any diplomat would have a stick jammed so far up their ass they couldn't sneeze properly. The fact that this unassuming woman gave Jack the slip is impressive, and she finds herself warming to her. "How'd you manage that?" she asks Akiko.

The ambassador lowers her head humbly at the far end of the couch. "I admit to using one of my meager talents to persuade him to fall asleep."

Jack's eyes widen into dinner plates. There's a sharp, angry tug on the invisible energy that binds Cora to him, flashing violently blue in her mind's eye and making her gasp quietly. The shock isn't just from the intensity of his emotion, but that she can feel it at all. What drove her to push him away yesterday was the idea that their bond might be dangerous if secured too tightly—breaking his heart now to save his life later. Severing the entanglements that had created the bond should cut it, too, right? Apparently not. The magical blue thread, which she could hardly sense an hour ago, flickers to life. Her heart clenches with the fear that all she's accomplished in trying to save him is to hurt them both for no reason. But she breathes through it, reeling in to avoid telegraphing her anxiety. Judging by his reaction to Akiko's confession, he's got enough to worry about.

Jack sits forward in his chair. "You did what?" he growls.

A sigh from the ambassador. She appears genuinely sorry, although for magicking Jack or for what she's about to say, Cora isn't sure. Maybe both. Akiko looks Jack full in the face as she speaks. "I assume you have read your agency's file on me. I also assume you found it largely redacted." Jack nods. "That is because I requested it so, to protect my family and the community I serve. But I see the time for secrets is past." She takes a swallow of her gin and tonic. And then things get strange.

"I am the last descendant of the sun goddess, Amaterasu," she says. "In Japan, her legend is powerful. Here, she is largely forgotten. It has been many years since my ancestor was consumed by Apollo's lust for life, but a devoted sect of believers in my home country has kept her line alive one paragon at a time, throughout the centuries."

To Jack, she says, "I escaped your watch by

using a lesser-known ability. Human circadian rhythms are linked so strongly to the sun that I can put them to sleep by dampening certain waves of light around them. Greater levels of stress or exhaustion increases the effectiveness. Your body needed little encouragement, Agent 97. " She bows her head to him again. "I apologize for the deception. It was necessary that I meet with my contact alone."

Akiko switches her gaze to Manny before Jack can reply. "I am telling you about my heritage so you will understand the importance of my mission here in America. The premise of my visit is false. This is no goodwill tour. I am tracking the contents of the box that is killing your vampires. It contains Amaterasu's mirror."

Jack and Manny continue their stares of confusion, but Cora's encyclopedia of mythology is eager to provide the relevant information.

"The mirror that coaxed the sun out of hiding," she says. "Amaterasu hid in a cave after a fight with her brother, and there was nothing but night. They got her to come out by hanging up a mirror, then throwing a party. When she heard the hubbub, she peeked out, saw her reflection and was so transfixed by how beautiful she was that the other gods could seal the cave, forcing her to rejoin the world." She glances at Akiko, whose delicate eyebrows are arched in amazement. "Is that right?"

"It is, agent. I am impressed with your knowledge of our legends. It is rare to find anyone outside of Japan who knows the story of my ancestor."

Cora dips her head. "Thank you, ma'am. I'm not sure how the mirror is killing vampires, though."

"The mirror contains the power of the sun. Anyone who gazes upon it is overcome with its majesty."

"Wait," Manny cuts in, practically laughing. "Vamps are ashing themselves because they're peeking in the box and blowing themselves up with sunlight?" He smacks his forehead, sloshing a hefty dose of beer onto the carpet. "Oh my god, that is hilarious!" Then he sees how Akiko is looking at him. He wipes off his smile and says, "I mean, it's sad, too. Obviously."

The ambassador slides her eyes from Manny to Jack. She seems determined to re-win his loyalty, for which Cora has a stab of empathy. "The situation runs deeper than a diplomat searching for a stolen artifact. My role in the supernatural community of Japan is policing our vampire community. This may be strange to you, but we have a quiet, disciplined population due to the mirror's presence." For the first time since she's started speaking, she hesitates, and Cora leans in closer at the pause, eager for the rest of the story. "Our vampires worship the mirror for its power to end their unlife, similar to other religions that venerate death. Centuries of blood sacrifice and trials of exposure resulted in the mirror granting protection from the sun's harmful effects to its worshipers. This gives them the ability to walk during the day, but only on our home soil where the mirror's belief lives." She flicks a burning look to Manny, who has the decency to look chastised. "As Agent Forty-Two has noted, the mirror's benefits do not work among non-believers. Here, it is a weapon of destruction for the vampire race. One that is taking many victims while it remains unchecked."

As Akiko goes on to talk about the importance of retrieving the mirror before further damage can be done to the American vampire population, Cora notices a faraway itch at the back of her mind. It's the same one she'd get when she was synthesizing ideas for an essay test at school. Her attention follows the trail from the description of the mirror's powers to the original legend. There are several variations of the story, of course, but the basic principle is the same: Day couldn't be separated from night because it unbalanced nature, throwing the world and other gods out of whack. Amaterasu had to return to keep the fabric of reality from disintegrating.

That's when the penny drops. "Holy shit," she whispers, eyes widening.

The conversation stops dead, and three heads turn towards her.

"Something you want to share with the class, Riley?" Manny quips.

Cora hesitates. If she's connected the dots right, she's not keen to reveal the result in front of the ambassador. Akiko acts like she's onside, but she's still an unknown quantity.

"I don't know if that's a great idea," she says with a significant glance at Manny. "The ambassador's been in SCD custody for less than twelve hours and look what happened. She lied to us about why she's in the country, and she knocked out our best agent so she could have a secret meeting with a vampire. How are we supposed to trust her with sensitive information?" To Akiko, she adds, "No offense."

Akiko bobs her head. "None taken. I would disappointed if you did not doubt my allegiance. These are uncertain times."

You should've brought Diogenes' Lantern with you instead of stashing it in your gun safe, Cora's practical side offers. *You going to mention that?* But she stuffs down the annoyingly right voice. In the hierarchy of Bad Shit, what she's sitting on is more important than her misadventures at headquarters.

But before she assembles a retort, Manny's chiming in. "I'll vouch for her," he offers. "You guys didn't see her with Finn. She's passionate about her people, and back in Japan, she's basically doing the same job as us." Cora and Jack both turn to Akiko, who nods confirmation. "I know I'm not the most seasoned agent," he continues, "but I have a good feeling about her. I mean, why would she turn up with this mission, being who she is, at exactly the right time and place if she wasn't meant to help us?" He gives a lopsided smile. "In my experience, that kind of luck is the right kind."

Much as she likes Manny, to Cora, "a good feeling" is a flimsy defense and no way to conduct world affairs. In this chaos-rich environment, it's monumentally dumb to take anyone's word on anything, much less a stranger's. Then again, the assurance about Akiko's character is coming from Mr. Lucky himself. Maybe it's enough to trust his judgment when it comes to serendipity. Gods know they could use some friends.

She sighs. At the end of this logic train, her opinion isn't important. She's the lowest-ranked agent in the room. Only one person gets to decide how they go forward.

"Boss?" she says, without taking her eyes off Manny.

Jack waits three full seconds before replying in his most official tone. "I don't see that we have another option. Forty-Two, that means you're answerable for the ambassador's loyalty. Do you understand the consequences if you're wrong?"

"Yes, sir. It starts with a cozy suite in the Roosevelt and gets worse from there."

"As long as you're willing to accept that, I'm willing to trust Akiko with whatever information we need to discuss. Please continue, Agent Six."

Cora readjusts herself in the squishy couch, fighting off the jitters by exhaling slowly with her eyes closed. But when she looks up to start talking, she automatically meets Jack's eyes, which makes her mental notecards flip out of her hands. *Dammit*. She'll have to wing it.

"Remember what the Lorekeeper said about Arachne's prophecy?" she begins. "It needs a mirror." When Jack's hard expression doesn't change, she turns to Akiko, who's listening politely but without comprehension. "Madam Ambassador, what would happen if the mirror were used in a ritual involving the Gauntlet?"

The paragon's face blanches. "That cannot happen," she breathes.

"Why not?"

Akiko's first explanation comes out in Japanese. She makes a frustrated gesture and tries again in English. "If the barrier could be disrupted, the mirror would allow the transference of energy by reflecting the worlds into one another. The power of the sun would create a magical bridge since it shines on both Perat and the Otherworld. But the concentration of magic is unbalanced between them. The contents of the magical plane would flow into the mundane world without resistance across the sun bridge."

Cora groans and drops her head into her hands. That's pretty much exactly what she'd thought, but she'd been hoping it wasn't true.

"Whoa," whispers Manny. "Lightspeed osmosis."

Akiko nods wordlessly. Then she looks to Cora with hope high in her eyes. "This is pure theory, of course. Such a thing is not possible."

Cora shakes her head. "I'm sorry, ambassador, but we're a hundred and ten percent sure that's exactly what Eris intends to do." She casts a glance at Manny. "We have to make sure the vampires A, don't find the mirror in the first place, and B, don't hand it over to Queen Chaosbritches if they do."

Manny nods emphatically. "You said it, dude. I better call Ninety-Nine and get some backup approved. We're gonna need more hands."

"No!"

The second Manny's phone is out of his pocket, Cora's bolted across the room and snatched it out of his hand.

"Dude, what gives?" he shouts.

She dances out of reach with the stolen phone. Everyone's staring at her like she's grown a third arm. There were better ways to handle that, she knows, but there's no way she can let him call Patel.

"Cora," Jack says slowly, "what's going on?"

Panic tries to silence her as the pressure ratchets up. She squeezes her eyes shut against it, then lets the story out in a rush. "I accidentally found Diogenes' Lantern while I was on Santa Watch and I tried to take it to One Hundred after what Tithonus said about it being useful for our side but when I got there I had to break into her office because something was fishy and the place had been tossed and there was all this blood in the carpet and I think she's been missing a long time so whoever did it had to have SCD clearance and the power to cover it up so I took the lantern into Ninety-Nine's office and tested it on him and it didn't light up." She stumbles panting to the end of the run-on-sentence and pries open her eyes. "That's why I came to New York," she finishes. "I had to tell you in person."

The adrenaline rushing in her ears is all Cora hears in the silence that follows. Her fingers twist tighter around Manny's phone, the edges biting into her flesh making the wait for a reaction easier to bear.

Akiko is the first to speak. Her voice is low and steady, the way you'd talk to a jumper on a ledge. "I am sorry, Agent Six. I do not understand the significance."

Cora starts to explain, but the words cram up against each other and won't come out. Then, in the gap, Jack clears his throat, pulling the room's attention to him. He's sitting back in his armchair, elbows on the armrests, his slender fingers steepled in front of him as he stares at a blank spot on the wall. The turning gears of his mind are practically visible, his anger drained away after being presented with a truly interesting set of data. Cora can't help thinking how much he resembles a Middle Eastern Sherlock Holmes.

"A Greek myth," he says. "The lantern illuminates in the presence of an honest man, according to its owner. Given that Agent Six is onside, the lantern's lack of a reaction to Patel would mean he's been compromised."

"Ah."

There's another expanse of silence as each person churns through their own thoughts. The quiet after the bomb is dropped. Manny in particular is troubled, Cora notices. His brow is deeply furrowed, his smile erased, his characteristic easy manner turned dark. It's disturbing and dramatic, and it gives her the willies.

Cora switches her focus to Jack, who's staring intently at nothing. "I admit it sounds crazy," she says. "Do you want the crime scene photos I took?"

"That won't be necessary. I'd suspected

something before we went to Faerie. The way the reports and assignments were being handled drew my attention. But the creed case built up too much steam; I wasn't able to investigate." He lowers his eyes from the wall to look directly at Cora. A couple of her organs do backflips. "I'm afraid Tithonus' warnings about Patel were correct."

"Dammit," Cora grumbles. "I thought he was just being a racist old bug." Her shoulders slump and her chest feels like it's caving under the weight of reality. Eris already has one of the relics she needs, and she's incredibly close to having the second. Plus, if she's seduced Agent 99 to the dark side, there's no telling how many other supposed "good guys" are working for her. Or what else they've missed by trusting their boss. "I wish I had more information," she says. "I should've stayed at headquarters, scraped together more intel before I came here. Sorry, guys."

"If I may," Akiko says softly. "I think you behaved admirably. You did not panic. You took charge of the situation, and now you are forming a plan with your allies." She gives Cora a reassuring smile.

Jack nods in agreement. "You wouldn't have been safe in DC," he says. "No matter how good your shields are, he likely knows you've made him. You did the right thing coming here."

The affirmation hits her with a metric ton of relief. She'd expected Jack to crack down, to punish her for hurting him—the way normal people react to rejection. She obviously underestimated him.

Maybe things aren't as ruined as she'd thought.

"So...," Manny says. He pulls on his beer, emptying the second half in one go. "What do you think, Ninety-Seven?"

Jack is quiet for so long Cora wonders if he's ignoring them. She tries to predict what's going through his mind. Could be doesn't believe her. Could be he's trying to come to terms with 99's betrayal. Could be he's so many moves ahead she can't imagine. Could be a lot of things with him.

Another few seconds pass, then, with all seriousness, he says, "I think we're in deep shit."

Manny bursts out laughing. It's so genuine after the dark cloud that descended on him earlier that Cora can't help laughing, too. The ambassador even quirks a smile. The hard edges that had formed between the four of them as they swapped information softens. The catharsis is tangible, and Cora senses Jack's energy shift along their bond, despite its weakness. He couldn't have done a better job of reuniting them if he'd given a rousing speech about duty, humanity, and freedom. Sometimes, one well-placed cuss word is all you need.

When the giggles die away, Cora wipes tears from her cheeks and says, "Seriously, though, do you have a plan? Everything I came up with sucked and didn't account for Manny's exploding vampires being the lynchpin of Eris' bonkers plan."

Jack unfolds from the armchair and starts pacing. "Forty-Two, when and where is the next Dracula Council?"

Cora snorts, waving a hand for a time-out. "Wait, wait. The what now?"

"The Dracula Council," Jack repeats dismissively, eyes on Manny.

But Cora can't let it go. "Like, 'I vant to suck your blood' Dracula?" she snickers. "Do they all wear capes and have an oddly receding hairline?"

"It is the formal title for the clan heads of New York City," Akiko supplies, casting a cautious glance at Jack. "A romantic elder in the early days of occupation became obsessed with Mr. Stoker's character. He began to insist that the Count was the ideal evolution of their race and began using the name as his title. He went so far as to style his hair and dress according to the film portrayal in order to more fully embody his hero. To the embarrassment of many, the title took hold, held up by humanity's love for the character. The classical appearance is no longer maintained in the modern era, though the honorific remains."

"Dang," Cora laughs after a moment. "Vamps are weird."

Jack ignores her snickering and turns to Manny. "Well?"

The younger agent turns to Cora, who tosses his phone back to him with an embarrassed smile, then he hurriedly checks his calendar. "The next Council is tomorrow." He pulls a face. "At the Met."

To Akiko, Jack says, "Isn't the presentation gala tomorrow night?" She nods. "That can't be a coincidence. If you both had contact with the same Founder for a meeting, they knew the ambassador was coming. And if they know this relic was giving Japanese vampires immunity to the sun, Kincaid is frothing at the mouth to get his hands on it." He strides up and down the room, deep in thought. When he finally stops moving, he simply says, "We're going."

The other two nod, but Cora isn't following. "Going where? For what?"

"If the Draculas are meeting at the Met the same night as Akiko is presenting the Japanese art collection, we're going to be there, too. All of us."

Cora scoffs. "You're kidding, right? We're going to prom?" But Jack's face doesn't twitch. "Oh, god, you're serious. What the hell am I going to wear? I forgot to pack a change of underwear, I left DC so fast."

Akiko dips her head respectfully. "I believe I may have a gown serviceable for you, Agent Six."

It's nice of her, but Cora doesn't relent. The idea of going to a fancy party in a tight skirt is damn near offensive when there's vampire asses to be kicked. She grabs the next available straw. "Where am I going to sleep tonight, anyway?"

"If you do not mind the company, I would be honored to share my bed with you."

Cora shoots daggers at Manny, who's doing his best not to let his sniggering become audible. Turning to Akiko, she says, "Thank you, ambassador. I'll take the dress, but I think I can find a less suggestive place to sleep. There's got to be at least one room a government agent can commandeer in this place."

Jack nods. "Everything's in order, then. We'll reconvene here tomorrow at seventeen-hundred to check in and head to the Met together for initial security checks. Agents, I suggest you make arrangements and get some sleep. We'll be in for an interesting evening."

Effectively dismissed, the four of them stand, stretching their tired limbs. Akiko retreats to the bedroom, and Manny steps into the kitchen to start calling formalwear rental places, leaving Jack and Cora alone in the living room.

Cora pulls out her phone and makes for the hall, about to follow Manny's example, but Jack puts a hand on her wrist before she can dial. A minute blue spark leaps from her skin. She tenses for an uncomfortable conversation, but the expression on his face is one of curiosity, not antagonism.

"How did you get in here?" he asks.

Cora laughs, part relief, part embarrassment. She gently removes herself from his grasp and dials the hotel concierge, turning the doorknob with one hand and putting the phone to her ear with the other. With a mischievous smile, she says, "I told them I was your wife."

The sputtering noise he makes as she steps into the hallway is deeply satisfying. Sofi would be proud.

THIRTEEN

"Wow. Just wow."

It's been less than twenty-four hours since Manny last set foot in the stately marble hall of the Met's sculpture garden, but now, from his post at an anonymous section of wall, he hardly recognizes the place. Decorators have transformed the venue with all the trappings of Christmas, including real holly garland and twinkling white lights, complicated snowflakes glittering from the ceiling, and Johnny Mathis crooning on the stereo. Tables covered with red and green velvet groan under swathes of holiday food laden with sugar, salt, and delicious fat. In the center, New York's upper crust mingles in opulent knots of finery around the precious Japanese artifacts they've come to admire, intermittently breaking away to dance to slow carols, chat in loud whispers, and drink too much spiked eggnog. The entire scene brings a happy tear to Manny's eye. It's like watching a bizarre, beautiful play. Having spent every Christmas at the YMCA since he left home, and a strict rule of "family only" before that, he's never seen this kind of holiday pageantry.

A tug at his elbow switches his attention from the crowd to his "date." Manny had assumed he and Cora would be working the room separately while 97 watched the ambassador, but Jack said they'd be less conspicuous if they paired up. The stealth approach.

It's half working. While Manny's flying under the radar—every man in the room is wearing practically identical tuxedos—several people have openly pointed at Cora. The dress Akiko loaned her is a strapless, metallic green number with a silver jacket to cover her shoulders and sidearm. Her copper hair is pinned back loosely, and a dangling pair of emerald earrings draws attention to her unusual grey eyes. In a sea of blondes in black dresses, she stands out like a piece of art even in this museum. Of course she's been complaining swearily about the attention, but Manny noticed her smirk at Jack fumbling his coffee when she came out dressed like that.

"Dude, check this out," he says to her, making an emphatic gesture at their surroundings. "I seriously can't get over it," Then, much quieter, he says, "Wow."

"You keep saying that," Cora replies around a mouthful of deviled egg. "You're drawing attention to yourself." While one of her hands is observing proper high society decorum by staying on her escort's arm, the other is stealthily pilfering hors d'oeuvres from a handy catering table.

Manny chuckles. "I'll stop when it's not impressive anymore. Besides, they're all too busy pretending they're having fun to notice a couple of unsophisticated grunts. Which is us, by the way."

She nods and plucks a shiny red thing off the table, and pops it in her mouth, eyes thoughtfully scanning the room as she chews. The registry claims a hundred and fifty people in attendance, although it feels like more. Manny suspects there are a few uninvited guests.

"Anything on the radar?" he asks.

"Nothing nearby except us and a handful of vamps, but that's about what we expected. Do you think anything'll happen tonight?" she says. "Anything bad, I mean."

Manny shrugs. "Doubt it. There's security all over the building, plus the three of us. Somebody'd have to be really stupid to try anything."

She nods again and reaches over a plate of white fudge to a savory dish. "It'd sort of be a shame, though, us being here without any action." She selects a skewer from the tray and offers it to him with a smile. "We could get lucky."

The innuendo hangs in the air, buoyed by the melody of "Baby, It's Cold Outside." Cora's eyes go wide, but Manny laughs it off. He'd have to be blind and deaf to miss the vibes passing between her and Jack; whatever weird romantic crap they're dealing with, he's happy to watch from the sidelines. He holds up the blob on a stick she's given him and examines it. While he considers himself a foodie, the socialite palette is unfamiliar to him. Everything's too petite and fancy and expensive for his tastes. Give him a giant, stale bun full of mystery meat from a street cart any day.

"What is it?" he asks.

"No idea, but it's delicious." She pops another one in her mouth. "Bacon and some kind of cheese."

"It's smoked Gouda and applewood bacon wrapped in phyllo and sprinkled with pink sea salt. Considered quite good, if you enjoy cow lactation and shaved pig."

Both agents look up to see a pale bald man walking towards them. Manny smiles broadly as he recognizes Finn. He almost didn't without the security guard uniform; the tailored navy blue suit and faint sparkle to his skin enhance his angular features, making him look like an haute-couture model. Cora releases Manny's arm as he extends a hand to the vampire. They shake, but Finn's eyes aren't on him.

"Are you going to introduce me to your lovely companion, Forty-Two?" he says with a salacious grin.

There's something about the way he says it that gives Manny the creeps, but he makes the introduction anyway. "Agent Six, this is Finnegan Kincaid of the Founder clan," he says, waving the bacon ball casually but keeping his voice low to avoid mundanes eavesdropping. "My favorite vampire. He's the one who gave us the info about what the Dracs are up to."

Cora wipes her greasy fingers on a napkin and extends a hand to Finn. Instead of shaking, though, he presses his lips delicately to the back of it. Cora half-laughs with an nervous smile. They lock eyes for a moment, and her ears turn pink.

Warning bells to go off in Manny's head. He glances sharply over to where 97 stands behind the ambassador as she receives guests at the center of the room. Jack's staring right at them. Even from this distance, Manny can read the senior agent's displeasure. Not good. He looks back to the flirtation happening in front of him and suddenly wants to intervene. *So this is what it's like to want to beat up a guy for hitting on your sister*, he thinks.

There's a break in the music as the tracks change, and he does the first thing that comes to mind. "Would you do me the honor, Agent Six?" Manny says, smoothly taking possession of the hand Finn's caressing.

The vampire blinks and Cora starts to protest, but he doesn't wait for either of them to refuse. He gently but insistently leads her towards the dance floor at the center of the room as Frank Sinatra starts singing "The Christmas Waltz." Other couples filter from the sidelines to join them, emboldened by their example, effectively separating the predator from his prey. As the dancers close around them, Manny sees Finn grin, then bow gracefully to him before dissolving into the crowd.

An awkward second follows as Manny finds his

feet in the tempo of the song. He's a terrible dancer, but this can't be as bad as the witches' ball two years ago. He counts his blessings that Cora plays along, putting one hand on his shoulder and letting him take the other. Together, they bob across the floor in a tight three-count square the way he learned in grade school.

But Cora isn't content to dance in silence. "What the hell was that about?" she demands through a fake smile.

"Would you rather have Jack come over and tell Finn what's up?"

She blushes purple at her ears. "How did you know about that?"

"I didn't know you were trying to hide it." She groans quietly. "Anyway," he continues, "you don't want to get involved with that. Finn's quite a ladykiller."

"Figuratively speaking, of course."

Manny lifts an eyebrow.

"Oh." She lets a few measures pass, then says, "Can we talk about something besides my love life, please?"

He chuckles. "Sure," he says. He extends an arm to let her roll out and back in. When she's tucked back into place, he says, "Have you seen the Draculas?"

Cora's eyes light up. "They're here? All of them?"

He nods. "Not a big deal you didn't notice. The text descriptions don't do the real-life versions justice, and they mute their auras in public, so I'd bet your radar marks them as regular vamps. See if you can pick them out."

Her attention darts around the busy hall, and Manny lets her fish for a minute before pointing out the vampire elders that have come to pay their respects to Akiko. First, he spins to point her towards the dessert table and drops to a conspiratorially low voice. "The tall black guy in the pinstripe suit and glasses stealing the last macron off the table? That's William Ellison. He's the head of the Aristocrats. Cultured and monied, if a bit prissy." Another box-step turn. "The white lady in the black corset and blue hair staring at her smartphone is Lauren Not, head of the Techs. They're the youngest clan but rising fast."

Cora chimes in after another turn. "And the pile of black robes and a mask that looks like a preschooler made it—the one talking to Jack. That's the Inconnu, right? The Hermit elder that does the weird experiments?"

Manny grins. "Good study skills, Riley. Yeah, that's him." He squints around the room, searching for the remaining two Draculas. "You'd think Nexus would be easier to spot with those red and green glasses."

As they whirl around for another one-two-three set, though, Cora stiffens in his arms and tears herself away before Manny has time to react.

"Gun!" she shouts, her skirt ripping up the back as she runs.

The crowd's reaction is less than ideal—no one notices. The guests keep milling about with their drinks in hand, laughing and talking, completely oblivious to the petite redhead barreling through their ranks until it's too late. She elbows through two knots of bystanders before taking a flying leap at a dark-haired guy twice her size, hitting him at the knees. He goes down, and a chromed handgun skitters out of his fist across the marble tile floor, stopping inches from the Japanese ambassador's feet.

That's when the guests start screaming.

Manny over his shoulder, but Finn's gone, so he bolts out into the crowd alone. He raises his badge and starts ushering people to the nearest exits, encouraging them to walk instead of run, to stay calm—all the crowd-management techniques he knows. But they're taking his help the same as they took Cora's warning, which is to say not at all. A hundred and fifty people, mundanes and supernaturals alike, stream to the front door, jamming themselves together in their haste to get out. The hired security untangles them as quickly as they can, ushering a few to the side for statements. By the time Manny gets a bead on Cora again, they're all gone.

The entire thing takes less than five minutes.

Manny jogs to where Cora is sitting on the shooter's back. He's a gorilla of a man, wearing the traditional black duster and newsboy hat of the Bruiser clan. Cora's yelling his Miranda rights at him and trying to hold him down, but he's slowly pulling himself across the floor to get at his weapon.

"I hope you're not thinking about doing anything

stupid," Manny says. The Bruiser's face is priceless as the agent scoops up the gun using his unraveled bow tie. There won't be any prints—vampires don't leave any—but it's better that Manny's aren't on there. He swaps his sidearm into the back of his tuxedo pants and tucks the confiscated weapon into the holster. Losing his gun deflates the would-be assassin; he stops squirming.

Cora slaps cuffs on the vampire and stands up, straightening her ruined dress with strands of copper hair falling in her face. She's grinning. But then she looks around the empty room and her face falls.

"Where's Jack?" she asks.

In the kerfuffle, Manny hadn't given a single thought to his boss or the ambassador; he'd been too focused on directing the crowd to safety. No blood or anything on the ground, though. They must've gotten away clean. At least, he hopes so.

"I'd bet money he's spirited Akiko away to a predetermined safe house or some other cool spy thing," he says.

The crease in Cora's forehead smoothes out and she nods. Turning her attention to the Bruiser laying face-down on the floor, she says to Manny, "Would you believe this is the second guy I've had to tackle in two days?"

"Sure, why not?"

"Would you believe the first one was a mall Santa?"

Manny snorts. "I would. My first takedown was a Santa, too. It's sort of a rite of passage in the SCD."

He points at the mook on the ground. "Let's get him moving. The Dracula Council can wait." There's a dangerous edge to his voice as he adds, "I've got some serious questions for this guy."

Cora nods in agreement, and the two of them help the hefty vampire to his feet, but he's not the grateful type. He refuses to look at either of them, glaring furiously into the distance. With Manny on one side and Cora on the other, they march him towards the back door.

They're stepping out of the sunken part of the sculpture garden when the vampire pulls up short. Manny's about to berate him for not cooperating, but Cora speaks up before he does.

"Oh, hey, Finn! You're just in time. We caught this guy trying to whack the Japanese ambassador." She nods her head at the shooter. "Do you know him?"

The Founder approaches, balefire lighting up his blue eyes. "What are you doing here, Vinnie? Only clan elders were invited tonight."

Vinnie sneers. "You know why."

Before either agent can blink, Finn's fist smashes into the front of the Bruiser's face. The crack of bones breaking echoes morbidly through the tiled room. Manny redoubles his grip on Vinnie's massive arm to hold him back, but there's no retaliation. He hangs his head silently, black ichor dripping from his nose onto the pure white floor.

"Jesus, Finn, what the fuck?" Cora hisses.

The Founder peers imperiously at the chastised Bruiser. "We have to take him to the Council. The elders will decide the punishment for his transgressions."

"Uh, no?" says Manny.

Finn replies with an icy stare that makes Manny flinch. If he didn't know better, he'd swear the guy tried to tap his mind using blood magic. But that can't be right—Finn's never done that to him before. It's far more likely that he's telegraphing his anger at the assassin's balls-out treachery, which Manny definitely empathizes with.

"The Council's not exactly known for its reasonableness, Finn," he reminds him. "Besides, this is a criminal matter. I get that he's a vampire and broke your laws, but it happened in public and he was apprehended by agents. Let us do our job."

Finn takes a single step forward. Neither Manny nor Cora move. There's a drawn-out, uncertain moment, then the vampire's eyes narrow, and he spreads his hands in the air. "I offer a compromise," he says. "Bring him to the Council for judgment, and I'll make sure that whatever his punishment is, he'll meet the demands of your agency's justice first."

It's Manny's turn to narrow his eyes. He's known Finn for a while now, and he's proved himself to be a loyal informant. His motives are right out there on the table—a rare thing in a vampire and the quality Manny appreciates most in him. But a nagging thought is trying to decide between trust where it's been earned and paranoia.

As with most things in Manny's life, however, the positive outweighs the negative. *You're getting way too caught up in this conspiracy thing, dude,* he thinks. *Take your friends where you can get them.*

"You got yourself a deal," he says to Finn. He's rewarded with a regal smile that makes the glitter in the vampire's skin twinkle under the museum lights.

To Cora, Manny says, "You down with that, Six?" She nods. "You do know this means we're going into the Dracula meeting without Jack, right?" Her eyes widen. "And that we're responsible for the interrogation and diplomacy he was going to handle."

He feels like a heel as color drains from her cheeks, but she doesn't waver. "Yeah, let's do it." She squares her shoulders and turns to Finn. "Lead the way, Mr. Kincaid."

The Founder nods and takes Vinnie's arm. Manny lets the prisoner go with minor protest. He knows Finn's better equipped to handle the Bruiser if he decides to be dumber than he's already been tonight, but it irks him that the agents aren't in control. The quicker they get done with this formality, the better.

Manny lets himself drop behind as they follow Finn to the council chamber. Pulling out his phone, he fires off a text to Jack: *Caught shooter. Finn assisting. Doing Drac Council w/ Cora. If haven't reported by midnight, send help.*

He ends the text with a smiley face, but as he pushes "send," he's not convinced help won't be necessary. There's something off about this entire night. Then again, maybe the Council will go great and they'll get this jackass to justice and locate Amaterasu's mirror before Jack comes out of the safe house.

Manny grins to himself as he jogs to catch up with Cora, the sense of dread in his chest dissolving to a familiar lightness. Hope really does spring eternal. And he hopes his luck will hold out tonight.

FOURTEEN

The Dracula Council is not what Cora wanted it to be. She'd expected pomp and circumstance, low lighting and flashing eyes, tangible power crackling in the air. Or at least horribly clichéd red capes and widow's peaks. After Manny explained the *éclat mort* situation on the way to the Met, she'd even have accepted a row of glittery Edward doppelgängers. Instead, it's five rather normal-looking people in office chairs arranged down one side of a conference table talking quietly amongst themselves. All that makes the Council stand out from an executive board meeting is the heavy-duty bodyguard standing behind each of the elders. Hardly the summit of dark, bloody monsters it was built it up to be.

No introductions are offered as Cora, Manny, and the sulking Vinnie are ushered into the bland room in the back of the Met. Fortunately, Cora recognizes all but two of the Draculas, thanks to

Manny's guidance on the dance floor. At the far right of the conference table sits the Inconnu. He appears to be speaking to Lauren Not sitting beside him, but the Tech is glued to her phone. At the far left end is William Ellison, the Aristocrat macron stealer. He's gesticulating in his conversation with a short Latino wearing a T-shirt under his suit jacket who has a chromed gun casually out in front of him. Cora marks him as the Bruiser leader, Daniel Nexus—a shit disturber, but fairly trustworthy in the SCD books.

That means the dark-haired man in the center of the table must be Seanan Kincaid, head of the Founder clan and oldest recorded vampire in America. Despite his chic modern clothes that would fit in anywhere, there's a sense of otherness about him. Like he doesn't fit into the background. Where his colleagues are chatting and lively, he's not speaking to anyone. His eyes are closed, his head slightly bowed, his hands folded serenely at the table's edge as if he's praying. It makes Cora want to scan him with her supernatural radar to see what it would pick up, but she decides against it. There's no telling what reaction she'll get from a room full of ultra-powerful vampires if they sense they're being magically groped.

Finn pulls the door shut as the agents and their captive move to stand front of the conference table. He didn't knock, just walked right in. The elders continue their conversation without acknowledging them—until the door clicks shut. Then Kincaid's eyes snap open and everyone else falls silent.

Ten sets of vampire eyes stare at the new arrivals, giving Cora wild goosebumps. It feels like she's on trial or a gazelle paraded in front of a pride of lions. It's easy to be lulled into treating vampires like normal people, particularly given this banal setting, but their true nature, hidden close under the civilized surface, is decidedly cruel and violent. Although she'd insisted on taking point with the Council at first, Cora's grateful let Manny pull rank; it's going to take every scrap of his supernatural luck to persuade this crowd to his side.

Or will it?

Now that she's closer, Cora notices a striking detail she couldn't see from the doorway, and her heart leaps with excitement. She elbows Manny sharply and indicates Kincaid with a faint nod: The Founder elder's pallid skin is covered in silver glitter. Manny breaks into a wide grin that's quickly covered over, and Cora has to resist the urge to celebrate right there. If Kincaid's caught the French Vampire Disease, the chances that he's lost his ruthless edge are high. The mirror is as good as theirs.

Finn doesn't seem to notice the exchange as he moves in front of the party and addresses the assembled elders. "Honored Draculas," he begins, "I apologize for the abruptness of my arrival, but a matter of justice has arisen during the course of the celebrations, and I fear it cannot wait." He takes a step to the side that exposes Manny, who's holding Vinnie's elbow. "This vampire was caught by federal agents in an attempt to assassinate the Japanese ambassador being honored here tonight." Cora expects worried murmuring to follow the pronouncement, but the council stays silent. She's not sure any of them blink. If vampires even do that. Finn is unconcerned by the lack of response, however, and continues. "Agent Forty-Two and I have come to an agreement: This Bruiser will be sentenced by you, according to our laws, then transported to the agency's care for criminal proceedings. He will suffer mortal justice first, then be returned to us to fulfill the terms of our people's punishment." He sweeps his gaze from one end of the table to the other. "What say you, revered elders?"

Surreptitious glances are exchanged between the Draculas. One by one they nod to Kincaid. The Founder looks to Finn, his second in command and child, to hear Manny tell it, and waves him away. The gesture is overtly rude, a flick of annoyance, but Finn complies without objection. He gives a curt bow and removes himself from the front of the room, sliding towards the door and out of the way. Cora has a stab of sympathy for him; while she's not well-versed in the rules of vampire society, it's obvious he's paying for his alliance with the SCD.

Kincaid motions for Vinnie to be brought forward. Manny steps into the gap left by Finn, moving the captured vampire up with him. The Bruiser leader is scowling heavily, his fingers tracing the trigger on his gun, but he doesn't say anything. Everyone waits for the Founders' Dracula. Cora notes the hesitation with interest.

The Council is supposed to be egalitarian, but if it's Kincaid that put out the call for the mirror and Kincaid to whom everyone's looking for leadership, there must be a change in the ranks the agency hasn't gotten wind of yet. This does nothing to allay Cora's sense of being ignorant prey.

Solemnly, the elder Founder stands and leans forward with his fingertips pressed to the table. Where Finn's blue eyes are often alight with his emotions, his sire's are carefully neutral, revealing nothing. Practice over centuries, Cora imagines. Handy.

When Kincaid finally speaks, it's with a hint of old Irish that plucks at Cora's genes. Whether it reminds her of her father's soft accent, her Fae grandmother's strong voice, or simply a faraway country she's never visited, she isn't sure, but she finds herself leaning forward, as if being physically closer to his words can disclose a new secret. As if she hasn't had enough of those lately.

"Bruiser, stand before me," he commands.

Manny releases Vinnie's arm, and the mook steps towards the table with a growl. But when he turns to Kincaid, the defiance vanishes; he hangs his head, refusing to meet the elder's imperious glare.

"Look at me, Vincent."

The Bruiser raises his head.

"Did you attempt to kill Minamoto Akiko?"

Nod.

"Did you succeed?"

Shake.

"Why did you fail?"

"That woman saw me," Vinnie says, indicating Cora with a jerk of his head.

Kincaid breaks his gaze from locking down the Bruiser to find Cora. There's a peculiar tingle along her skin as his attention falls on her. She inhales deeply and draws herself up, refusing to be cowed by the intensity of his stare. In the silent moment that follows, Cora finds herself noticing how beautiful he is. Not merely handsome or anything as crass as sexy—like, aesthetically perfect. The arch of his eyebrows, the cut of his cheekbones, the line of his chest. She wonders what subsect of belief created him. What he looked like when he was human. Who he was then. Who he is now.

Don't fall for it, whispers a quiet voice inside. *It's blood magic. He's trying to enthrall you.*

Cora responds by throwing up her mental shields, ashamed she hadn't done it before. The elder narrows his eyes as the connection breaks, as if remeasuring her character, then swings back to Vinnie. Cora breathes a grateful sigh as an invisible weight slides off her. She tries not to think about how vulnerable she was just then and instead considers the tenor of the connection. Manny said *éclat*'s later stages soften the host's mind with sensuality; she can't think of a better way to describe what she shook off. Wait until the others hear about this.

Vinnie doesn't have any such defense mechanism. He's cowering under the Founder's glare, shoulders as hunched as his cuffed hands allow, his head bowed.

Kincaid draws himself up, and while he isn't much taller than Cora, his presence is huge as he pronounces the Bruiser's judgment. "Vincent Lazzara, you have shamed the Council and your people. For this, our laws condemn you to ash by starvation." He pauses dramatically to allow Vinnie a choked sob as punctuation. "Yet," Kincaid continues, "because I am merciful, I offer you a chance to redeem yourself through an act of great service. Do you accept? Or will you choose an agonizing, slow death for your transgressions?"

It takes the Bruiser a minute to compose himself enough to speak. It's sort of embarrassing to watch, Cora thinks. Aren't these guys supposed to be the asskicking vampires? Then again, he's getting the death penalty. She can't say she wouldn't be a blubbering mess in his shoes, either.

"I will serve," Vinnie says.

It is not a happy answer, and it makes Cora nervous. She scans the room, but the other Draculas are as unreadable as Kincaid. Manny's lost, too, and twice as concerned. And Finn....

Where did he go?

Cora's brow furrows as she notes she's lost track of their vampire ally. It's doubly unsettling because knowing everyone's location was a talent she counted as her superpower before she had a real one; whenever she went out, she always knew where each of her friends were. That Finn slipped away puts a knot in her gut.

That knot tightens to the breaking point when

she turns to find him standing at the door, hand on the deadbolt. A wicked grin curls one side of his mouth as he turns the lock with a decisive click.

Trapped.

"Forty-Two...," she starts.

But before she can back away from Finn, he's on her, gripping both her wrists in one vise-like hand and holding her in place. She gasps at his clammy touch and twists to get away, but she's no match for his supernatural strength. Another vampire, the Tech bodyguard, is on Manny faster than her eyes can track, locking his arms behind his back. But he doesn't resist. Cora wonders if he suspected foul play before she did.

"Don't struggle," Finn purrs in her ear. "I'll break every bone in your body before you can get away."

"Fuck you, traitor," she spits back. But she stops fighting. Assuming she could get away, it's clear he'll kill her with zero compunction. It's even more clear that he was never on their side to begin with. If they get out of this, she's going to give Manny a serious talking-to about how being too relaxed and groovy will get you killed. Although he's getting a big taste of it right now.

Finn laughs at Cora's anger and drags her to the front to stand beside Manny. The elder Kincaid is openly grinning now, triumphant over the two agents.

"What the hell, dude?" Manny spits.

"You're too trusting, Forty-Two." He sniffs proudly. "How does it feel to know that the killer you were tracking was the man helping you the entire time?"

Manny mouth falls open. "You ashed that last vamp?" His brow furrows with confusion. "But there wasn't any evidence of murder on the body. That means...." His eyes widen. "You have the mirror."

Finn's face is alight with pride, but he's cut off by the Aristocrat Dracula before he can brag further. Ellison coughs genteelly and all heads turn to him. "Allegedly," he says. "My clan has also secured a potential candidate. That is the purpose of tonight's meeting: to ascertain the authenticity of each mirror claimed to be the one we seek."

Nexus rolls his eyes behind red-and-green tinted sunglasses. "Oh, come on, Ellison." He picks up the gun in front of him and waves it casually at Finn. Cora flinches, but no one else does. Apparently this is normal. "This fucker tested it on Sian already. We know the one Kincaid has is real. You just want to wave your dick around in front of the Hermits for brownie points."

The Aristocrat is unruffled. "We cannot simply take his word. If this artifact is as powerful as the legends claim, it is worth testing again, here, for all to see and acknowledge."

Without prompting, every set of eyes—vampire and mortal—slides to the far end of the table where the black-robed mountain sits. The Inconnu's expression is unreadable behind the crude mask he wears to cover what's rumored to be a hideously deformed face. He nods once. Agreement given, attention returns to the captives at the front of the room.

"And now, agents," Kincaid says with relish, "you will bear witness to the turning point of the vampire race. The moment we transcend the mire of human belief and become untouchable in our power." He snaps his fingers, and two wooden boxes are set on the long table in front of him. "Vincent. Come forward," he says.

With growing horror, Cora understands what Vinnie's great act of redemptive service is going to be. And even if he is an undead criminal, he doesn't deserve this.

"Wait!" she calls out.

Vinnie stops in his tracks. Kincaid turns to her with both eyebrows raised. She's not sure if it's disbelief, a question, or if he's contemplating how best to kill her for interrupting, but she plows ahead.

"This is insane. Yeah, he tried to kill the ambassador, but he didn't. She's safe. I know your justice is different than mortal justice, but there's no reason to run mirror experiments on this guy. He's just an idiot who did something stupid. Nobody got hurt, and nobody has to."

The words drop into the thick carpet. For all the reaction they get, she may as well have never said them.

And then Kincaid starts to laugh. It's a sweet sound on the surface, but there are ugly undertones that grate against Cora's mind. One by one, the other Draculas join in. Then the bodyguards. Soon, every vampire in the room is laughing—except

Vinnie. Cora and Manny exchange a baffled look and wait for the mirth to subside. Cora's having flashbacks to standing in front of Mab and her Faerie court; bad guys laughing at your attempts at morality is not a good sign.

When the laughter dies away, the Founder's Dracula turns to Cora and says, "Foolish girl. You assume his punishment is a result of his intention." He leans closer to her over the table as if telling a precious secret. "He will be punished because he failed."

Cora's mouth drops open. "You sent him to kill her?"

Kincaid straightens. "His instructions were to retrieve the ambassador and present her to the council. I believe Dracula Nexus," he casts a sidelong glance at the Bruiser elder, "added the gun."

"Hey, I told him to bring her back alive," Nexus says. "She's no good to us dead."

"Why?" demands Manny from beside Cora. She glances at over to see his jaw flexing under his calm exterior. "What good is she to you?"

This only amuses Kincaid more. He's really enjoying himself. "Our research indicates that by washing Amaterasu's mirror in the blood of her descendants, it can be purged of the curse it carries when away from its homeland. Once cleansed, we will receive the same blessing as our Japanese brethren and break the shackles of our existence. We will walk in the sunlight once more, no longer be afflicted by the capricious whims of humanity.

All curses will be lifted." He closes his eyes in rapturous thought. "And when we are free, the Lady Eris will use the mirror to open the way for the lost to be reclaimed. The worlds will be made whole." He sighs lightly, then opens his eyes with a smirk. "You are too late to stop it."

Questions zoom through Cora's mind faster than she can process them. How did they find out about Akiko? Where did they learn about the mirror's powers? Is Agent 99 involved? Too many layers, too little time. Nothing she can say in this moment is going to change Vinnie's fate. Or hers and Manny's.

Kincaid raises a hand, and two bodyguards bring the boxes around the table and hold them in front of Vinnie, whose whining has dried up. "We will test Ellison's candidate first," the elder Founder says.

The Aristocrat underling steps forward. As one, the vampires in the room close their eyes—except Vinnie. He raises his chin in ready defiance as the box lid is lifted, revealing a large mirror in an ornate gold frame, the kind you'd see in your grandmother's bedroom. Vinnie looks into the open box. Several seconds pass.

Nothing happens.

Cora lets out her held breath, and the surrounding vampires take it to mean the coast is clear. Everyone opens their eyes. Kincaid is holding back a smug grin while Ellison shakes his head in disappointment. The Aristocrat bodyguard retreats to his master with their useless crate in hand, and the Founder bodyguard steps in front of Vinnie who's looking decidedly less confident.

"Now we will test my candidate," Kincaid says.

Again, every vampire closes their eyes. Cora finds herself leaning forward in morbid fascination as the lid of the box is lifted. If this is the real thing, what will happen? If it's not, what then?

The contents of this box are more sedate. Inside is a hand mirror with a dark, polished wood frame perched on a green silk pillow. Vinnie lowers his eyes to gaze at his reflection. How long has it been since he's seen his own face? Cora wonders. For a brief moment, the Bruiser smiles.

And then he bursts into flame.

Cora yips with surprise, she was so focused on the object. She automatically tries to cover her mouth, but she's held fast by Finn's powerful grip. It twists her wrist hard and forces her back against him to alleviate the pressure. By the time she's recovered, the fire is out and all that remains of Vincent Lazzara, enforcer of Clan Bruiser, is a tidy pile of ashes no more than a foot wide.

Two seconds pass before the remaining vampires open their eyes. Kincaid's grin is wide and wicked, reminding Cora of the horrible curly smile on the Grinch's face when he decides to steal Christmas. The Founder's eyes shine with an interior light that can only be magical. He motions for the pile to be swept up; the Hermit bodyguard does so quickly, tucking the remains into a plastic bag that she hands off to the Inconnu.

Cora peeks at Manny to see her horror replicated in his face. There's sadness there, too. He must be heartbroken to have this happen after years of working in the vampire community, to be turned on so easily and viciously.

The Draculas don't notice the agents' discomfort, however. They're too busy congratulating Kincaid in their civilly backbiting way. Handshakes and salutes are given in equal measure with contempt and snark. Par for the vampire course, apparently. Eventually, the commotion dies down, and the elders remember they have prisoners. They sit back in their chairs and wait for Kincaid to speak again. When he does, it makes Cora want to retch.

"Agents, I thank you for your assistance. Your apprehension of the unworthy Bruiser provided the perfect opportunity to authenticate our victorious acquisition." He lifts his chin. "I am afraid, however, that despite your great service to us, I cannot allow you to go free. Finnegan will escort you to my haven, where you will await the arrival of the ambassador and Agent 97." His eyes find Cora's, and although he's speaking to both agents, it's drilling directly into her head. "Until they see fit to join us, you will be my honored guests. After, we will share the glorious fruits of the paragon's sacrifice with the world—and together prepare for Lady Eris' arrival."

FIFTEEN

The noise and vibration of the phone in Jack's pocket are a thousand miles away as he runs, piloted years of field experience. Fortunately, Akiko is keeping up with his lengthy strides, so they're not slowed as they race to the parking lot behind the Met. There's no indication of pursuit, but he's not taking any chances. He recognized the would-be assassin from an old ABP as a low-level Bruiser, but after greeting the entire Dracula Council at the soiree, the underling set off no red flags. He saw the gun too late. And if he failed to notice that key detail, there could be a dozen other signs of sabotage he missed. He needs to make sure the ambassador is truly safe before stopping to assess the situation.

Akiko doesn't argue as he barks instructions. Turn here, keep your head down, get in the car. She obeys but pauses for a moment before she opens the passenger side door of the black SUV. Jack's about to reprimand her, but the flare of sunlight that erupts around her vaporizes the words in his mouth. He's quick to close his eyes, preventing himself from being blinded, cluing in to her intention a split second beforehand: She's dazzling onlookers from seeing their plates and escape route. He hears the car door slam, then he throws himself into the driver's seat, cranking the ignition with one hand and dragging on his seatbelt with the other.

It's a furious ten minute drive to the nearest SCD safe house. There used to be one in the Met itself, but half their asset protection system shut down a year ago. Jack can't bring himself to question if it was from budget cuts as Agent 99 had claimed or if it was an early move in whatever scheme he's concocting with Eris.

When they arrive, the Japanese ambassador is not pleased with his choice of location, but she keeps silent, frowning as Jack ushers her through a side entrance to Grand Central Station. They hurriedly step across the bustling mosaic tile floor to one of the dozen identical wings leading to the trains. The buttery glow of the bakery washes over them as they push through the glass double doors, and a fresh-faced teen boy greets them from behind the brass counter.

"Hello, how can I—"

"I need to inspect your inventory," Jack demands.

The reaction he gets in return for the code phrase is skeptical at best. Reasonable, considering the kid is faced with a frenetic Middle Eastern man in a tuxedo accompanied by an Asian woman whose makeup is sweating off. But then an older woman, heavyset with short grey hair, shoos the boy away. She nods at Jack and opens the break door next to the counter. He pushes past her, Akiko trailing close behind, and makes his way to the storage room.

It's not until the thick metal door is securely fastened behind them and the entire area has been given a thorough examination that he stops to rest. With closed eyes, he puts his back to a concrete wall, letting the cool stone leech the excess adrenaline out through his skin and retune his mind. It's been years since he's faced a moment like that as himself and not as Agent 97; he's not sure how he fared.

Do not worry, precious warrior, says Ishtar's sandy voice within him. *You have performed admirably. You are ready.* She's gone before he can summon the energy to speak back. As always.

When Jack opens his eyes, his world is full of angry paragon. Akiko's standing inches away from him, glaring, her dark eyes burning with indignation. It was one thing for that look to be turned on a self-important security guard at the airport; now that it's directed at him, Jack isn't sure he likes it. He pushes himself away from the wall with his shoulder blades and stiffens his posture, ready to endure a lecture. Among the many valuable things he's learned in the last year, it's how to conduct himself with angry women. Patience.

"What in the name of all the worlds and their many wonders happened back there?" the ambassador demands, stabbing a finger at the door. "Your duty—your sole duty—is to protect me from exactly this sort of incident. Explain how a man with a gun made his way within five meters of me." By the end of the sentence, she's shaking with rage, strands of glossy black hair falling out of its elaborate style. The blistering light in her eyes erases any semblance of humanity.

But where Jack's first reaction is to brush aside her concerns with authoritative bravado to preserve his pride, he's stopped short by a memory of grey eyes clouded with hurt. Pretending to have all the answers and maintaining the illusion of infallibility didn't work so well as he led Cora through the underworld; it nearly got them both killed more than once. He'd rather not make that mistake again.

And so, rather than bending excuses around himself for protection, he opts for the truth. "I don't know," he admits. "There were ten police officers, two additional SCD agents, plus a contact on the floor, and none of us caught on until it was too late." He spreads his hands in the air. "I take full responsibility for the failure of your security, Madam Ambassador." He pauses to consider what he's said, then bows his head deferentially. "I'm sorry."

To his relief, the fire in her eyes goes out. She drops her arm and tucks errant hairs behind her ear, all traces of her vengeful fury gone with two words. He's never seen anything like it. He's also not sure how to proceed. Vulnerability was certainly not rewarded in his house as a child or in his career with the agency. But it's transforming a furious paragon into an exhausted woman right in front of him.

"I accept your apology, Agent Ninety-Seven," Akiko says as she lowers herself to sit on a pile of industrial flour sacks. "It is not as if I did much to assist."

"The flare was quite helpful, actually. It kept anyone in the park or the museum from tailing us effectively. Although advance warning next time would be nice."

She smirks humorlessly. "I will keep that in mind."

Unsure of what to say next, Jack says nothing. Instead, he studies her as he perches on a stack of milk crates on the opposite side of the narrow stock room. The ambassador is half curled around herself, knees high from pointing her toes against the floor, barefoot from kicking off her ruined high heels; her elbows rest on her knees, hands supporting her forehead as she stares blankly at a case of blueberry pie filling. A few quiet seconds pass before Jack parses the body language into data he understands. He's pleased, in a small way, that he's picked up on these subtle clues. Another step in the right direction.

"Akiko, have you ever been in a fight before?" he asks.

She tilts her head, her usually stoic face

incredulous. "Of course. Surely you do not think the line of the Sun Goddess survived all these centuries without being skilled in warfare."

There's a flicker of doubt in Jack's mind. He was certain he'd noticed discomfort with the battle in her posture. Perhaps his approach is wrong. He tries a different tactic. It's risky, he knows. Direct, personal, and casual. But between watching other agents use it in interrogation and the magazines the SCD receptionist keeps shoving at him lately, he figures empathy is worth a try.

"What's bothering you?" he asks, leaning forward with his forearms on his thighs.

The question catches her off-guard. For a second, he's sure he's crossed a line of propriety. Which would be the perfect way to cap off this day. But her face clears and she sits up. She stays open. It occurs to him that she's been hiding, protected by diplomatic armor, since the moment they met. What triggered his suspicions earlier wasn't nefarious motives; it was her efforts to guard her real self. A second realization is close on the first's heels: She's a perfect reflection of who he was as Agent 97, the machine man driven solely by duty. His feigned empathy instantly becomes real.

So he's not prepared for the bluntness of her answer to his question.

"I have spent over a century protecting the vampire clans of Japan, agent. They are my family's chosen people. Here they are evil and tainted too heavily by human belief, but in my country, they are different creatures. Noble, honorable, loyal. I have dedicated my life to them as you have dedicated yours to humanity. So you will understand the importance of this when I tell you that the only life I have ever taken was that of my dearest ally, Hikari, a woman raised human and turned vampire under my care."

She looks down at her feet. "Agent Ninety-Seven, I must confess that I knew of Eris' plans to converge the worlds before Agent Six explained the Gauntlet ritual. Hikari came to me one night and explained the promises the mad goddess makes to any who will listen. In her greed and fear, Hikari attempted to convince me to surrender my ancestor's mirror. 'For the cause,' she said. But I knew what she was. My favorite charge had become a willing handmaiden to chaos, the enemy's eyes and ears in our world. She sold herself to Eris." Her jaw tightens as she lifts her chin. "I struck her down."

Akiko pauses to take several slow, deep breaths, but there are no tears or regret in her face. Jack notices he's been holding his own breath during the tale. He exhales quietly but doesn't dare interrupt, waiting as he files away important details.

"What happened tonight," she eventually continues, "reminded me too much of that. That man—that vampire—who tried to take my life has sold himself to Eris, as well. And though the night walkers play at politics, they are a people of one mind. Once one of their number joins the cause, all will." Her brow creases. "If the entire race is aligned with the goddess, then I no longer have a people to care for or to believe in me, agent. I do not know what I will become."

Jack is fumbling for something comforting to say when the matronly woman from the front of the shop enters. He stands, drawing attention away from the ambassador. "You must be Agent Eight," he says extending his hand. "Agent Ninety-Seven. Please excuse our unscheduled arrival. There was an incident at the Metropolitan Museum that required a quick getaway."

The junior agent shakes Jack's hand, her own dusted with sugar. She's nonplussed by his arrival or his rank, and she gives him a broad grin that could be an advertisement for Colgate. Jack remembers a tidbit from her file: Netta Smithwick, a grandmother who narrowly avoided a Red-Riding-Hood fate because she smelled the beast coming. That landed her a prize tracking spot in the SCD a decade ago; she semi-retired last year, aging body too worn for field work but insisting she could be useful as a "housekeeper." Her cupcakes aren't half bad, either.

"Nice to meet you," Netta says. "Sorry for the state of the room." She looks around at the boxes and piles of bakery essentials. "All the safe house gear is in here someplace, I swear. You might have to shift that puff pastry to get at it, though."

"Are we secure?"

She scoffs. "Oh, pshaw. Of course. So many people go by here in an hour that no one sees the store anymore. You'll be fine. But if you need more than a couple hours, you'd best switch to the High

Line house. This place ain't for long-term stays."

Jack nods in agreement. "We'll get moving as soon as I can get in contact with Six and Forty-Two." He indicates Akiko. "The ambassador's lodgings will need to be secured before we can return there. We have to assume all aspects of this case—and potentially Forty-Two's case, as well—have been compromised."

A treacherous thought insinuates itself into his mind. Knowing they're being monitored, he lowers his voice and steps closer to Netta, putting his back to Akiko, who's sitting in front of a hidden camera. "Have you heard anything from Ninety-Nine or One Hundred in the last two weeks?" he whispers.

Agent 8 matches his low tone. "Nothing unusual. Memos on agency events, new procedures, and whatnot." She purses her lips thoughtfully. "Though I noticed they're from Ninety-Nine these days. Haven't heard from the tip-top in ages." The older woman's face scrunches into a new pattern of lines as she considers this. "Everything okay?"

Women's intuition isn't considered a magical ability according to the agency, but Jack's convinced it should be. The way they peer right into the heart of a situation, see what's hidden, and connect random dots to form a legitimate picture has to be supernatural. But confirming Netta's suspicions is premature. It's bad enough that three agents know about 99's treachery; better to keep it quiet until they have a damage-control strategy.

Jack nods with a tight smile. "As fine as it usually is. I just want to confirm you're receiving communication from headquarters. Because of the background magic increase and the intel on Eris, there's been a new memo every day. We need every hand on deck, including yours."

Netta beams at the praise, making him feel like an ass. It's not that he lied to her—they do need everyone on high alert—it's that she's so damned proud to be an agent. He wonders how proud she'd be if she knew what he does about their boss.

"Well," she says at normal volume, "we close at ten sharp, so be ready to go by then. I'll be out front if you need anything. And there's sure to be extra cheesecakes that'll go to waste if you don't claim them." She gives Akiko a wink, then heads out, pulling the storage room door closed behind her.

Alone again, Jack turns to face the ambassador. The interruption was helpful in that it prevented him from diving into an emotional mire, but it's apparently waiting for him. Akiko looks up with a tearful shine in her ink-black eyes. There are questions there that, for once, he knows the answers to. He sits down next to her, knowing he'll get flour on his rented pants and not caring. He draws together his will and his words, then allows himself to speak freely, praying he doesn't offend her.

"Akiko, there's nothing to be afraid of. With the influence of Eris and the spread of *éclat*, your people need you now more than ever. While they may have chosen the wrong path, they can saved. You don't have to abandon your people to their fate. It's never too late for anyone, right up until the moment of death." He hesitates. "Or final death, in this case." He waves a hand to clear the air. "My point is that I've been there, lost and ostensibly irredeemable. And I was able to come back. I know that redemption is possible."

"How?" she asks.

It's the question he was hoping she wouldn't ask, although it's the logical one. He knows the answer, but he also knows how utterly incipient it's going to sound when he says it. He chokes down his pride and says it anyway.

"Love."

She laughs.

He winces. "I'm serious."

She stops laughing.

Jack takes a long breath, then continues, eyes trained on nothing. "In one form or another, love is what brought me back from the abyss I'd thrown myself into. I was hollow. A shell of a man without emotion or identity. Not a man at all, really. Then I saw a girl die for the chance to have an open heart. It broke me. And then the oddest thing happened. People I would've sacrificed without blinking cared for me when I tried to throw away my life. A woman protected me when I wouldn't save myself." His voice catches, abstract emotions he'd refused to acknowledge becoming concrete reality as he speaks. The words form a knot in his chest, but he can't stop there. "Love can do the impossible," he says, holding Akiko's gaze. "I'm living proof. But it's a kind of magic—you have to believe it can work."

Her eyes are wide now, but whether it's a

reaction to his uncharacteristic candor or because she understands, he can't tell. He hopes it's the latter. But he lets the moment pass. That's quite enough emoting for one day. He pats her awkwardly on the shoulder and stands, stretching muscles grown stiff from sitting in the chilly room.

Halfway through calculating their next move in terms of safehouses and protocol, Jack's phone rings. The noise rattles around, too loud in the cramped space, and he hurriedly fishes it out of his interior coat pocket. There's a missed text message, and the displays says it's Manny on the line. Probably wondering where they are and why he didn't respond to the text.

"Yes, Forty-Two?" he says as he picks up.

But the voice on the other end isn't the laid-back surfer dude he's expecting. It's an older man with a lilting accent. "Agent Ninety-Seven. I'm so glad to hear your voice," says the stranger.

Jack furiously scours his brain for a match. "Who is this?"

A low chuckle. "I'm the one holding your agents hostage."

He has Cora.

For an endless moment, Jack is crushed by a wave of guilt that he hadn't considered she might be in danger after the assassination attempt. Memories of his unsavory behavior as Agent 97 combine with his newly-minted imagination to show him horror after horror. Cora beaten and bleeding from a dozen wounds, chained to a stone floor and starving, surrounded by men with a singular purpose. His long fingers squeeze the phone until the pain brings him back. It's his lifeline to her with their bond so weak. He needs to keep it in tact.

"I'm going to ask you again. Who is this?" he says hoarsely.

"Oh, agent, I'm disappointed in you. We met this evening, actually."

The information fits the voice to a face. "Kincaid," Jack spits.

The name grabs Akiko's attention. Her head snaps up, her eyes narrowed. She starts to say something, but Jack holds up a hand for silence and she obeys, albeit with annoyance.

"I prefer Dracula Founder, agent. Respect is in order."

Jack's nostrils flare, but his voice is steady. "What do you want, Kincaid? Where are my people?"

A disappointed sigh. "You are so predictable." In a sing-song voice, the vampire says, "Bring the Japanese ambassador to Belvedere Castle within the hour or else."

"You've become quite a classic villain. I can practically hear you twirling your mustache."

"Did I mention that the 'or else' comes in the form of turning her?" A disappointed *hrm*. "I could have sworn I said that. I must be getting forgetful in my old age."

Shards of glass cut Jack's veins as he pictures Cora as a ragdoll blood slave, abused and wasted over centuries, a husk for undead desires. He chokes back the rising rage. "You wouldn't. You know the penalty for siring outside the confines of the treaty. You're bluffing."

The mild amusement in Kincaid's voice turns to iron. "Try me," he hisses.

Jack closes his eyes against the certainty that the elder is telling the truth. If Akiko's observations are accurate, they're playing for the other side. And where Eris reigns, so does chaos. There's no predicting what the vampires will do for the promise of ultimate power and unending life. He's got one more trick up his sleeve, though.

"I know you're after Amaterasu's mirror," he says. "What if I allow you to keep it in exchange for the safety of my people, including the ambassador?" Behind him, Akiko exclaims something foul in Japanese.

Kincaid's smile is audible. "An intriguing offer, considering you don't know where the mirror is located nor do you have any way of retrieving it if you did."

"You have no idea what I'm capable of."

"True. I haven't had the pleasure of testing you myself." He gives a short laugh of satisfaction. "I accept. Arrive within the hour, and we will finalize the terms of our agreement and transfer your people to your care." A note of threat slides into his voice. "But I warn you, agent. If you deal falsely with me, I will make the girl into the basest slave for the pleasures of my children. And when she is spent and unworthy, I will drink the boy to the point of death and turn him to feed on her until she is dry. One hour."

Then there's nothing but a dial tone.

Jack manages to not crush the phone in his hand by sheer willpower. He's dimly aware of Akiko berating him, and he expects to be physically assaulted at any moment, but all he can think about is the razor's edge of hope he's negotiated and how carefully he will have to walk it in order to save his people and their world.

SIXTEEN

The last time Manny was in the Founder's home, he was on an afternoon fieldtrip to Central Park for senior history. Then, Belvedere Castle was little more than a glorified landmark. The original 19th-century walls were covered in graffiti outside, and the 1980s restored interior was grey and drafty. It felt lonely to him, even as a surly teenager more interested in Miss Brunner's ass than his grades. Like the castle longed for occupants after centuries standing as an empty façade for tourists and the US Weather Bureau.

What he didn't know until his first year with the SCD is that it's been occupied by Seanan Kincaid and his family since before the last stone was placed. Between politics and blood magic, the vampires kept prying mundanes away and kept City Hall happy for their tenancy. Since befriending Finn, Manny's been aching to visit the castle again to see it without the glamour. To be the first agent invited into a haven. Being inside is a dream come true.

Of course, when he'd pictured it, he wasn't being escorted to a cell by four armed guards to await vampire justice. Or being elbowed by a woman twice his age with nicer hair every time he slows down to take in the scenery.

"Easy, lady," he says amiably. "Believe it or not, I'm sort of glad to be here."

"Shut up."

Manny shrugs—at least he's not cuffed, right?— and continues to drink in the differences in the castle since his last visit. The wood and stone and curtains are all there, exactly the same, but now he catches glimpses of new displays of weaponry and armor. And where before he'd thought of the castle as a sad, empty place, now it's undeniably alive with the bustle of dozens of vampires anxious for action. What gives him the willies is that every Founder they pass is struggling with varying stages of *éclat*— dreamy-eyed romantics one second, blade-sharp spies the next. An unsettling percentage are dressed like they're trying out for SWAT.

As they walk deeper into the haven, Cora draws Manny's attention by bumping into him to avoid a knot of leering boys in poet's blouses sprawled on couches off the foyer. She took his suit jacket to protect against the winter air during their short trip from the Met, but the fangbangers don't care that she's covered up. They pass a similar group of women, whose eyes widen as Cora passes amid their hushed whispers.

Rather than be intimidated, though, she juts out her chin and says, "What's your problem?" When no one responds, she follows up with, "Yeah, that's what I thought."

Manny represses a snort at the aghast expressions on the Founders' faces. He's dealt with vampires for a long time, and this clan's rep for leadership and power means no one talks to them the way she did. He's oddly proud of her for standing her ground, especially after the way Finn turned on them.

Cora scoffs as their escorts whisk them into quiet hall dotted with art. "What the hell, Manny? Aren't Founders supposed to be the biggest, baddest vamps in town? I'm seeing a whole lot of hipsters wearing black eyeliner and reading poetry between makeout sessions."

He nods. "Founders are the romantic ideal of vampires. Real warrior-poet types as good with a sword as a pen. Powerful and charismatic, but also sexified." He pauses for a thoughtful moment. "I think it's what makes them such easy hosts for the virus. It builds on what's already there."

She chuckles, but her response is cut off as they're stopped in front of a polished wooden door indistinguishable from the half dozen others in this corridor. The guard in front nods to the other three who dutifully salute and head back to the entrance hall. Manny and Cora exchange dubious looks. One sparkly newbie vamp against two armed agents? He's tempted to try it. But Cora shakes her head as if reading his mind. The idea evaporates. She's right, of course. While they're allegedly Kincaid's guests, they can have no illusions about their situation. Two mortals, metahuman or otherwise, against a hundred or so superpowered undead isn't odds even Manny's luck can tackle. And they get worse immediately.

"All right, hand 'em over," the guard says, resting one hand on a gun in his belt and waving with the other. "Weapons and phones."

Manny's already got his sidearm out when Cora says, "Is that really necessary...," her forehead creases delicately and she takes half a step forward, "What's your name, sir?" She lets the suit jacket fall open to reveal her collarbones above the emerald gown.

The guard can't help staring at her neckline. His eyes bore holes in her skin. "Justin," he says thickly.

Cora flashes a dazzling smile, drawing his attention to her face. "Justin." She leans closer. "Dracula Founder said we're to be treated as honored guests in his house. Is it normal for your guests to be stripped of their belongings when they arrive? Surely this isn't necessary."

The vampire straightens and regains a modicum of his composure. "No, m'am. But I have orders."

Cora's response makes Manny's eyes pop. She sticks out her lower lip, widens her grey eyes, and says, "You can't see your way to letting us keep them? The way some of your brethren gawked at me out there has made me awful nervous. I'd hate for the Dracula to blame you for my," she bites her lip lightly, "violation if I were unable to defend myself." She steps forward again, now almost touching him, gazing into the guard's pale face with huge doe eyes.

If he could, Justin would be sweating buckets. Manny's even sweating a little. What is she doing?

There's a moment of pained indecision in which the guard checks the hall for eavesdroppers, then with a quiet whine, he says, "Meet you halfway? Keep your guns, but I gotta take the ammo and phones. At least you can make a good show if anything goes down. Nobody likes getting shot."

Cora makes a sour face but smoothes it over by winking saucily at him. "You're a peach, Justin. I knew I could trust you."

Manny's astonishment doesn't wear off until a full minute later, after the door to their holding cell is closed and audibly locked behind them. He blinks hard a couple of times as he takes in what turns out to be an inviting, lavishly-decorated bedroom crammed with antique furniture, thick carpets, and tasteful decor.

Cora makes a beeline for a small, round table in the center of the room with a large tray in the center. She lifts the silver cover and mouth-watering steam pours out. "Whaddya know?" she says with delight. "There's a real chicken dinner in here."

As tempting as the food smells, Manny's still working out what he saw in the hallway. "Dude, how did you do that?"

"Do what?" she says, pausing halfway to a dinner roll. He points over his shoulder to the door. She laughs. "Oh, that?" She scoffs and waggles her fingers in the air. "Vaginamancy."

He chuckles. "I didn't know you were that kind of girl, Riley."

She sets the lid back over the food. "Pretty sure all girls are, somewhere down inside. While I much prefer clever wordplay and occasional threats to get results, feminine wiles work remarkably well." Another shrug. "I'm no expert, though. I'm a first-level vaginamancer at best." She puts both hands on her hips and gives the bedroom a critical scan. "You know, I can honestly say this is the nicest jail cell I've ever been in."

"I'm learning all kinds of things about you today, dude," Manny says. "How many do you have it to compare to?"

Cora crosses to the four-poster bed against the far wall and hops up to stretch across the burgundy duvet. "Two, but one of them was Hel's dungeon, so it counts as double awful."

Manny laughs and lets it go in favor of investigating the room. It's a short endeavor. After a couple of laps around the laden bookshelves and chessboard table, finding nothing but boring antiques, he flops into an oversized brocaded chair and sighs loudly.

Cora sits up on the bed, legs crossed inside her torn skirt, and rolls her eyes. "Nobody makes a noise like that unless they want something."

"I was just wondering when you're going to spring us," he says with a lopsided grin. "That's why you're not worried, right? We're two seconds away from freedom at any time with a sidestepper."

"I don't think so," she says slowly. "I did a sweep before they brought us inside, and there aren't any doors for a good quarter mile."

Manny waves a hand. "Ah, whatever. Background magic as high as it is, you can cut one wherever you are." He raises his eyebrows. "Right?"

But the way she's gnawing on her thumbnail tells him that he's about to be disappointed.

"I can't," she says. "Not in the field, anyway. We'd need the Interdimensional Staging thingie back at headquarters." As his face falls, she hurriedly adds, "Besides, even if there was a door in this room, we'd have no way to know where it goes or how to get to anywhere recognizable once we were on the other side." She lowers her eyes. "Sorry, man. There's actually not a lot of call for my powers, rare and cool as they are. Most of the time, I'm basically a regular cop." She chuckles mirthlessly. "You're by far the more valuable agent this go-round, my friend."

Manny lets his head fall back against the chair and stares at the ceiling. Until right this second, he hadn't realized how much he'd been counting on Cora for an escape. If he'd known they couldn't grab a door and book it from wherever they ended up, he would've tried harder to finagle out of being captured in the first place.

And yet, he's not worried. Not that he gets worked up over much anyway, but this is certainly the right moment for it. Surrounded by vampires trying to become daywalking mini-gods by helping the goddess of chaos wipe out humanity? Good time to panic. But it's not happening. Somehow, he's convinced everything's going to work out fine. Whether that's naïveté or healthy optimism is up for debate.

Cora, however, doesn't share his peace. She's picking at the bedspread, her forehead creased in thought, shoulders hunched as if the world rested on them. Doesn't make it better that, in a way, it does. Manny knows that she's been in worse jams than this since joining the agency, but even when reality isn't being screwed with, rookies always break down before they toughen up. Gods knows he did.

With a pang of empathy, Manny moves to sit on the high bed beside her, kicking off his salt-crusted shoes onto the thick rug and crossing his skinny legs in front of him. "Don't worry, dude," he says. "It's going to be okay. Good guys always win."

She gives him a half-hearted smile. "Not in every story." she says. "And not every hero lives to see the end."

Manny blinks. "Dang, girl, that's harsh."

She shrugs. "It's the truth."

An opportunity to dig deeper waves at Manny in the ensuing silence. But he hesitates at taking it. While they've definitely got the big brother, little sister vibe going on, he's not sure he's allowed to ask Cora super personal questions. Then again, he'd rather her be mad because he tried to help than watch her beat herself up because he did nothing.

"Dude, you want to tell me what's up?" he asks.

"You're different since you got back from Faerie. Like, depressed different."

She rolls her eyes. "Ugh, am I that transparent? First Sofi, now you. How come everybody can read my freaking mind?" He shrugs with a smile she doesn't return. "It's stupid," she says morosely.

"Try me."

With a dramatic whine, she drops back on the bed to stare at the lace canopy. "I haven't even told Soph about this, so you have to swear you won't tell."

"I swear."

"Or laugh."

"That, too."

She takes a deep breath, then lets loose. "When I got my sidestepping powers, everything was great because I was finally 'special.' But after a week at the SCD, I learned I wasn't actually because in the agency *everyone* is special. So, despite the Eris clusterfuck, I'm stuck running down misdemeanors at Christmas, and nobody gives two shits about anything except my reporting skills, despite me being the one to break the whole damn case in the first place." A tear runs down her temple and into her hair. "I thought I'd be the glamorous heroine," she says with a frustrated stab at the air, "that I'd wow everyone with my awesomeness. That I'd be the best. I thought I had a destiny with a capital D, but it turns out I'm a measly supporting character who's accomplished her goals already and has no clue where her plot is going." Sniff. "I'm no more important now than I was living in that shithole town brewing coffee for rednecks." She wipes at her face and laughs self-consciously. "Told you it was stupid."

Manny lets a few beats pass before he says, "Not stupid at all."

"I bet you think I'm a brat. I certainly do."

"You want to know what I think?"

"Sure, why not. Can't be worse than what I think about myself."

He takes a slow breath through his nose and squints critically at her. It's rare that anyone asks for his perspective on anything deeper than a case file. And what's running through his mind is firmly in the "tough love" category.

"You sure?" he asks.

She nods.

"Okay, dude." He gives her a wry smile to try to soften the blow. "Two things. Number one, the story's not always about you. You're literally in the middle of saving billions of lives, plus who knows how many worlds, including ours. I'd say that's more important than your existential crisis." Cora makes a strangled noise and covers her cringe with a throw pillow. He resists the urge to apologize and barrels on. "Number two, you're a supernatural rockstar and a goddamn living legend, Riley. Yeah, it's tough to figure out who you are and what it's all about, but you're trying way too freaking hard. Relax. Do you." He squeezes her knee reassuringly. "Greatness will come, dude. You don't have to chase it."

It takes a second for the sniffling under the

pillow to subside, then Cora's damp, red face peeks out. Manny braces for impact. Last time he tried to help out a fellow agent with personal problems, they not only told him where to stick it, they attempted to provide hands-on instruction. But she merely gives him a watery smile. He raises an eyebrow at her as a visual question mark.

"Don't worry, I'm not going to yell at you or throw anything," she says as she sits up, hugging the throw pillow. "You're right. This is such a teenage drama queen thing to be upset about." She huffs and mops her face with the sleeve of his suit jacket. "I just thought everything would be different after I left home. Like I'd never doubt the reason for my existence again."

Manny waves a hand. "Nah. That doesn't go away. It's the human condition. Keeps life interesting. Personally, I deal with it by pretending it doesn't exist and continuing to protect, serve, and be awesome."

She manages a weak laugh.

"There we go," he says with a smile. "Don't let the brainweasels keep you down. You're so much better than them."

She sighs heavily and smiles back. He nods.

The moment passes, and Manny turns to survey their cushy prison again, ready to tackle their escape. "What odds will you give me that we can talk Justin into letting us go?"

But Cora ignores this and prods him in the knee with one finger. "Hey, I just told you my mortifyingly self-centered secret," she says. "You have to tell me one of yours. Can't have you running around with dirt on me and not have any on you."

He smiles indulgently. "Sure, why not. It'll pass the time until Jack and Akiko ride in with whatever plan they're surely concocting. What do you want to know?"

"Why did you get so bent out of shape yesterday? You looked super upset about Agent One Hundred going missing, but you didn't say anything."

It's a sucker punch that makes him wince. He didn't think anyone had noticed his reaction to the news. Memories and emotions he's been stuffing into a bottle marked "deal with this later" clamor to be released. And because he reacted, he's got to tell her. He mentally rehearses line after line to find the right delivery, but tact isn't his strong suit. Straight to the point it is.

"Because she's my mom," he whispers.

There's a measure of satisfaction in watching the revelation roll across her face. Her mouth drops open, working silently for a second before words come out. "Dora Boxer is your mother?" she eventually says. "I mean, I should've guessed because of the last name, but shit." She squints at him, presumably searching for a family resemblance. Then she gasps and covers her mouth. "Oh, gods. And I said all that stuff about...." Her eyes gloss with tears.

With a strength he doesn't feel, he shrugs, rolling his shoulders like stones. "You didn't know. No one does." He tightens his ponytail. "Hell, I didn't find out until recently, myself. I've lived with my aunt and uncle my whole life, and they kept her a secret. But she called me out of the blue about six months ago. Said she was sorry it'd taken her so long to get in touch, and we needed to talk in person. She called a couple more times, but we never did meet up. I was riding that rollercoaster when she," he hesitates, "went missing."

Before he knows what's happening, Cora's wrapped him tight in her arms. "I'm so sorry, Manny," she whispers. "We're going to find her. I promise."

A single tear rolls down his cheek under the cover of her shoulder. "Thanks," is all he can say.

They stay that way for a good minute or two. He doesn't try to escape. When she releases him, he smiles gamely, then sniffs and tightens his ponytail. Cora scoots back to a more professional distance, although they're still facing each other cross-legged on the bed like a couple of girls at a sleepover. Slowly, his thoughts realign, storing away his fears about Dora for another time.

"So," Cora says matter-of-factly, changing the subject clumsily. "We need an exit strategy." She ticks off points on her fingers. "We've got no ammo, no phones, and my powers are useless. You got any ideas for a daring escape?"

He smiles unconvincingly. "Hope?"

"Hope is not a plan, Manny."

"It's always worked for me."

She rolls her eyes and glances around the room. "Maybe we could build a wooden horse out of bookshelves and...," she starts.

As if on cue, there's a knock at the door. Manny looks at Cora with both eyebrows raised. What jailer knocks to let the prisoners know he's coming?

The outside bolts on are drawn back, and the door swings inward to reveal Justin, accompanied by a heavy-duty Latino in riot gear with minimal skin glitter.

"Dracula wants to see the girl," says Riot Gear Vampire. His tone brooks zero argument.

Manny argues anyway. "What for?"

"None of your business."

There's no way Manny's going to let this undead gorilla drag Cora off into the dark to please a blood-drinking monster with delusions of grandeur. But without his gun, holy water, or a stake, it'll be impossible for him to keep this kitted-out monster from doing whatever he wants. Won't stop him from trying, though.

He takes a step forward, earning a hiss from Riot Gear Vampire and a show of teeth.

"Whoa, whoa, hey now," Cora says, sliding off the bed and into her shoes. "Don't fight over me, boys."

The two break their standoff as she crosses to Manny's side. She shrugs off the suit jacket, revealing freckle-dusted shoulders and more cleavage than Manny is comfortable with. He fixes his eyes respectfully on her face.

"It's fine, Forty-Two," she says with a mischievous glint in her eyes. "I'd be delighted to chat with Dracula Founder. I'm sure the conversation will be," she flicks a glance at Justin, who squirms a bit, "stimulating."

The understanding that dawns on Manny does nothing to make him more comfortable. Using ladymagic on a freshly-turned foot soldier is one thing. Trying it on a clan elder who practically invented charisma is a whole different ball game. She's either brave or crazy.

He tries to convey the danger in his face, but Cora's smile doesn't waver. She leans in as she returns his coat, whispering, "Let me do this. You saw how sparkly he is back at the Council? He's all *Twilight*ed up—he'll be an easy mark. Plus, I could use the ego-boost to get back on my game."

Manny grumbles but clears the way to the door. "Just don't do anything you'll regret, okay, dude?" he says. "No intel is worth your pride." Pause. "Or certain other agents being righteously pissed because I didn't stop you."

"No promises," she says with a saucy wink. He groans as Cora steps gracefully into the hall to meet her escort. "Ready when you are, big boy," she says. Riot Gear Vampire grunts and puts a huge hand on her shoulder to steer her in the right direction.

Before she disappears from view, Cora calls back to Manny. "I'll be back soon! Don't eat my half of the dinner, okay?"

"No promises."

Her laugh echoes down the corridor. And then she's gone.

Manny shakes his head as he tosses his suit jacket over the back of an armchair. He's decided to lay down for a well-deserved nap while Cora's gone when he notices that the door is still open. Justin's standing there, eyes roaming hungrily around the room. It occurs to Manny that most low-ranking fangs live in shared quarters; the guard's probably never seen this kind of luxury, and as militarized as the vampires have become, he doubts they're allowed much free time. This guy must be bored as hell. A flutter of hope wings through his mind, tracing out a new escape plan.

"Hey, dude," he says, nodding to the side table. "You play chess?"

SEVENTEEN

The circuitous route to Kincaid's quarters fails to be interesting; the Founders' haven is practically identical to Hel's underworld castle and Stonehammer's subterranean fortress. Cora wonders if all badass supers hire the same interior decorator. Like a fairytale Martha Stewart. But her good humor doesn't last as the walk continues down yet another featureless hallway. Between the stony silence of her escort and the hushed whispering of other vampires they pass, Cora starts to have flashbacks of being marched to the principal's office to be reamed out.

When they finally stop in front of yet another wooden door, the guard pushes her in front of him without warning, and she stumbles forward. Her skin immediately starts to itch like crazy. She wills herself into not scratching but takes a protective step backwards. The burning subsides, affirming her suspicions: The reinforcements around the old timbers are made of cold iron. The damn Dracula Fae-proofed his room. Good thing she's only a quarter Fae. It puts her teeth and mind on edge, though. Why would he bother when the Fae are onside with Eris, too? Unrest in the ranks already? Whatever the reason, it does mean Kincaid won't be as easy a mark as she'd hoped. Carefully, she raises her shields. It's harder than usual because of the iron, but it's worth the effort to avoid him groping her bare mind again.

When she's done, she realizes the guard hasn't knocked or rung a bell or anything. He's just waiting, staring into space. She's about to ask when there's a faint click from inside and the door swings inward, wide enough for her to enter but not for the guard. No one greets her. Nothing is said. She casts a final look at her escort who stares back menacingly, then shrugs and slides through the opening, avoiding the metal bindings that make her skin crawl as she passes.

If the castle is less impressive than she'd hoped, Kincaid's room is even less so. Where she'd pictured extravagant decorations, expensive furniture, and a succubus girl or two in barely any lingerie, instead she sees a sparse, grey space that puts her in mind of illustrations of monks' quarters. Less Gary Oldman's hedonistic Dracula and more Friar Lawrence from *Romeo and Juliet*. Bookshelves line the left wall, filled with volumes older than she is. Nearby are two plain armchairs in front of a coffee table, a tall desk with cluttered shelves in the center of the room, and a simple bed to the right. The entire exterior wall is covered with heavy black curtains, presumably covering the windows. Beige carpeting is all that says this is a modern home; the rest screams "medieval abbey." It's strangely similar to how she imagines Jack's apartment.

Cora steps inside as she assesses the room. She despite the dimmed overhead lighting, she can see everything in it—except Kincaid. The hair on the back of her neck lifts. She's this close to backing out and saying screw it when the heavy door swings shut behind her, the old-fashioned latch dropping into place with a clink. She whips around to see her host standing to the side of the door, hand against the hinges.

The elder Founder gives a low chuckle. "My apologies. I'd anticipated a less expeditious response to my summons. I'm afraid you've caught me in transition," he says, holding out an arm to let her inspect him. He's changed clothes since the Met, swapping his high-society getup for plain black slacks and an untucked button-up shirt. The hair around his pale face is damp, and he's holding a towel. No wonder Cora didn't see him; he was washing his face at the sink behind the door. He motions to the armchairs. "Please. Won't you sit?" He crosses the room himself without waiting for an answer, casually draping the towel over the back of his chair.

Cora stays where she is, glued to the spot from a blend of healthy suspicion and calculated manipulation. Make him wait. She's positive that an elder of his reported abilities could've used telekinesis to close the door, if only for dramatic flair, but he chose to do it himself. And this is the first she's hearing of vampires needing a bath. Why the idiosyncrasies? Bits of legend and scraps of data float offer themselves up to give her a clue on his angle, but she's coming up dry. This lore isn't her strongest, and the effects of *éclat mort* confuse things further. It's obvious he wants something; she's just not sure what it is. Only one way to find out.

She moves to take the empty seat across from Kincaid. It's closer than she'd like—their shins are practically touching—but she lets it be. Her willingness to mix wiles with wits could save billions of lives, as Manny so helpfully reminded her. This is no time to get squeamish. Without a gun, friends, or useful powers, feminine wiles is all she's got left, no matter how basic. The goody-two-shoes girl inside of her—which, if she's honest, is most of her—cringes at exchanging sex for information, but her secret agent side approves. Besides, it's not like Kincaid is a Nosferatu-style vamp with pruny skin and nails that'd make Edward Scissorhands jealous. That'd take a lot more preparation than getting up close and personal with this Chris Pine wannabe.

Cora's emerald gown has seen better days, ripped up the skirt and creased everywhere, but she'll work with it. She straightens her spine and adjusts her shoulders to enhance her cleavage. It's a minor tweak that doesn't go unnoticed. The elder's blue eyes flick downward and back up again. A little spark of victory leaps in her heart, and she starts assembling questions in the background as she lets him carry the conversation.

"Thank you for joining me, Agent Six," he begins.

"Cora," she insists with a smile. "Call me Cora."

There's a twitch in his expression. "Cora," he repeats. "I'm sure you're wondering why I asked you here."

It's a loaded statement, designed to get her to reveal more than she's ready to. A test. She'd anticipated verbal fencing, but not so soon. Fine. She'll play.

Cora casts around the room, feigning innocent curiosity. But what she says is intended to cut. "I'm assuming it's got something to do with the mirror you stole."

As she swings her gaze around, she notices that the desk behind him isn't empty like she'd thought. The tall shelves that make up the back house a motley collection of objects she couldn't spot from the doorway. If she weren't concerned about her radar being detected, she'd check for magical artifacts. A couple of them are familiar—like the chunk of golden wool holding a red stone—but it's hard to tell in this mood lighting. She remembers what the Lorekeeper said about relics vanishing from the Roosevelt archives. Could this be where they're ending up? If she could get closer....

She returns her attention to Kincaid. He's not overtly smiling, but there's an air of authoritative amusement surrounding him. It's probably hard not to find mortals funny when you're hundreds of years old and can punch through concrete.

"Yes, the mirror," he says. "I've heard that you're insightful and quick. I am not disappointed. You certainly see straight into the heart of the matter."

She shoves down the cop response to demand how he'd heard about her. Instead, she draws on movies and books where being demure is a good thing. She lowers her eyes and smiles. "I'm flattered, sir. I don't do well with small talk, which makes me a poor conversationalist." She looks back up. "It's nice to meet someone who appreciates it."

He nods. "When I was a lad, I was the same. Mortal life is so short. Everything is rushed." He settles back in his chair. "But after the first hundred years, I learned to appreciate small things that pass the time. You will, too."

Then he gives her a strange look that drops ice cubes into her veins. It's somewhere between a smirk and a leer, like he's been keeping a secret that he's about to reveal. It occurs to her that she might not be as clever as she thinks. That it's entirely possible he can read her mind through her shield and is playing along, waiting for his moment. Her bare neck suddenly feels exposed and flush with blood.

But she doesn't let the doubt show. She leans forward, elbows on her thighs, knowing the top of the strapless gown leaves little to the imagination at that angle. Another flick of his eyes. She covers a grossed-out shudder with a suggestive smile.

"What else do you do to pass the time, Dracula Founder?"

Now it's his turn to waive formalities. "While we're in this room, my name to you is Seanan."

Progress. Her smile brightens, although nothing more happens. Must've been too subtle of an innuendo. She'll have to step it up.

"I'm a collector of rare objects and magical antiquities," he says to answer her question. "You undoubtedly know that already from your agency's files. They're quite extensive and well-researched, I understand." He turns in his chair and waves at the desk. "These are my most recent acquisitions, awaiting inspection." Cora starts to ask the obvious question, but he gives her a sly grin. "The mirror you seek is safely stored elsewhere. Naturally." Then he leans forward conspiratorially and says, "I understand you're quite the folklore expert. Would you like to see my modest collection?"

Again with the info about her. How does he know? Did Eris tell him? But this isn't the time for an interrogation. That can wait until he's locked up in SCD custody.

"Of course," she says eagerly, then gives him a sly look of her own. "Assuming you trust a government agent whom you've kidnapped and stripped of her weapons, thereby committing treason."

Seanan doesn't rise to the bait. He simply stands and offers his pale, graceful hand to her. Pianist's hands, she thinks before taking it. Unlike Finn's, the elder's hand is warm, soft, and strong as he helps her up. They walk over together, then he respectfully lets go, turning on a study lamp on top of the desk to better illuminate the objects.

They stand in front of the collection as if they were in a museum. Although Cora's face is calm, alarm bells are going off inside. Of the dozen pieces in the shelves, Cora recognizes ten, even without her magic radar. What is Seanan doing with these artifacts? Or rather, what is Eris doing with them through him? Could the final piece of the Gauntlet-crashing ritual be in front of her? She sweeps over the objects again, but there's nothing resembling any kind of fruit. Her anxiety subsides as her disappointment rises. While she's glad she only has to worry about rescuing one relic from a castle full of bloodsuckers, it would've been sweet to procure two.

There is one thing in particular that stands out, primarily because it's not an ancient magical object: a wooden frame tucked between shelves. The portrait inside is monochrome and yellowed with age. Cora leans in for a better look, then lets out a startled gasp. She takes a step back, but Seanan's hand rests lightly on her back and stops her from retreating too far.

"The likeness is uncanny, don't you agree?" he says serenely, eyes on the frame.

The woman in the photograph is younger and thinner than Cora, but otherwise, she could be looking into a mirror. They share the same fine features, big eyes, and broad shoulders. No wonder the minions were whispering about her.

"Who is she?"

"Karen. My wife of a eighty-one years."

"What happened to her?"

"She walked into the sunlight when the burden of modern belief became too heavy to bear."

There's a bitterness in his voice begs her to look at him, but instinct tells her not to. In her peripheral vision, she watches his eyes rim black, and she clamps down on the urge to gag. Ichor tears are not hot. And the "you look like my dead wife" thing is creepy as hell. Not a good combo.

She tries to change the subject by continuing to study the table while Seanan composes himself. There's a golden fleece fragment, a couple magical rings, a bottle full of dark liquid. But the warmth from his hand low on her back is a growing distraction. Rationally, she knows he's routing power into making himself appear less undead for her benefit, but he radiates more than body heat. Like the intensity of his emotion is leaking out. Curiosity about what and why that is outweighs the logic of safety, and she opens a microscopic crack in her shields, allowing herself to taste the magic that's slipping up her spine.

It's the opposite of what she's come to associate with vampires. Rather than inhuman, bitter, or violent, what she picks up is achingly sad. The way you imagine a puppy feels when it's lost in a rainstorm—but for decades instead of overnight. There's a crimson tint to it and the tang of pennies, but at its core is endless loneliness. It's unlike any energy she's felt before, yet it's so familiar after years of aimless living back home. She widens the gap in her magical armor to know more, eager to touch a mind that understands. It rushes to fill the space, making her eyelids flutter and her breath thicken. It's magic that needs to be made whole, incomplete on its own. It needs her. Wanting to the point of tears. A desire she's never felt.

Not even from Jack.

The thought bursts at the surface of her mind, disrupting the trance. She tries to slam her shield closed, but it's too late. Fingers of dark craving slink around the curves of her mind, softening its edges and her will. Slowly, she turns around, putting her back to the desk. She raises her head to see Seanan's blue eyes huge and expectant in front of her. This close, in the pool of bright lamplight, she notices a crucial detail that had escaped her.

He doesn't sparkle.

Cora's heart stops. Time stops. Everything stops. How could she have missed it? She ransacks her memory for clues. There he is at the Council, glittering under the fluorescent lights, same as the other infected Founders. There he is a moment ago washing his face....

Washing his face.

Her eyes dart to the discarded towel over the back of the chair. With the lamp brightening the room, what she'd missed then is screaming at her now: a cream-tinted smear even a makeup-adverse girl like Cora knows is foundation and a liberal dusting of silver glitter.

He faked it.

That's when Cora knows she's in over her head. She'd bargained on squeezing a virus-dulled sexpot for intel, not matching wits with a centuries-old tactician set on owning her. He's not infected—the sensual haze of his mind is genuine, but from his lost love, not as a symptom of the disease. Seanan Kincaid is wholly himself, hi mind untainted and sharp, his power uncorrupted.

If he senses the shift in her thoughts, he doesn't show it. She glances around, trying to find an easy way out, but there isn't one. Resigned to the confrontation, she eventually looks directly at him. It's a mistake. The connection when their eyes meet is paralyzing, intensified by gods know what kind of magic, and Cora has to steady herself against the tabletop behind her to keep from swooning. Through the sticky haze engulfing her mind, she notices she's put her hand down on one of the table's objects. She closes her fist around the cool metal as an anchor, anything to keep her in the real. It works for a moment. But then he steps forward, eyes locked on hers. She drops the thing into a pocket cleverly tailored into the dress and sends up silent thanks for practical women as he reaches for both her hands.

"Cora," he whispers, emotion thickening his accent, "I wish to make you an offer."

She sees it coming from a mile away. From the second she recognized the woman in the portrait as her doppelgänger, she knew why he'd asked her to come. But she was too curious, too sympathetic, and more than a little lustful after denying the man she actually wants in an idiotic twist of nobility. She let her guard down, and now she's screwed.

Seanan pulls her close, wrapping an arm around her waist. "Your beauty wounds my heart, *mo shíorghrá*. But you are so much more than beauty. From the moment I first touched your mind, I have sensed greatness in you." She inhales sharply. How deep in her mind has he seen to push that button? "With you by my side, there is nothing I cannot do," he continues. "You will have eternal life and power beyond imagination. I will make you a queen in the world that is to come." His lips curl sensuously. "Isn't that better than playing house with a man more in love with duty than with you?"

Tendrils of desire pierce Cora's heart, warping her sensibilities. Everything he's saying is laser-targeted to her most vulnerable points: her longing for greatness and her yearning for real love. Her knees want to buckle from the relief of being understood so completely. But there's a streak of iron in her mind that stands strong, reminding her that this isn't real; her mother's Southern practicality overruling her whimsical Fae side. She clings to it desperately.

"There's always a price. Nothing's free in stories," she whispers. She stiffens in his arms as a show of resistance, but it presses her into his chest, making her shiver. "What do you want?"

He smiles and strokes her cheek, his eyes shining with victory already claimed. "Just fear me, love me, do as I say. Be mine, body and soul, and everything I have is yours. Forever."

Temptation stares her baldly in the face. It's magic, yes, but it's also the promise of power not limited by rules and location and men in black suits. Her current talents make her rare in the world of the supernatural, but what more could she be as a sidestepper with vampiric power? What new paths could she forge, what new destiny could she manifest? The lure of a heart that needs her dangles before her, too. She could be a cherished other half, not a tagalong sidekick. It's refreshing to be so explicitly desired after the exhausting dance of guesswork that Jack's put her through. She knows he's is toying with her. But she's unconvinced he's entirely wrong.

The tension trickles out in a near-silent whimper. Her lips part and her eyelids flutter as she wrestles between what she knows, what she wants, and what she's being magicked into wanting. A distant part of her observes out how vampire-victim she's acting at the exact second Seanan seizes his moment.

It's not just his hands that are warm. Cora gasps hard as he puts his lips to hers, hard and hungry. She instinctively kisses back, her own arms snaking around his waist, hands up his back, suddenly all in and hungry for more. His fingers tangle in her copper hair, and he moves from her mouth to her jaw, trailing kisses down her neck toward her collarbone. She tips her head to one side with a soft moan as her skin flushes in response. Both afraid of and desperate for the next moment, she puts a hand into his hair has he lowers his head to her throat.

Teeth brush the delicate skin at the vulnerable spot between her neck and shoulder. His mind slides around hers, sharp and insistent, the impending union punctuated with a low growl.

The sound echoes down passages of Cora's mind, ringing in forgotten corners until it strikes against a memory. It tips over, spilling out as a girl without magic or a clue what to do standing in a field growling at her own damsel-in-distress mentality after battling her way out of paradise for a second chance at life.

I'm the hero of this story, goddammit, the girl says. *Time to start acting like one.*

All Cora can manage is a hard shove, but it's enough to break the spell. It catches him by surprise, he was so convinced she was in his thrall. And she was. Right up until she remembered who she is: a woman whole in her own power, not a pretty object to be bought with promises and draped over an arm.

Kincaid stumbles backwards, disrupting their connection long enough for Cora to reseal her protective shield, but he quickly recovers, his blue eyes now blood red with predatory fury and radiating power. That's when Cora runs out of courage. It was all she could do in the moment to get him off her; now an elder vampire aligned with the goddess of chaos is about to tear her to shreds. He snarls, flashing extended canines, and she raises fists she knows are useless and braces for the attack.

Knock, knock, knock.

Both of them freeze.

Knock, knock, knock.

Cora looks to the door, then to Kincaid. "You going to get that?" she says.

The elder doesn't move. "What?" he barks over his shoulder.

"There's something going down outside, boss," says a voice through the door. "The dogs are fighting."

There's a subtle shift in Kincaid's posture that takes him from specter of imminent death to merely dangerous. His eyes shift back to blue, and he sniffs as says, "Thank you, Harley." He fixes Cora with a withering stare. "I need you to escort our guest back to her chambers."

"Yes, sir."

Kincaid seizes Cora's arm with a grip so hard she squeaks in pain. There's a corpse chill to his skin now that numbs her to the bone. He half-drags her to the door and yanks it open, but before he releases her, he leans in and whispers in her ear. "You have chosen poorly, agent. I will enjoy using you in every way imaginable. Lady Eris has promised me your life for my service. After she has consumed the human world, no matter how you resist, you will be mine, and I will turn you slowly. You will watch from the prison of your mind as your body is vandalized over years. And when you think you cannot withstand any further desecration, your friends will feed on you, alive, until nothing remains but gobbets of offal on my floor."

Then he shoves her into the guard's arms and retreats, slamming the door so hard the wood cracks down the center.

EIGHTEEN

Vampires and werewolves weren't always enemies. Like all supernaturals, their basic natures have been altered over time to reflect human belief: Because humans wanted to believe that monsters needed enemies aside from man, that's what happened. The races grew hateful and violent, often skirmishing in plain sight, pressing ignorant humans into their ranks to fight in the battles they'd created.

In New York City, the rift was particularly tragic. The Founder clan didn't only bring vampires to America; they were accompanied by a contingent of lycan guards. This original pack stood watch during the day while they were defended at night. They cared for one another the way neighbors do, searching for a way to thrive in the burgeoning city—a place to call home.

Eventually, they settled in Central Park. The Founders insinuated themselves into Belvedere

Castle while the Pack claimed the green spaces around the reservoir as their territory. The city grew up around them, morphing ever faster as more humans imported beliefs from faraway places and the digital age spread ideas like a cancer.

As they city changed, so did the two races. The Founders became arrogant and factious as the Pack became resentful of their thankless vigils. A few resisted, but they became the minority, chased away or killed for their "old-fashioned" ways. Most relished the new power brought by popular film and novel trends. Conflict soon followed. Any Founder setting foot outside his haven's door risked death. Any Pack member caught alone did the same. Within a single generation, the vampires and werewolves of New York City had become caricatures of their former selves: thugs, thieves, and transients in the place of noble savages and princes.

A small part of Jack pities them, but the closer he gets to Central Park, the more the ugly scars across his chest itch and the less he cares about the history. The entire return drive from the safehouse has been filled with dread. There's roughly a ten percent chance they can make it to the Founders' haven without incident. He wishes Manny was with him for the ninth time; he's not confident that his own luck is enough protection in that narrow margin.

The ambassador is not making it easier. Akiko's been arguing with him since he got off the phone with Kincaid, demanding he formulate a different plan to retrieve the abducted agents and preserve the mirror. He's largely ignored her, preferring to let her shout herself out as he computes possibilities, risk outcomes, and ratios.

After about twenty minutes, though, she hits her limit. Her sudden silence is more jarring than any of the insults she's hurled at Jack, and he checks to see what's changed. She's on her phone. In the moment between dialing the number and putting the phone to her ear, he reads the caller ID: *Samir Patel*.

Jack's arm is out like a lightning flash. He snatches the phone with one hand while rolling down the window with the other. It's gone into oncoming traffic before she can react. There's a moment of stunned silence, followed by more Japanese swearing.

But he's done being reprimanded. Trying to call 99 was the last straw. He pulls sharply into a streetside parking spot, slamming the SUV into park, then turns fully in his seat to face Akiko.

"I understand you may not be thinking clearly due to your anxiety about a family heirloom being used in a world-ending ritual," he says, "but let me explain a few things to you, Madam Ambassador." He keeps his voice slow and level, despite the anger bubbling inside him. "This is not your show. It's mine. Your safety is one of many duties I am tasked with, and I will not allow you to come to harm because you refuse to trust me. Samir defected. I'm willing to give you the benefit of the doubt and assume you forgot because you're too distracted by anger to remember that he's in Eris' pocket." He leans forward slightly. "But you are not my only priority. I would be more than happy to take you directly to the New York office for safekeeping while I retrieve my agents."

Akiko's face shifts from shock to indignance. She lifts her chin haughtily. "And what of your duty to humanity, Agent Ninety-Seven? You are trading two lives for seven billion if you allow the vampires to keep the mirror and hand it over to Eris."

"If it were the final piece she needed for the ritual, I'd agree with you. Six and Forty-Two could fend for themselves, and I would fight until my last breath to have the mirror returned safely to you. But that is not the case. One relic is being retrieved as we speak by the best tracker in the agency; the other is in the wind, findable by either side. We have more than enough opportunity to stop Eris on other fronts. We can afford to surrender this particular battle."

The frosty temperature inside the car has nothing to do with the winter outside. But he doesn't defend himself further. If she continues to fight, he'll take her directly to the field office and deal with Kincaid's wrath alone. If she comes around, he'll bring her to the castle; he could use the help. It's up to her.

Akiko exhales hard through her nose and breaks her stare. "You are a loyal friend, Jack Alexander," she says, with unconcealed irritation. "I will not stand in your way. But I swear to you that I will do everything in my power to retrieve the mirror after your agents are secured. I must restore the honor of my family." She closes her eyes for a moment. "And the dignity of our chosen people."

"Thank you," he says simply.

Then he starts the car and pulls back out into traffic, heading towards what he's sure is the worst idea he's ever had.

"Agent Ninety-Seven, this might be rude of me to ask, but I feel obligated to do so. Do you have a plan?"

The ambassador stands next to him on the sidewalk that borders Central Park West near Hunter's Gate. They're not looking at each other but out into the deceptively beautiful snowscape. The SUV is parked nearby, and they're as close as possible to the Founders' haven without driving directly onto the lawn, but there are another four hundred yards of gardens, jogging track, and open grass between them and Belvedere Castle. All of it is Pack territory.

Worse than the high probability of an encounter with werewolves is the fact that Jack has no plan. There was a time when this would send him into a tailspin of mechanical failure, but he's acclimated to it over the last year. Being involved with Cora has done a surprising amount for his reaction to the unexpected.

He's about to admit this to Akiko when a hot voice fills his mind.

This is your first test, my warrior. I am with

you. Do not fear. Across the grass to victory.

This time, he doesn't argue. *Yes, Lady Ishtar.*

"Agent?"

Jack shakes himself. "Yes?"

"Do you have a plan?"

"I have twelve percent of a plan."

"That is barely a concept."

"Would you rather I lie and say yes?"

A beat passes. "No."

"Then I recommend you draw your weapon and follow me as closely as you can."

There's a gleam under the streetlight as she unsheathes out the dagger he's given her. Seven inches of steel dipped in pure silver with a leather-wrapped handle—the knife of a werewolf hunter. It was a gift from Agent 100, left on his apartment doorstep after he fought off the lycan infection that nearly killed him; the infection he contracted perhaps a quarter mile from where he's standing. He can't use the weapon himself—it burns like fire ants under his skin—but he kept it as a reminder. When he found out he'd be traveling to New York, he'd packed it as a matter of course, in case of an emergency. Like this one, for example.

He nods approvingly at her without tearing his attention from the park. Visual scans are turning up nothing unusual. A handful of dedicated nighttime joggers, a couple of persistent squirrels. But he can smell them—the Pack, the Founders. Their scents float on the surface of the breeze blow across the frozen reservoir. Jack grits his teeth and shifts uneasily. There's no good time to do what they're about to do. Better to start and get it over with.

While he was honest with Akiko about how little he's planned, he doubts she'd be comforted by knowing the contents of that twelve percent. It amounts to one word.

"Run," he says.

Jack bolts, the paragon close behind, keeping his eyes glued to the black spot he knows is the turret of Belvedere Castle. Powdery snow flies behind them in fans as they tear across the park, ignoring paved paths in favor of direct lines. Blood surges in Jack's ears, quickened by adrenaline. The longer he runs, the more the wolf inside him wants out. He draws on it to increase his speed. His vision narrows, darkening at the edges with desperate exertion. Fifty yards, seventy-five, a hundred, two hundred. The castle walls quickly loom over him, both intimidating and beckoning him forward. They're getting there. They can make it. They'll be okay.

He's not sure when he becomes aware that he's running alone, but when he stops to look, Akiko is gone.

In fact, everyone is gone, including the joggers and the squirrels. Jack finds himself standing alone and panting in a wide clearing between fir trees. His lungs burn with the effort of his sprint, but he gulps down air anyway for the scent, directing his senses into confirming what he already knows: A circle of werewolves is tightening around him. Ten so far, and more are coming. The Alpha is with them.

Jack knows he has approximately ten seconds before the Pack arrives and all hell breaks loose. He looks over his shoulder at the vampires' haven. Cora's inside. The energy bond between them is distressingly pale and thin, but he can still feel her. If he runs, he can make it inside. What happens then, he has no idea, but it's absolutely what he wants to do, even if it costs Akiko's life.

No! Ishtar's voice cracks across his thoughts like a whip made of fire. It reverberates so loudly in his skull that he winces and clutches at his temples. *You will stay and fight, Jack Alexander. You have sworn an oath to me, and this is the service I require. Face your Pack.*

When he opens his eyes again, he's surrounded.

The Pack is different than it was five years ago. He recognizes a scant three of the fifteen members, and most are in full wolf form. When he was here last, to be changed in public was severely punished; no one was allowed anything except human form unless absolutely necessary to avoid confrontations with mortals. For them to flaunt the old laws this way....

The scout from the Met parking lot shuffles forward, his muzzle firmly in Akiko's back. He nips at her heels when she stops walking, but she doesn't react, her face reassuringly stony. The beta growls his frustration, but there's a singular bark from the other side of the gathered wolves, and he retreats back to his place in the circle. Jack nods approvingly at Akiko. She's been disarmed—he can see the handle of the silver dagger sticking out of the ground near a tree—but she's not showing any fear. It's her best defense.

Hidden in the snow-dusted trees, there's a wet, crunching sound that goes on for the better part of a minute. Then the circle of wolves parts briefly and a stocky white man with disheveled amber hair lopes up to Jack, stopping millimeters away from touching him. The Alpha. His gold-flecked brown eyes are huge under bushy eyebrows, and his breath smells like rotting meat. He's totally naked but shows no sign that it troubles him, not even goosebumps. He's dwarfed by Jack's unusual height as he sniffs and snuffles the agent's clothing and cold-reddened skin. It's an aggressively vulnerable action this far inside an opponent's guard, and it would be easy for Jack to slip away or knock him down. But he stands perfectly still while he's examined. The last thing he wants in this moment is to give the Alpha a reason to kill him where he stands.

Apparently satisfied, the werewolf steps back and gives Jack a final evaluative look, then turns to the Pack and says in rough English, "Well, brothers? Our lost runt has returned home. How should we welcome him back?"

A chorus of howls erupts from the circle, punctuated with excited yips. The Alpha laughs. Jacks heart sinks. It's too similar to the last time he stood in the Pack's circle, but he's determined to keep himself from panicking now the way he did then.

When the howl drops off, the Alpha turns to Jack

with a grin. All of his teeth are unnaturally pointed. "You heard them. I'm afraid the Pack has spoken, *ragga*," he says. The lycan word for "traitor" doesn't come out of a human mouth easily, but Jack understands it fine. "Your brothers will see you punished."

There's no need to calculate the odds. Jack knows he's screwed. He can see Akiko behind the Alpha, flanked by two wolves, staring resolutely ahead as if she's ready for death at any second. All that's standing between that fate—for her, him, and the agents inside the vampire's haven—is Jack's ability to talk his way out of a fight.

"Leon...," he starts. But the Alpha growls viciously at his mortal name, and Jack hurriedly backtracks. "Rhand. I assume your scout reported back what I said when he met me yesterday." No sign of acknowledgement. "I'm no longer part of your pack. I'm not fully lycan. You have no right to punish me."

Rhand takes a step forward. "You pledged to us. Hunted with us. Slept with us. Howled with us. You were under oath—a brother in all but blood until you were discovered." He sniffs disdainfully. "A liar and a coward."

Jack wants to hit him right then but instead forces himself to lower his head respectfully. "I was undercover with the agency. It was strictly an intel-gathering mission, but someone blew my cover. If you and your brothers hadn't been acting like riotous gangsters instead of upstanding members of supernatural society, I wouldn't have come at all. I was trying to help you."

The Alpha ignores the explanation. "You carry my blood in your veins, whelp. You are Pack whether you claim it or not. You belong to me."

Familiar red mist starts to envelop Jack's mind, but he continues fighting the urge to lash out, keeping his voice steady. "Don't act so noble. You mauled me and poured your filthy blood into my wounds to contaminate me, then threw me out saying you'd kill me if I came back. Something about how being a brother without a pack was the worst punishment you could give me. I spent months in the ICU fighting for my life, and when I did get back on my feet, I was completely insane." He takes an aggressive step towards Rhand. "I don't belong to anyone except myself."

"I have changed my mind," the Alpha says. He gives a startlingly wolfish grin for a human face. "I've heard you've grown powerful since you left us. Given the news that the worlds will soon be reunited, I'd be a fool not to welcome you back into the fold. We will need all the strength we can gather to establish our people's territory in the new order."

Jack stares as the data slots into a coherent picture. "You're asking me to rejoin the Pack so I can help you take your cut of what Eris has promised you?"

Rhand stabs a thick finger into Jack's bony chest. "I am not asking," he says. "I am your Alpha, and you must obey."

The red mist thickens, making it difficult for Jack to avoid panting. The lycan taint in his blood itches for the change he cannot make. What Rhand's saying is both true and not. He is Jack's Alpha, but he was cast out; the urge to obey is fractionally less than his resistance. But Jack's ability to process this logic grows dimmer by the second, swiftly overtaken by a single thought: The Alpha is standing between him and Cora. Eris may be using the Pack to twist their bond, but he doesn't care. He has to get to her.

Before the Alpha can blink, Jack lashes out with both fists, connecting with Rhand's collarbones. The crack reverberates in the air despite the insulating blanket of snow surrounding them. The Alpha stumbles backward, putting several feet between them, and a vicious growl goes up from the circle of werewolves, but none of them move. They recognize this for what it is. Even Akiko steps back towards the trees to make room for the fighters.

Rhand wastes no time in shifting form. Blood splashes across the snow as his fingers split to make room for claws and his jaw cracks wide to grow fangs. Jack doesn't give him a chance to continue, hurtling forward and bowling the Alpha to the ground. Talons tear through his coat and suit down to the skin of his back as he's wrapped in arms made entirely of muscle. But he hangs on. Keeping the werewolf off balance and unable to achieve into full wolf form is the only way for him to survive.

But where the lycan strength and speed in Jack's blood have won him countless brawls in the past, it's not enough against a true werewolf. Rhand is easily twice as capable, even in his weaker human form, and he effortlessly regains control of the grapple, flinging Jack away in a high arc with one hand. The agent lands heavily on the ice-packed ground, all the air knocked from his lungs.

"Get up!" cries Akiko. "He's changing!"

Jack peers through the stars in his vision to see the Alpha wolf roll up to standing on two feet, the moonlight casting a dull sheen on his thick black fur. Panic seizes him, making it harder to catch his breath. He shoves himself up and to the side in time to dodge a charge that takes Rhand bounding into the circle. His brothers howl with glee as they catch him, then he turns and leaps back into the fight.

It's only a matter of time. Without silver or the ability to change form himself, Jack's a dead man. Flashes of the fate that awaits Akiko, Cora, and Manny taunt him as he sprints out of the way of another bullrush. It should've hit him. But he gets the impression that Rhand's toying with him, running him down to nothing to prove how insignificant he is before devouring him alive. Always been a classy one, that Leon.

You have another weapon, precious warrior. Use it.

He'd completely forgotten.

Jack spools up his energy as fast as he can, setting aside a stab of doubt. The bond is damaged but not broken. He has to trust it will work or die in the attempt. He stands in the center of the makeshift fighting ring with his eyes closed and fists at his sides—an easy target. The Alpha howls victoriously to see his prey has stopped struggling and barrels forward for the kill.

But when he arrives, there's no one there.

Confused, Rhand stumbles and crashes face-first into the snow, skidding several feet from his own momentum. When he flips over to survey the area, Jack is standing over him with a silver blade leveled right between his eyes.

"Submit," Jack hisses through clenched teeth. The short-range teleport to retrieve the dagger drained him of magic, and the silver burning his flesh is maddening, but his aim holds true. "Submit," he says again, louder this time so the entire Pack can hear.

Silence. For a full minute, fresh snow falling in Central Park is the only sound Jack hears. And then the black muzzle parts, not with a growl of defiance, but with a whimper of acceptance. Submission. He's won.

Jack releases the breath he'd been holding and straightens to his full height, lowering the silver dagger to allow Rhand to get up. He casts a glance over the attendant werewolves, turning in a complete circle to meet their eyes individually. One by one, the members of the Pack kneel. Some on human knees, some in a dog's bow. By the time he's facing Rhand again, even the huge black wolf is kneeling.

After a moment, he realizes they're waiting for him to say something. He looks to Akiko, who nods perfunctorily, and he tosses the silver blade to her. She catches it neatly by the handle and sheathes it in one swift movement. It might not be the smartest move to disarm, but he's confident it's the right one.

Bleeding and breathless, Jack spreads his arms in what he hopes is a magnanimous gesture. "My brothers," he says. "We have much to discuss."

There's a rumble that travels all the way around the circle. Two words, spoken in both human and lycan tongues, unmistakable and terrifying to him.

"Yes, Alpha."

NINETEEN

One in five. That's what they taught Cora's all-female class on the first day of sex ed. In a room of girls she'd grown up with, the statistic struck hard. Three people—three friends—would be a victim. By graduation, that prediction had come true. But it didn't stop there. As years rolled by, the numbers in her small-town cohort rose. Quietly. Furtively. Unreported except for tearful confessions to those who'd been there. One in four. One in three. One in two.

One hundred percent.

As she numbly trails the guard back down the haven's twisting passages, Cora finally counts herself among her peers. When she was younger, she waived blame for bar patrons who groped her and boyfriends who insisted on sex when she refused. Nothing she experienced compared with the flat-out rape her best friend suffered, so she didn't count it. But the Kincaid incident is different.

This time, she'd wanted it. Ached for it. Right up until she didn't. And when she said no, he went from lover to attacker. If the guard hadn't interrupted, she'd be dead.

She's vaguely aware that she should feel lucky, but all she feels is guilty. Could Jack sense everything through what's left of their bond? Does he know what she almost chose? How she failed? Her jaw quivers with the effort of holding back tears of shame as they approach the room where Manny's waiting. After his whole "you're awesome" speech, she's let him down, too. And her mother and father. Everyone that's told her she's strong and able.

Before the door to the holding room swings open, Cora gathers her grief and what-ifs into a tight ball in her chest and resolves to keep the events of the last hour a secret. She lifts her chin and wills her face into her usual open and amused expression. No one can know how weak she was. Is.

Manny's reading a book in an overstuffed chair when she arrives, and he stands to greet her with his usual warmth. But she must be more transparent than she thought. His smile falters and becomes knitted eyebrows and worried eyes.

But he doesn't ask.

And she doesn't tell.

The two agents wait until the door clicks shut before they both start to talk at once, meeting at the middle of the room.

"What did you find out from Kincaid?"

"Did you eat my dinner while I was gone?"

Manny smiles, sets down the book, and makes a chivalrous a half-bow. "Ladies first," he says.

Cora rolls her eyes but welcomes the silliness. It puts a crowbar separation between her and dark reality. "Unfortunately, the one real piece of intel I got is awful," she says. Manny quirks an eyebrow, and she makes an apologetic face. "Kincaid's not infected."

Manny blinks several times. "What."

She sighs, trying to distance the information from how she learned it. "Yeah, he's been wearing glitter-foundation to fake it. Gods know how long that's been going on."

"Why?"

"I'd guess it's so the other vamps will underestimate him, maybe to bring out his enemies who assume he's gone sappy and emo. It'd let him strike from a position of power whenever he wants. It's a pretty good con, actually."

"It's a huge problem is what it is," Manny scoffs.

"I know, right?" She shrugs. "Other than that, I didn't learn much," she says, glossing over the rest of the story. "The mirror's on the premises, but he didn't say where. Turns out elder vampires are good at keeping secrets." Then she remembers what else she discovered. With a sly grin, she reaches into the dress' hidden pocket and holds out a closed fist. "But I did find something in there." She waggles the fist playfully. "Guess."

"Kincaid's iPod filled with Britney Spears and N*Sync?"

"What? No!" she laughs. "Gods, you are so

weird."

Rather than letting him guess again, she opens her fingers. There's a plain gold ring sitting there. Other than its wide band and large diameter, there's nothing interesting about it.

"What is it?" he asks.

"No idea. My magic radar doesn't give me details. It's magic as hell, though. Pretty sure everything in his room is," she says, trailing off at the end.

Manny glides smoothly over the awkward silence. "You put it on yet?"

"Do I look like a Baggins to you?" She shoots him a sharp look. "Don't answer that."

Cora shifts her gaze to the ring and holds it up with two fingers to squint at it in the light. Ring lore is one of the hardest subjects she's tackled in her mythological education. They're all so similar, both in function and appearance, that it's hard to tell one from another. What makes it extra complicated is that it's possible this could be the One Ring because of those damned hobbit movies. They changed the dwarves—why not magic rings?

The ring isn't past her fingertip when Manny stops her. She gives him an offended frown, but he shakes his head solemnly. "You know better than to put on strange magical jewelry, Riley."

"But you just said—"

"I was kidding, dude. But who knows? Maybe you found the one artifact that can seal the Gauntlet forever. We can traipse on home, lock Eris up, and have a round of beers for a job well done. Have Cid test it when you get back to headquarters."

Cora huffs melodramatically. "Okay, Dad." The ring goes back into her dress pocket. "You're no fun, you know that?"

Manny looks stung. "Hey, I'm a fun guy," he says. "For example." He reaches into a pocket and holds up a closed fist of his own. Beaming from ear to ear, he says, "Guess what *I* found."

She doesn't miss a beat. "The key to Kincaid's German midget porn stash?"

"Geez, no! What is wrong with you?" he snorts. He opens his hand, releasing a bunch of keys that dangles from his thumb. They jingle lightly against each other.

It's Cora's turn to raise an eyebrow. "And those are...?"

"Man, you were supposed to be impressed." He drops the keys onto the bed with a mock pout. "I nab the keys for the entire damn haven, and all I get is sass."

Her eyes widen. "The guard's keys? How did you get those?" She looks at the door to their room-slash-cell. "Can we get out of here?"

"Our door isn't locked." Her eyes get even wider. He shrugs. "Anymore, anyway. Kincaid said we were supposed to be honored guests. All I did was point out to Justin that locking us up wasn't exactly in keeping with that."

Cora doesn't mention that she did the same thing when they arrived, albeit with limited results. "But the keys...," she says.

"Let's just say our guard is a betting man who's

bored out of his skull and sucks at chess," he says, mildly embarrassed.

Cora shakes her head in amazed disbelief. She knows Manny's been kicked out of casinos for winning too often, but this is ridiculous.

"Oh, and poker," he continues with a sheepish smile. He points at the round table at the center of the room. The covered trays sit on the floor, replaced by a messy stack of cards, two beer bottles, and—

"Our clips," Cora breathes. "How...?" she starts, but he just shrugs. "You are the luckiest son of a bitch in the world, Manny. Remind me never to bet against you," she says with a disbelieving laugh. "I assume you have the ultimate escape plan, between the literal keys to the castle and getting our ammo back."

"Actually, no. I mean, I had a couple ideas, but I was waiting for you."

The reminder hurts, but she masters it before it shows on her face. "Well, I'm here now. Tell me what sort of Houdini act you've got in mind. Does it involve beating up vampires and blowing stuff up? Because I could seriously go for some of that."

Manny chuckles. "I was thinking more like we could walk out of here. Although, now that I say it out loud, that's pretty dumb. We'd need help, and Finn turned on us. I don't know if I have any allies left in the building."

"You've got Justin," Cora says, pointing to the door to indicate their guard. "And a buttload of supernaturally good luck. That's got to count for something, right?"

"I'd feel better about relying on my powers if I hadn't been betrayed and locked up by friends in the last two hours," he says with a rueful grin.

She reaches over and prods him in the knee. "Weren't you the one reminding me how stories work not an hour ago, Mister Luckypants? Bad guys always get their comeuppance. Finn's either going to get horrifically murdered for being a douchebag or he'll redeem himself and turn out to be a good guy. Given that he's playing a double agent in a vampire story, my money's on horrible murder."

He shrugs. "You're probably right. But I hope you're wrong."

Cora gives him a reassuring smile, then picks up the keys, wishing for a solution to their problem. There have to be two dozen room keys here, and they're each neatly labeled. *Freezer 1*, *Ballroom*, *Laundry*, and so on. The brain-softening glitter herpes is turning out to be useful, after all.

One key in particular catches her eye. "Wait a second," she says. "I believe I've found our plan." She grabs the key by the end, letting the others fall to the bottom, and holds it up for to Manny to inspect.

He squints to read it, then grins hugely. "You think?" he says.

"I do."

"Right into the treasure room?"

"And out the back door."

Manny barks a laugh. "That's pretty ballsy, my friend. I like the way you think." But then his face falls. "What about Jack?" he says. "I don't know if he'd want us pulling that kind of stunt. At least, not without him."

She considers it. He's right, of course, but he'd sent Jack a text before they headed to the Council hours ago. It's possible Jack's hot on their trail. She wishes, not for the first time, that she hadn't tried to sever their magical link, that she'd put more faith in it and in him.

The moment she has that thought, a wave of cerulean energy smashes against her mind with the force of a Mach-five migraine. She gasps and screws her eyes shut, but the light doesn't dim. She's temporarily paralyzed with pain and confusion, yet part of her knows exactly what's happening. It seizes the cord that connects her to Jack and rides out the influx of magic bursting through it. Where yesterday she had trouble sensing him while standing at his side, now she's breathless with information about him. Fear, guilt, rage. Weakness, desires. Her—endless images of her. They rush past as fine threads of energy wind into the frayed bond, strengthening every tear in the fabric.

And then she's released.

Endorphins flood in to protect her fragile mind in the aftermath and sweat stands out on her forehead. For a second, she's forgotten how to breathe. A deluge of questions chokes out everything but the undeniable conviction that all is not lost—the bond is mending.

Eventually, Manny's voice filters through Cora's trance. "Dude," he says. "Are you okay?"

She opens her eyes one at a time, the ordinary light of the room chasing away her desire to sink back into the magic. She blinks several times, then nods at Manny, her lips curling into a grin.

"Jack's here," she whispers. "And he is *pissed*."

It's amazing what a difference half an hour can make, Jack muses to himself. Twelve percent of a plan has become a full hundred, complete with options and moving parts. Even the Founder guards who came out to "greet" him and the ambassador on the lawn of Belvedere Castle are part of it. He can see the intertwining threads as clearly as if they'd been drawn in the air.

But the battlerage hasn't left him. The aftermath of defeating Rhand as Alpha, the rush of victory and thrill of the fight, isn't wearing off. The red edge of it tints his thoughts and vision, overriding other sensations, his whole being prepared to leap back into action. He writes it off as adrenaline, anticipation for the impending confrontation with the Dracula. There's work to be done, and all of it is dangerous. He needs the boost. Senses sharpened and mind whirring, he's enjoying the rush of fresh power where his sidestepping abilities are useless.

Akiko walks beside him as they're ushered into the haven, drawn up so tall with pride that it's a wonder she doesn't float. Jack tried to talk her out of coming along. With their new allies, there's no need for her to be put in further danger. But, as she so convincingly pointed out, having the descendant of a sun deity could be helpful when facing down vampires. If all goes according to Plan A, though, it won't come to that.

The two of them are escorted into the haven by four low-level Founders wearing battle gear. Jack adds that detail to the other out-of-order items he's compiling. Outer doors barred with silver instead of steel, rooms devoted to weaponry instead of books, visitors from other clans mixing freely in public spaces. Further evidence that Akiko's fears about their allegiance to Eris are true. The vampires are preparing for war.

As they're ushered into the main hall, the scene is no less disturbing. Jack and Akiko's guards haul open the heavy double doors to reveal that the entire room, barring a narrow strip down the center as an aisle, is crammed with vampires. Jack estimates a hundred and twenty, meaning the crowd is composed of more than Founders. His eyes skim over the would-be soldiers to the front where Seanan Kincaid presides over the assembly from his casual perch in a high-backed chair decorated with gold filigree. Finnegan stands next to him, arm draped protectively over the top of his sire's throne and his head on a swivel. Both are dressed for combat—the elder in a chain shirt and battle kilt, his child in black operator fatigues.

As the doors swing open, every vampire in the room turns to look, laser-focused on the new arrivals. No one speaks or moves. Jack is certain his heartbeat is audible. The fine hair all over his body raises under their gaze, the lycan taint in his blood riled at the presence of its enemy. He concentrates on gathering his energy into a peaceful center to ground himself. A single tendril refuses to be gathered; the cord binding him to Cora, which is brighter than before. He gives it an experimental tug. There's a solid pulse in return that makes his heart soar and the rage first subside then redouble. She's here. She's alive. She's close.

Akiko nudges Jack in the ribs; he's been standing in the doorway a few seconds too long. He wonders if the vampires noticed, but steps into the room as if they didn't.

The Dracula waits to acknowledge them until they're at his feet. His chair is raised on a platform so that even at Jack's tremendous height, he's being looked down on. Both Kincaids have amused expressions on their faces as the agent and paragon are required to look up at them in a semblance of respect.

"Welcome to our humble abode, Agent Ninety-Seven," the elder says, then nods to Akiko. "Madam Ambassador. My clan and I are honored to receive you."

"Save the speeches, Kincaid," Jack says. "You have my people. Release them to me."

Red eyebrows go up. "Very well. You've fulfilled your end of the bargain." He glances lasciviously at Akiko, ignoring the ugly word she mutters, then snaps his fingers at Finn. "Fetch the agents," he says without looking around.

There's a twitch in the younger vampire's face, but he simply says, "Yes, sire," and withdraws through a door behind the platform.

Jack watches him go, an ray of hope slipping into his mind. He'd planned for resistance. Vampires aren't known for their fair dealings, but it's possible that the *éclat* has contaminated their minds enough to be useful. Perhaps he really will leave here with all his people unharmed.

A second snap of Kincaid's fingers shatters that hope.

Faster than Jack can react, an armored Founder clamps onto Akiko's right arm. She gasps as her bones grind together, and the goon grins horribly and starts to drag her away. She twists and flails with her free hand, swearing mightily in her native language, but she can't break free of the supernatural grip.

Jack's coiled to spring, plan dashed and ready to fight his way out, when Kincaid's voice cracks across the scene.

"Gently!" Everyone stops as if the command were a spell. Then, softly, he adds, "The ambassador is to be treated with the respect due the savior of our people. Shedding her blood now gains us nothing."

Jack glares at him, willing away the stirred-up battlerage. "That wasn't our arrangement, Kincaid," he says. "The mirror for my people."

"Yes, that's true. But I've changed my mind." The Founder gives him a bemused smile. "Surely you didn't think I'd let you abscond with the source of our cure after you so willingly delivered her to us, did you?" His smile widens into a grin. "You did?"

He laughs, short and sharp. "You've become painfully naïve in your autumn years, Agent 97. I expected better from you."

There's a momentary struggle in Jack's mind, but years of polished conduct win out. Kincaid's taunting him, daring him to strike first so he has an excuse to kill him and his agents, then claim Akiko. He has to play this right. Stick to the plan.

Jack straightens, heartbeat quickening, and takes a measured step forward. It's not enough to be a real threat, but it's enough to suggest one is coming. It does the trick. The room falls silent. The elder tilts his head to one side as if intensely curious.

"All of my people will be leaving here with me, including Minamoto Akiko," Jack says, ensuring his voice carries. If this doesn't go well, he wants everyone to know why. "You can keep the mirror. Do whatever you like with it. You can hand it directly to Lady Eris for all I care." A murmur shoots through the crowd at the mention of the goddess' name. Evidently word of the agency's involvement hadn't gotten this far. Good. Maybe that'll scare some of them back into reason. Jack keeps his eyes trained on Kincaid, jaw and will set. "But the ambassador, Agent Six, and Agent Forty-Two are leaving here with me, unmolested and unpursued." He allows himself a wry smile. "Or else."

Kincaid smirks at the reflection of his earlier threat. "Or else what, agent? Your weapons are useless against my kind, and I could break your neck before your next sentence." He raises his eyebrows encouragingly. "What do you have up your sleeve that could possibly intimidate me into giving in to your demands?"

The lone howl from outside is barely audible at first. It builds as more voices rush to join in, seeping through the thick castle walls. It changes the texture of the air in the throne room as each vampire understands what they're hearing. It closes in fast from every direction.

The haven is surrounded by werewolves.

A susurrus of uncertainty in the crowd becomes a chorus of nervous fear. Out of the corner of his eye, Jack can see that every vampire face is turned expectantly to Kincaid.

But the Founder's expression doesn't change one iota, his air of patient amusement lingering as the lycan cries rise and fall. Jack can't help being impressed. The elder vampire surely knows what hell's being called down on him—he's survived the shift from allies to enemies and lost family to the wolves—but he's unmoved. There's flicker of uncertainty in Jack's mind, and he clamps down on it. He's got to trust Rhand.

"That's your plan, agent?" the Founder says. "Werewolves at our doorstep?" He leans back with studied casualness and waves a hand at the room in general. "The doors are barred with silver. There are guards at every entrance. The walls are four feet thick. You are surrounded by vampires. Explain to me why I should be moved by such an empty threat."

"Because it's already happening."

A quiet beat passes. Then two, then five, then ten. Nothing happens. The baying wolves fade and disappear. The smile on Kincaid's face turns into arrogant victory.

The silence is more frightening to Jack than the blood-curdling howl. The Pack's entrance into the castle should have been noisy. He'd instructed them to crash the rear gates, sacrificing a willing brother to the silver doors, and joining him in the throne room to enforce his renegotiations. The lack of screams tells him something has gone wrong. A dozen possibilities run through Jack's mind, cramming together into an increasingly desperate picture of failure.

When it's clear that the moment has passed, Kincaid stands and regards Jack and Akiko with something close to pity. "I'm sorry, agent, but your friends are not coming to rescue you." He bends at the waist, face inches from Jack's. "And since you have the audacity to threaten me in my own home, I believe I will keep all of you. Turning three children is as easy as turning one." His eyes slide up and down Jack's frame. "Oh, the things I will do to you."

A pair of hands seize Jack's arms and yank them behind his back. He twists and knocks the guard to the floor, but two more are on him instantly. Next to him, Akiko struggles with her own assailant. Her entire body is faintly outlined in a pulsing glow that pushes back the vampires around her. Jack realizes she's spooling up her magic—power that, if released, could wipe out the Founder clan in an instant. As much as he doesn't want to be captured, and as little love as he has for vampires, he can't allow wholesale murder, even in self-defense.

"No!" he shouts.

Akiko looks up, startled. It breaks her concentration, and the glow fades. The vampire behind her, free from the ultraviolet burn of her aura, resecures his hold on her wrists.

The ambassador gives Jack a furious glare. "I will see every one of them in ashes before I allow them to become servants of chaos."

Jack shakes his head. "Trust me," he says. Although he's not sure she should. Plan B is messy.

Kincaid sneers with satisfaction at his prisoners. He's about to give another command when the door at the back of the room opens, and Finn reappears. Alone.

The elder's brow furrows angrily. "Where have you been?" he demands. "Where are the agents?"

Finn says nothing. He only gives a vindictive smile and presses his back to the wooden door, holding it open wide.

And then the world is full of wolves.

The Pack pours through the doorway, some too big and cracking the wooden frame as they barrel into the throne room, foam dripping from their fangs. Fifteen enormous werewolves bound towards their prey, starting in tight formation, then breaking into groups of three to better cover the battlefield.

The first victims don't have time to scream. Jaws like bear traps clamp around limbs and heads, crushing and cracking bones like matchsticks. Black ichor and grey ash smears fur and flagstones, turning the hall into a slaughterhouse floor in seconds.

Others are quicker on the uptake. The Founders haven't lost their battle instincts, despite the changes from the last century of belief. Even *Twilight* vampires are accomplished fighters, after all. Many draw silver daggers from their belts, but others attack with fangs and talons of their own, shifting from beautiful human to monster of the night in seconds.

Yet more of their number fall. The element of surprise works in the lycans' favor. The hulking beasts bite and slash their way through another score of vampires before the first werewolf is wounded. A snarl of pain and fury echoes against the castle stones, giving new vigor to the Pack's offensive.

Jack and Akiko are secured in place as the fight rages around them, protected from being fatally involved themselves by Rhand's massive body between them and the fray. The former Alpha bats away vampires like annoying moths and takes several cuts with silver blades from the better fighters to keep the new Alpha from harm.

The plan worked.

From the raised platform at the front of the room, Seanan Kincaid watches as the werewolves mow down his people. His face shows no emotion. Not alarm. Not fury. Nothing. Seconds tick past as he stands that way, ignoring the agent and paragon in front of him, attention wholly absorbed by the fight.

Then, without warning, he's gone.

Jack whips around in time to see a streak of black hair and pale skin materialize under a fountain of lycan blood across the room. Before he can ascertain who's been wounded or how, there's another flash of black and crimson on the other side of the hall. Then another. The hair on the back of Jack's neck rises as he realizes Kincaid has joined the fray. The elder Founder darts between victims faster than the werewolves know they've been hit, faster than Jack's sharp eyes can track. The first delayed yips and howls of pain follow as one, then two, then three werewolves are mutilated by the ancient vampire, his lesser clanmates leaping on the easy prey he leaves in his wake.

Rhand sees his brothers start to fail and rears up on his hind legs, fully twelve feet high, and lets out a bellow that vibrates the tall windows of the castle. He flings himself headlong into the knot of bodies, red-eyed and lost to rage, leaving Jack and Akiko exposed at the front of the room under a cloud of ashes.

Neither of them hesitate. Jack pulls Akiko to him as she attempts to charge her aura of sunlight. He scans the room with lightning-quick analysis, tugging urgently on the blue cord of energy that leads to Cora, formulating an optimal plan for escape, retrieval, and survival.

When his eyes land on the door behind the throne, he notices Finn's standing in the doorway, motioning urgently at him.

Akiko is moving before Jack is, practically dragging him as she sprints towards their ally and the promise of temporary safety. He doesn't resist.

They're heading right to Cora.

PART III
MIRROR, MIRROR

TWENTY

When I was a boy, there were so many overt lessons taught to me about the qualities and values that made me a man. I never thought about the lessons I absorbed under the surface until I lay in a hospital bed fighting for my life. For the right to stay a man instead of become a monster. Every one of them rose up and fought against the wolf trying to take over my body. They rallied together to preserve my self. They won. Over weeks and months, they won. But the cost was so great that I returned to the living world a man in form only. Inside—in my mind, heart, and soul—I was a cold summation of platonic ideals.

A man values duty above all else. A man is efficient and practical. A man is honorable and strong. A man must work. A man does not feel. That is what I was taught as a boy. That is what I became as a man. As a machine.

A year ago, the machine broke down. I was left

with the shell of who I had become covering a quivering mass of painful memories and abandoned desires. Six months later, I functioned well enough to convince those around me that I'd recovered. I fooled myself for a time, too. I thought I was whole again. I had no concept for how much further I had to go—until her. Each day she's in my life, another chain breaks. Freedom I didn't know I lacked. Even in this current purgatory, she's there, reminding me there's more to being a man—to being human—than ideals.

Standing in the ringing quiet of the hallway in the Founders' haven, battle raging on the other side of a barred wooden door, I close my eyes and focus on Cora. I stretch my awareness along the magic between us, plucking it like a sounding line. It thrums with blue energy, pointing me to her, and I smile within myself. The bond had all but died the night she left me standing alone on my doorstep. I was so angry, so hurt. When she appeared unannounced in New York, I wanted to hate her—or worse, to feel nothing. To turn the mess of emotions into something useful, detached, and efficient. But without the mechanical voice of Agent 97, I can't. And now that I'm free of Limerence's ownership, too, there's nothing concealing the deeper truth: While we can abuse and ignore it, while we did not ask for it, the bond is firmly in place. It doesn't matter what we want. It doesn't matter how we treat one another. This is old magic, with rules and purposes of its own. It will have its way. Though she may not want anything to do with it, for my part, I will treat the bond as it's intended, as it was forged—with love.

There's a gentle tap on my shoulder. I look down to see Akiko staring up at me inquisitively. It's the second time I've drifted away thinking of Cora since we arrived at the castle. The ambassador must be wondering about my sanity, but she doesn't ask.

Finnegan, however, isn't as respectful. He finishes securing a set of locks and bars on the door to the main hall, then claps me on the back as he moves past. "No time for day dreaming, boyo," he says. "We need to move."

I don't argue. The mêlée in the throne room is intensifying, and I can smell blood. It prickles at my skin, demanding I turn around, dive into the fray, and fight with the pack I now lead. But there are more important things to attend to. I push down the wolf and grip the thread of cerulean energy as my guide and my anchor.

The three of us break into a jog, heading to another doorway at the end of the long hall. Finn moves to turn left at an intersection, Akiko following, but I stop. They're going the wrong way.

"Wait," I call after them. They stop but with reluctance. "We need to find Cora and Manny." I tap the bond, searching for her, like a game of hot and cold. Ah, there. "They're down here," I say, pointing to the other arm of the corridor.

I'm the subject of a pair of confused stares. "How can you know that?" Finn asks. "That's the complete opposite direction from the room they're being held in."

I respond by jogging towards the signal, the energy growing stronger and brighter with every step.

Finn matches my stride in seconds, and he paces me as we run. "Agent, we're heading directly to the treasury. Any fighters that haven't made their way to the battle yet will be posted there. You're running us straight into a trap."

In my emotional haze, I hadn't considered the possibility of additional resistance. Or the fact that the captured agents have no idea I've arrived and likely have their own escape plan. We might not be the only ones running into a trap.

I stop again, and the others draw close with expectation in their faces. There was a time when that would bring me great satisfaction—knowing everyone is depending on me to direct them. Now, it's more wearisome than gratifying. The downside of ridding myself of Agent 97 is that I don't always have an answer.

A thought I'd disregarded during the invasion of the castle uses the pause to thrust itself forward. My danger sense bridges two moments, making a logical connection. I quickly scan the area, then turn my attention to Finn. We have precious few seconds to spare, but this can't wait.

"Speaking of traps: Why did you let the werewolves in?" I ask. "It's odd to me that you'd open the gates to mortal enemies, knowing what would happen, much less be unhurt yourself."

The Founder's eyebrows draw together and his jaw tightens. But rather than lower his head in shame, he lifts his chin defiantly to answer. "The Omega, Heedless, and I were friends before his Change. We've saved each other's lives more than once since then, and keeping our friendship hidden from my clan has not been easy. When I recognized his voice in the howl, I ran to the side entrance and he explained your plan. In the absence of his Alpha, he ensured my safety in return for my help."

"That you have been searching for a way to dethrone your sire has nothing to do with it, I am certain," Akiko adds. "You are an opportunist."

Finn glowers at her but nods curtly. "I will do whatever it takes to keep our people from falling further. We have already lost so much."

Every instinct I've honed in over a decade in the field tells me that this man is our enemy, one with complicated, secret agendas leading us to a messy death. His story is too clean; his motivations are vague; his allegiances, unclear. But there's something in his eyes that gives me pause. Like he's asking for permission. Or forgiveness. Why he would need such things, I don't know.

Approaching footsteps cut off further questions. All three of us turn sharply towards the intersection ahead. I motion for the vampire and paragon to move to either side of me so that we occupy the full width of the hallway. Tactics for vampire combat begin to fill my mind as I allow the battlerage to trickle back into my muscles. We crouch down, ready to spring on our attackers from a strong foundation. I signal again, indicating for the others to wait. Let them come to us.

"Holy shit, Ninety-Seven?!"

The first person around the corner is a rangy man in a disheveled, ash-dusted tuxedo with light brown hair hanging in his eyes. He holds a rough-hewn chair leg in one hand and a handgun in the other. I have to shake my head hard to clear the descending red mist before I recognize him.

It's Manny.

Quick around the corner behind him is Cora, wielding the same weapons, her borrowed emerald gown inexpertly ripped to raise the hem from floor to knee, her grey eyes ablaze. Relief floods through me at the sight of her safe, washing away the last of the wolf I'd been subconsciously relying on to find her.

Her eyes catch mine, and she starts to smile. But when she recognizes the rest of my party, the smile evaporates, and suddenly both agents have their guns raised.

"Jack, get away from him!" she shouts.

"Finnegan Kincaid, down on the ground!" says Manny, striding towards us.

Both Akiko and I turn sharply to the Founder. Anger is written boldly across his features, but he does as directed, interlocking his fingers behind his bald head and kneeling slowly. Manny holsters his gun and retrieves handcuffs from his belt in one motion, then twists Finn's unresisting wrists into them behind his back. He hauls the vampire to his feet, and as he rises, I can see that the agent's expression matches his captive's.

The ambassador steps straight up to Manny.

"What is the meaning of this, Agent Forty-Two?" she demands. "This man is our ally. He assisted us in escaping from the elder Kincaid and was helping us to locate and rescue you."

Manny shoots a questioning look at me over her head. "This is the guy who kidnapped us, boss. He knew about the attack on the ambassador, led us to the Dracula Council, then turned on us the second he had the chance." He tightens his grip on Finn's arms. "Who knows how long this son of a bitch played me?"

Akiko gasps as if she's been slapped. The weight of the vampire's betrayal physically sags her shoulders. "Why—" she starts.

But the sound of more footsteps cuts her off. The battle in the throne room must have overspilled its boundaries. I count six people running, none of them wolves.

"This can wait," I say, shifting into crisis management. As much as this revelation makes me want to rip out Finn's lying tongue, our survival comes first. "Bring him with us. Traitor or not, he can be useful." Then I turn to Finn and ask, "Where can we hide?"

He shakes his head. "The rooms down this way are admin and tech. They're locked."

"Don't worry about that," Manny counters. "I've got it covered."

Finn points with his chin towards the left fork of the intersection. "The treasury's down that way. If you want the mirror, that's where it'll be. Plus, it's the most secure room in the entire castle. Good hiding spot, if we can get in."

I narrow my eyes at him. "You said it's heavily guarded. Are you really still trying to play both sides when you've been caught?"

"You don't have to trust me, agent," he sneers. "If you have a better plan, I'm sure the pissed-off vampires closing in to kill you would love to hear it if you wait a few more seconds."

He's right, of course. We're wasting valuable time out in the open. I curse and motion for the group to follow behind as I start moving. Better for me to be out front if we're going to encounter more resistance.

Cora, however, has other ideas. She pulls up alongside me, jogging to keep pace, stake levelled on top of her sidearm as if it were a flashlight. Her face is serious and analytical as we clear the hallway together. Our movements are silently coordinated, high-low and left-right, as if we've been partners in the field for years. It strikes me that this is the first time we've worked together this way. I can sense the bond between us brighten at the thought.

It takes two more turns and a full minute for us to reach the treasury. As we round the second corner, I brace for a fight with a new contingent of Founder guards but find none. Either they've joined the fight in the throne room or they weren't here to begin with. Perhaps the lowered common sense and inflated confidence of the *éclat* infection is working in our favor.

We stop in front of the iron-reinforced double doors at the dead end of the last hallway, and I take over Finn's security as Manny flips through a keyring. If it were any other agent, I'd ask where he got them. With Manny, there's no point.

"Got it," he whispers with excitement.

The right side of the door falls open, and the five of us creep inside. Cora's the last in, and she pulls the door closed as six sets of pounding footsteps round the corner in hot pursuit. They come to a faltering stop, accompanied by swearing. There's a muttered argument as the Founders grasp that their quarry is gone, primarily along the lines of "where the hell did they go." Not even breath moves on our side of the door as we wait in total darkness for them to leave.

We don't move until the vampires have retreated out of range of my heightened senses. Held breath is exhaled, echoing dryly over the stone walls. I turn from the door to the interior, the large room completely black, processing our next steps. Then Cora, likely disoriented in the dark herself, bumps into my side, brushing my hand. I expect the blue spark this time; what I don't expect is how large it is. Like a static charge built up steadily but unreleased, it makes an audible *snap*, sending out a bolt that illuminates the treasury for a half second. She gasps—although I'm not sure if it's from the unusual magical discharge or from what we saw in the flash.

"One moment," Akiko says from the far end of our line.

A beat passes, then a warm yellow glow cut through the gloom. It intensifies until a ball of light fills her cupped hands and reveals a broad circle around her, spreading quickly to cover the rest of the group.

"Shit, turn that off!" Finn hisses. He's leaning away as far as possible, trying to defend himself against the light.

The paragon gasps, dousing her light immediately. "Forgive me," she says in the dark. "I had forgotten your people are not immune to my powers."

"Jesus," he mutters. "This is the twenty-first century, you superpowered idiots. There's a light switch on the wall behind Forty-Two."

Cora does a poor job of suppressing her laughter, and I make no effort to hide my smile in the dark. But when Manny flips the switch, the humor drains out of all of us.

The overhead lights come on in rows to reveal that we're standing in front of a massive collection of artifacts. Stories-high shelving covers every inch of the walls, leaving the broad floor empty except for four equally-spaced tables, which I note are bolted to the ground through a vast Arabian-style carpet. It reminds me of the archives at the Roosevelt, if it had been arranged for proud display rather than efficient storage.

What has struck us speechless, however, is not the size of the room or the impressive quantity of objects it contains. It's the fact that every single artifact is contained in an identical wooden box. There are no labels, no writing, no identifying markings of any kind. Just row upon column of square crates staring blankly down at us.

It's Manny that breaks the silence. "At least it's not full of vampires?" he says.

Cora laughs, but no one else does. We're facing hours of searching, using time we don't have, in a haven filled with vengeful monsters aligned with a mad deity who needs the very item we're looking for. If we're going to do this, we need help.

I turn to Finn, who's fidgeting with his handcuffs beside me. "Do you know which box the mirror is in?" I ask.

"Like he's going to tell us any secrets," Cora says.

"Dude, not cool," says Manny at the same time.

I hold up my hand, and they fall silent. Finn stares defiantly back at me as I say to him, "Founder Kincaid. I'm offering you a chance to redeem yourself to the agency and humanity at large. You will answer for your involvement in the abduction and assassination attempts, but for the moment, I choose to believe that you're driven by the well-being of your people. That gives you a measure of grace in my eyes." The vampire's expression shifts subtly, his back straightening. I've got his attention. "Help us locate Amaterasu's mirror, and I promise to do what's in my power to help your race recover."

Before Finn can answer, Cora is beside us. "Jack, you have no idea what he's up to." She points at the ambassador. "He thinks that if they drain Akiko's blood onto the mirror, it'll remove the UV curse so they can become daywalkers, like Blade. Even if he does find it in this mess, we've brought her right to him." She glares at Finn. "What's to keep him from calling up his buddies on the Founder Phone, overpowering us, and dumping our blood on the damned thing, too?"

I look back at Finn, eyebrows raised. "Well?"

"I suppose taking my word on it won't be enough."

"Not by a long shot."

"What about mine?" says Akiko.

"Madam Ambassador?"

She ignores me and locks her gaze on Finn. "Will you take my word that no matter how much of my blood is spilled on the mirror, the curse cannot be lifted? That no power can be gained that you do not already possess? That I will give my life to prove it, if necessary, for the sake of curing this obsession?"

Finn's eyes widen, rimming with black ichor. "Yes," he whispers. Then he lowers his head, and Akiko puts her hand on it in benediction. The next words are so quiet I nearly miss them. "I am sorry, *hogosha.*"

TWENTY-ONE

On the other side of the room, Manny clears his throat inelegantly. His face is dark under a furrowed brow, a startling change from his usual self. It seems he's not so quick to forgive Finn's duplicity as the ambassador.

"That's all very touching, but do we have an actual plan?" he says, stabbing a hand at the racks of identical boxes. "We still have a shot at finding this thing. Cora and I saw it at the Council meeting, so that'll help, but we need a starting point."

I look to Cora, but she shakes her head. "Already checked. There's too much magic in here for the radar to be useful. It's basically one giant yes."

I look to Akiko, but she also shakes her head. "The mirror does not call to me. I can identify it through magical communion, but it takes time. I am afraid I am no more helpful than anyone else at this stage."

I look to Finn, who's already exchanged

penitence for smugness. "It's organized by type. I don't know where they stored this exact mirror, but I can point you at the accessories section, no problem." He turns to the side to show me his wrists. "But you have to let me go."

Manny's eyes are heavy on my back as I unlock the vampire's handcuffs. I make a mental note to speak to him when we have a moment. As someone who's been burned by treating informants as friends, I want to ensure he doesn't harbor the same bitterness as I did. Innocence isn't traditionally desirable in a government agent, it should be preserved in Manny. I doubt he understands how valuable his perpetual optimism is. Until now, I'm not sure I did, either. Even if he won't stop calling me "dude."

Free from his bonds, Finn indicates the middle rack of the southern wall. "The bottom half of that one is where the mirrors, bags, and hair things are kept. If I remember correctly, there are at least six mirrors in storage."

I nod, then check my internal clock against what I know about vampire tactics, lycan battlerage, and probability. "We have approximately fifteen minutes before we risk being discovered," I say. "Then we need to get the hell out of here."

I'm grateful that they head to the boxes without asking for details of our escape. I'm still working on that.

Before I join the search myself, I turn to Finn and say, "Stand guard. I don't want to be sweeping you off the floor on the off chance we find the thing and you're the one who opens it." He moves toward the door, but I catch his elbow and draw him close enough I can whisper in his ear. "I'm trusting you on this, vampire, but gods help me, if there's one grain of betrayal left in you, if you risk the lives of my people by turning on us again, I will end you."

His blue eyes widen with satisfying fear. He nods quickly, and I let him go.

Well done, dearest one, Ishtar says. *You are progressing beautifully.*

I sweep her voice from my mind as I cross the room, yet traces of her remain. Before tonight, any time the goddess spoke to me, I accepted it as the price for the foolhardy oath I made to her in the underworld. After defeating the Alpha and taking over the Pack, I assumed that I'd completed the service she required and that I'd be free of her. But she's still here, prodding me onward. I want to know why. For the moment, though, I have more than enough to manage without wondering if a ten-thousand-year-old goddess is riding me like a warhorse toward an awful fate.

The others have a system in place by the time I join them. Manny's hoisting crates to the floor while Akiko uses my silver knife to pry them open and Cora checks the contents. I allow myself a private smile at their efficiency. Whatever else I feel about 42 and 6, they're excellent agents.

"Any luck yet?" I ask.

"Just the usual sort," Manny says over his shoulder.

From the floor, Cora says, "I found a bag of

holding!" She holds up a velvet drawstring bag about the size of a basketball. It appears to have once housed an entire colony of moths. Seeing I'm not impressed, she jams her arm into it up to the shoulder, but the bag doesn't change size. "Eh, eh?" she says encouragingly.

I shake my head. "We're not taking anything except what we came for. We're tracking down a stolen object, not stealing others." Her face falls and she puts the bag back in its box. Hurriedly I add, "I'm confident we can get a warrant to search this place for the Roosevelt's missing artifacts. Ninety-Nine will—" But I don't finish the sentence. I can't. I recover somewhat lamely, saying. "I'll talk to Tithonus and see what we can work out."

The other agents return to their work with sad eyes, leaving me to my thoughts. I'd forgotten about him. About what he's done. I've been operating as if nothing was wrong, but now that we're close to returning home, I don't know what will happen when we get there. What has Samir been doing while we're away? Does he know he's been discovered? What will happen if we bring the mirror into headquarters? Who else in the agency has turned? The world is dangerously unbalanced beneath me as I try to parse the proper course of action.

Two voices break my trance.

"Got it!" say Akiko and Cora in unison.

There's a comical moment where they look at one another, then look at the objects in their hands, then look up at me. Both women are holding simple hand mirrors, the sort commonly found on vanity tables until the mid-1900s, with dark wood frames. I kneel down to examine them more closely. Of course they're identical, right down to the grain of the wood and flaws in the glass. I recognize the method from a larceny case I worked as a rookie: a high-level glamour to conceal the artifact in plain sight. Highly annoying. I knew this wouldn't be an easy task, but I'd predicted less of a runaround.

"Open the rest of them," I say. "We need to make sure we see all the mirrors before we proceed."

It doesn't take much longer since we've located the right section of the collection. With three minutes left on my internal timer, seven mirrors, safely in their boxes to avoid hurting Finn, are laid out in a line. Every one a copy.

"Somebody's fucking with us," Cora mutters. "They had to know we were coming." She shoots an acid glare at Finn guarding the door.

"I do not think so," replies Akiko, turning one of the boxes over in her hands. "In fact, I would be disappointed were there no magical security on the objects. If I had to guess, they are linked to the haven in addition to this glamour. It is possible that if we remove the mirrors from this room, they will self-destruct or simply transport back to their places." A faint smile touches her lips. "It is actually quite elegant."

Cora huffs. "Great. Now I'm mad and there's no one to be mad at. Fantastic. Can't you use ancient sun-lady powers to figure out which one's yours?"

"I can. However, it is a tedious and energy-intensive process that requires time we do not have. I predict an hour per object as I am off my home soil during the night."

There's a pause in the conversation, and I slowly realize that they're looking at me. I tear my eyes from a whorl in the carpet that I'd been staring at while I was thinking. The answer is obvious. In fact, we have the best possible team for this job.

"Forty-Two, you're up," I say. "We've got two minutes and one shot at this. I'm counting on your luck to pull us through." I wave a hand at the assembled objects. "Choose."

"But choose wisely," Cora quips. She's rewarded with a shoulder-nudge from Manny, who picked up on something I didn't. There's a twitch in small, petty part of me, but it passes. Jealousy is the least helpful of my reclaimed emotions.

The women move to stand next to me as Manny steps up to take in the array. I'm aware that I've never seen him actively use his powers before; they've always been haphazard, more serendipity than magic. He closes his eyes and raises his hands like an orchestra conductor, breathing deeply. Three seconds pass, then, without so much as a vibration in the air, he opens his eyes and drops his right hand onto the seventh box.

"This one," he says.

I smile encouragingly when he checks for my approval. But as I'm reaching for the selected box, ready to lay out my escape plan, Finn turns abruptly and shouts from the doorway.

"Get down!"

None of us have time to react before the bats flood the room. Finn is knocked to the ground in an instant as they burst the wooden doors and stream inside. For a blurred moment, we're surrounded by dozens of flying creatures, screeching and circling in a cloud like black smoke. As I start to move, the swarm tightens, turning the cloud into a cyclone. By the time the others are moving, the bats are gone, leaving a single man standing in the center of the treasury, black ichor and crimson blood smeared across his face and chain mail shirt. Behind him, other vampires are rushing down the hallway towards us.

Seanan Kincaid strides forward, eyes blazing red, coming directly at me.

The rush of hot wind over sand fills my mind, stirring up my blood. *Yes, beloved!* she crows. *Fight! Win! Prove yourself worthy, and I will rain glory and blessing upon you in your triumph.*

There is only one answer I can give. *Yes, my lady.*

I push Cora and Akiko behind me, ignoring their shouts of protest. If I can defeat the Alpha of the most powerful werewolf Pack in America, I can save us from a half-spent, delusional elder vampire. As long as the others hold back the rabble and don't become collateral damage.

"The door!" I shout. But Manny's already running towards Finn with Akiko close behind.

As she runs to join them, Cora says, "Watch out, he's not infected!" then lunges into the fray.

I snap my attention to Kincaid as he advances,

unwilling to believe I could have missed such a vital fact. Then I notice the wide smear of clean flesh across his cheek, devoid of *éclat*'s sparkle, and the malicious smile that spreads across his face confirms the truth. My mind frantically recalculates tactics based on this new information, but there's no time. Instinct takes over, and I step forward to meet him, crouching low to change my center of gravity.

The first punch comes faster than I expected, in a burst of supernatural speed and strength, directly into my midsection. I'm thrown back a full yard, connecting with the study table holding the mirrors. It rocks and strains against the bolts keeping it pinned to the floor, but the boxes on top have no such security. Hearing the magical glass shattering is more horrific than feeling my abdominal muscles tear. My body will repair itself. The mirrors won't.

I shove myself up, but Kincaid is already on top of me. I hold up an arm against his slashing claws, no longer noticing pain through the rush of adrenaline and the descending red mist. The lycan power in my blood demands to be released again, and I let it run. It coils steel into my muscles, allowing me to match his unnatural strength. I thrust my forearm against Kincaid, pushing him out of my guard, and replant my feet.

Over his shoulder, I see a knot of people thrashing against each other and I long to leap around the elder in front of me and help my pack. But the logical side of me points out the lack of human blood spilled. They're okay. For now.

Kincaid lunges at me just as I refocus on him, fangs fully extended and driving towards my exposed neck. I duck my head in and step to the side, but his reflexes are sharper than mine. Lightning-fast, he changes course with me, latching onto my wounded arm with both hands to draw us back together, nails digging into my flesh. I hiss and shove my knee into his stomach. It forces air out of him, but it does nothing to loosen his grip. Together, we whirl in a circle from the momentum, crashing again into the table of mirrors, our feet stomping on the broken glass spilled over the carpet.

With a surge of power, Kincaid uses his leverage on my arm to bend me backwards over the now-empty table and pins me there. I struggle to get free, but he's pressing down using the magic in his blood, and I can't budge him despite my enhanced strength. The second my muscles weaken, he'll crush my creaking ribcage, tear open my throat, and drain me dry.

"A gallant effort, agent, but I'm afraid it's not enough," he says, red eyes flashing. "Your pets are dead or fleeing. The ambassador is delivered to us. Your friends will die a horrific death, and you are about to join them." Then he leans down until our noses are practically touching. With a cruel grin, he says, "The only one spared will be the woman. She will be my queen. I will use every scrap of her mind, body, and soul until nothing remains but an empty, obedient shell. I will ensure she knows her torment is because of your arrogance in thinking you could alter the course of fate. It will be your name she curses through the centuries, not mine."

Rage takes over. There is no me, no voices, not even the wolf. The red mist swallows me whole, filling my blood, my nerves, my muscles, my bones. My lips twist to bare my teeth and my head tips back to make room for the howl, the sound of a rabid dog.

Kincaid's eyes widen in disbelief as I thrust him away. He stumbles, and I spring up, already swinging. My fist connects with the center of his chest, clashing bone against steel. The chain mail does nothing to protect him from his sternum cracking. He cries out and continues to stagger backwards. I wheel my entire body around, leg gathered like a piston, and shoot it precisely into the same spot. The rage rejoices, sharpening my senses to such a point that I can hear the meat of his body tearing and filling with ichor. The momentum is too much for Kincaid to compensate, and he starts to topple over.

I snarl with satisfaction, clenching both hands into iron-hard fists, ready to finish the fight. But before I take another step, I notice that the Founder hasn't hit the ground. He's being held up from behind.

By Akiko.

The Japanese ambassador's formal kimono is covered in ash and ichor, torn to the point of indecency, but her eyes shine bright and her arms are strong. Kincaid leans heavily into her. A quick calculation tells me that between fighting the werewolves, fighting me, and knitting his bones and flesh together, he's using the last dregs of his power. He must be ravenous, desperate to feed and replenish his stores. This is my best chance to finish this.

"Get away from him, Akiko," I say through clenched teeth. "This will end now."

"He can be saved!" she shouts over Kincaid's shoulder. "They all can. They do not understand what they are doing."

I glance around her to see the others still engaged with the Founders at the treasury door. They're holding their ground, but tiring. Finn, fending off three attackers, his former brothers. Manny, hair wild and arms sagging. Cora....

I take a threatening step forward, but neither the elder nor the paragon flinch. "Get away from him," I repeat. "We'll never get out of here alive if he's spared."

But Kincaid is too fast for her. In the space of a breath, he's switched their positions, catching her arms behind her with one hand and pulling her head back with the other. She doesn't even have time to scream. I can only watch as he plunges his fangs into the soft tissue between her throat and collarbone.

Suddenly, I'm blinded. Bright white sunlight fills the cavernous room, followed by howls of anguish and the smell of burning flesh. I blink furiously and rub the spots from my eyes. When my vision returns, what I see makes me rub them again, unsure it's real.

Kincaid is convulsing on the ground, clutching at his ruined face with charred hands, chunks of grey ash falling to the floor. The other vampires at the doorway, including Finn, are doing the same. Cora and Manny stand over them, wide-eyed and confused. And in the center of it all is Akiko. Her breathing is heavy and stitched, making her entire body tremble. She's unharmed except for a wide ribbon of glittering gold streaming down her chest from two ragged holes in her throat.

"Sunlight in the blood," I whisper.

She gives me a tight smile. "You see why I cannot lift the mirror's curse." Then she looks down at Kincaid, who is weeping and growling through cracked holes in his face. His burned skin is not healing, but he's rallying. She looks back up at me and says, "Take the mirror and go, agent. He will soon recover."

"I can't leave you here, Madam Ambassador. You're still officially under my care."

"I release you." I try to protest further, but she cuts me off. "Your duty is greater than my life. The mirror must be kept from Eris, and your people must be safe." Then, to my surprise, she bows deeply to me. When she rises, she says, "I trust that you will do what is right, Jack Alexander."

"Uh, Ninety-Seven...," says Manny from the doorway. "We've got more company coming."

Running footsteps clatter down the hall towards the treasury. I glance at my people, covered in blood and ash, then at Kincaid, who's starting to get to his feet, if a bit shakily.

I decide.

"Let's go, agents. Akiko's going to handle this."

Cora and Manny jog to me with confused expressions but don't ask any questions. I point to the ruined collection of mirrors on the floor.

"Is our ringer intact?" I ask Manny.

He squints at the mess, then brightens. "Oh, yeah, totally," he says, bending to pick up one of three unbroken objects.

"Excellent. Now, both of you come stand next to me."

There's curiosity in Cora's eyes, but she tosses her makeshift stake to Akiko without question. The ambassador catches it neatly, bows to us, then heads towards the door to meet the fresh wave of attackers, bloody sunlight turning her kimono into vampire-proof armor.

Cora and Manny step to my side at a respectful distance, but I draw them in until we form a small circle with the mirror box in the center. I lay my arms across their shoulders, pulling us together as close as physically possible, their arms secured around my waist.

Cora catches my eye. "Are we—" she starts.

"Yes. And I need your help to do it."

For a brief second, she narrows her eyes, and I feel her test the magical tether between us. There's a pluck, then a hum, then a sensation I can't describe—soft outside and steely inside. There's an extended, empty note as the vibration dies away. Then her energy spools up. My own instantly responds, charging and winding faster than I've ever done it on my own. Our bond thrums merrily, as if it's happy to finally be used. We feed magic through it into a shared store that's rapidly brimming over, spilling down my branch of the bond, ready to power the jump.

But for a perilous moment, I'm not sure it will work. Though we're both sidesteppers, teleporting is my unique ability; will her assistance matter? She did hijack my first jump, and we've fused our energy before to power an instant sidestep in the underworld, but this is different. The odds of safely arriving where we intend are astronomical, and I haven't tried teleporting with passengers. If only I'd done more tests after Faerie....

Cora must sense my rising doubt. She squeezes me briefly, sending a surge of reassurance through the bond that clears my head instantly. She trusts me to rescue us. I can't let her down.

I recenter myself and picture our intended landing site in as much detail as possible. The white walls, the plastic furniture, the metal structure at the center. Then I close my eyes and begin routing magic into the jump.

Inhale...

Exhale...

Inhale...

My hands grip shoulders, my entire body tenses. Distantly, I hear Manny hiss as my fingers dig into his shoulder. Cora tightens her grip around my waist.

There's a sound like a twig breaking. The rush of

a cool breeze on a hot day. The sensation of altitude gained and swiftly lost.

Exhale.

TWENTY-TWO

The sensation of landing isn't enough to make me open my eyes. Possibilities including unfriendly locations and mistranslated bodies taunt me. If I've failed, I don't know what I'll see when I look up.

But my body doesn't wait for me to work up my courage. After the first jump in Faerie, I've known teleportation is exhausting—a power sink I'd never experienced before. This is so much worse. The drain from transporting three people and a magical box across two hundred miles crushes me until my knees buckle, starting a cascade of muscle failure throughout my body. My inner gyroscope spins crazily behind my closed eyelids, making me want to vomit and pass out simultaneously. I have a momentary flashback to my first hangover, then my entire body sags, heading for the floor.

Four strong arms keep me upright. Cora and Manny are okay. It worked.

Bright fluorescent light stabs into my brain when

I open my eyes, giving me an instant migraine. When I'm finally able to see clearly, the first thing I note is that we've successfully arrived in the Interdimensional Staging Room back at the SCD. Its white walls and empty space are solidly reassuring.

Otherwise, all I can see is Cora. She's sweating through ragged breathing, and she does her best to support my significant height with her petite frame. As I focus on her, I can see that she's hardly drained at all; she must have reabsorbed whatever magic I didn't burn for the jump. Knowing that I can share our resources without hurting her is an enormous relief, although she's palpably distressed at my condition.

"You with me?" she asks with a worried smile.

"Always," I say hoarsely.

She blushes. "At least you didn't get stabbed this time."

"Small miracle." I try to laugh but cough instead. Cora tries to shoulder more of my weight. I shake my head. "I'm fine, promise. I just need to sit down."

There's an argument in her eyes, but she keeps it to herself. "Whatever you say, boss."

Cora helps Manny hoist me up straight, and they walk me to the control desk. I sink gratefully into a white plastic chair as if it were an overstuffed recliner. I lean my head against the cool wall and take several deep breaths. It stops the room from spinning, but not the headache. I suspect it's from magic burn. This is the first time I've used enough power to trigger it, and from what I understand, no amount of aspirin will help.

"Hey, can you hold this for a second, dude?" Manny says, handing the mirror box to Cora once I'm settled. Holding his hair back, he leans over the trash can next to the desk and vomits neatly into it. Cora bursts out laughing. Manny comes back up wiping his mouth with the sleeve of his suit jacket. To me, he says, "Does it always happen like that?"

I shrug with a half-smile. "I have no idea. New powers."

"Huh," he says. "Better work on it. Barfing does not rule."

Cora hands the box back to him, then gives me an appraising look. I peel myself away from the wall and do my best to be attentive. There's a mild buzzing in my brain accompanied by the sensation of ice water being slowly streamed through my blood. My energy is starting to refresh itself. I silently give grudging thanks to Rhand that my lycan healing factor works on both my body and my magic.

"So, we're going to Cid with this, yeah?" Cora says. "Surely our resident Q has a magical doohickey that can identify the mirror."

I nod and reach over to punch a button on the wall com. "Agent Seventy-Five, if you're in the building, call ISR ASAP."

Within two seconds, Cid's reedy voice is on the line. "Ninety-Seven, is that you? What're you doing here?"

"Back from New York early," I say dryly. "I've got

a science project for you. Is the lab clear?"

"Pretty sure I'm the only one left in the building. Come on over."

The com crackles out as I release the button.

"Let's get moving," I say to Cora and Manny. "The quicker we find out what we've got, the better. But," I glance meaningfully around at the room to remind them about the recording devices, "we need to stay alert."

They nod, then I hold out a hand, and Cora pulls me to my feet. Something passes between us when we touch, and there's a marked boost in the regeneration of my energy. Our hands glow momentarily blue. She gives me a private smile and a wink. "You're welcome," she says quietly.

Manny heads for the door, box in hand. "Get a room, you two," he says with a chuckle.

For a second, Cora's face is a reflection of my own stunned embarrassment, like a toddler caught with his fist in the cookie jar. Then the ISR door slides open. We look away simultaneously, and she releases my hand, leaving me to wobble as I get my feet. Manny leads the way out and down the hall towards the lab. We follow, pretending nothing happened, knowing full well what did.

"One more time, just to make sure I understand."

Cora huffs at Cid. With exaggerated slowness, she says, "We think we found one of the relics Eris needs to bring down the Gauntlet, but it's under a glamour, and we need you to break it. Why is that so difficult to understand?"

"Sorry, I guess it's not. Got caught up in the 'whole sun goddess protecting the vampires' part of the story."

The two of them stand next to each other on one side of a stainless steel table as they argue, the open mirror box between them, Manny and me waiting and watching on the opposite side. I am pointedly not mentioning Cid's distraction being due to him staring down the front of Cora's mangled ball gown. It takes full concentration to keep myself from lashing out protectively. Manny must notice my irritation because he nudges me and smirks. I don't rise to the bait, which makes him grin more broadly. It seems like everyone knows what's going on between Cora and me except us.

"Okay, got it," the quartermaster says. He maneuvers his standing wheelchair to face the table, giving the crate his full attention. Gingerly, he lifts the mirror out and sets it on the table. "Grab me the quantum fluctuation monitor over there," he says, pointing vaguely at a shelf.

"The what?"

"The black box with the lights on top."

Cora retrieves the machine and hands it to him. Cid flicks a switch on the side of what looks like a walkie-talkie with toy siren lights glued to it and waves it over the mirror. Piercing static erupts from the speaker, and six of the ten red lights come on. The quartermaster *hrms*, then turns the mirror over and repeats the process with the same result. He tweaks a knob on the front, then does it again.

This time, more lights go off. His eyebrows go up.

"Well?" I ask tersely.

Cid looks up as if startled that anyone's there, black curls bouncing out of his face. "Oh, right." He taps on the machine in his hand. "Says we're dealing with a Level Eight enchantment. Heavy-duty stuff. Getting some interference, though." He gives Manny a sideways look. "Shouldn't be a problem. I'll toss it in the nullifier, clean it up, then we'll test it against the Roosevelt's artifact database."

"How long is that going to take?"

He shrugs. "Hour? Maybe two?"

I master the urge to demand faster results. This is too important for impatience. I want this done right, and rushing won't help. I also admittedly could use a solid hour of rest. I'm unsure how long it's been since I slept.

"Fine," I say with a nod to Cid. "I'm going up to my office to work on the case report. Call me the second you've got anything."

The quartermaster isn't listening. He's already got the mirror in his hands, gently caressing the glossy dark wood and muttering to himself as he glides to the back of the lab toward lead-lined antimagic booth.

I turn to Manny in his torn tuxedo and Cora in her ruined formal dress. They stand to attention. Both are covered in blood, ash, and ichor; both are exhausted but ready for orders. There's a tight heat in my chest as I realize that I'm humbled by them, these agents—these friends—who trust me to lead them, sure they're doing the right thing purely because I say we are.

Emotion thickens my voice, but I pretend not to notice. "You two are dismissed. Go and get some rest. I'll call you when I hear from Cid."

Manny salutes. "Aye, aye, captain. If anyone needs me, I'll be under Scott Kim's desk, sleeping." He throws a mischievous smile to Cora, who squints back at him, then heads for the bullpen.

Leaving Cora and I alone in the lab.

I rush to fill the silence, taking refuge in formality. "Agent Six, I recommend you follow his example. If the test returns positive results, we have an even longer night ahead of us." I turn and head for the door without waiting for a response.

"Oh, no you don't," she says, catching up with me. "No more of this lone wolf crap, okay? Let me at least help you with the report. You only know half the story, anyway. It'll save us both time." She lowers her voice as we walk briskly down the hallway. "And besides, I think there's more to talk about than New York, don't you?"

The tremor in my hand is hardly noticeable as I press the elevator button up to my office.

Cid was right: No one else is in the building tonight. When I sit behind my desk to start my computer, I know why. I stare at the screen as reality sinks in.

Cora waits patiently in the visitor's chair for ten full seconds before she cranes around to see what I'm looking at. When she sees it's only the desktop, she says, "Okay, I'll bite. What's wrong?"

"It's after midnight. It's Christmas Day."

"Oh."

Both of us stare into space for a while. I can't speculate about what's going on in her mind. Mine is warring between painful, scotch-fractured memories of last Christmas and the promise I made to my mother that I wouldn't work through another holiday. How did I let it get away from me? I accepted the security detail knowing it would cut close, but I was supposed to be back in time to be at my mother's for breakfast, the ambassador safely on a plane home. Now I don't know if Akiko's alive, and I'm in my office calculating how to proceed with our senior agents missing or gone rogue.

I shift my attention to Cora. Her grey eyes are shining, her nose reddening. She meets my gaze and gives a game smile. "Merry Christmas, Jack," she says.

I can't bring myself to return the pleasantry. I turn back to the computer and open a fresh report. The temperature in the room drops a couple of degrees, which I deserve.

"Tell me what happened between the gala and rescue," I say, in a more official tone. "Then you can sleep while I fill in the rest with my account. No need for us both to be up."

But instead of cooperating, she leans forward in her chair until her collarbones rest on the edge of the desk. She stares at me balefully for a second, then says, "First off, it wasn't a rescue. Manny and I were already loose by the time you found us. And second, why don't we talk about what the hell is going on with our powers instead?"

I sigh quietly and push back from the computer, resigned to not finishing the reports. Perhaps it was naïve of me, but I thought I'd be able to avoid this conversation. I'd hoped the excitement of finding Amaterasu's mirror and the anxiety of Samir's betrayal would be enough to get her—our—mind off what little of "us" there is. I'm not eager for her to hurt me again. But she's right. We have to stay out in the light or risk being twisted in darkness. I come around the desk and take the chair across from her. She sits up and turns to face me, eyebrows raised. We're a foot apart, yet the magical bond between us hums as if we were touching. Several seconds pass.

Cora finds her words first. "Do you remember the last time we sat staring at each other all intense like this?" she says with a smile.

The memory of that moment in Cloud Nine replays itself, and I chuckle. "I remember you calling me a fucker and threatening to punch me for leaving you behind."

"Hey, you deserved that."

I nod. "I did."

She chuckles lightly, and the tension between us dissolves. "What do we do about this, Jack?" she says, leaning back in her chair. "Real talk. Because I thought I did the right thing the other day, trying to put distance between us for safety purposes. But if your over-chivalrous rescue attempt is any indicator, it didn't do any good." She looks away abruptly. "And neither did my behavior with

Kincaid." She presses on before I can ask, although I'm not sure I want to know. "We keep putting ourselves in risky situations for each other. The bond is still there. Even without," she waves a hand vaguely, "anything official going on."

A series of emotions rises up inside me as I listen. Frustration. Confusion. Gratitude. Forgiveness. I have to squeeze my eyes shut against the uproar they're making in my mind. It's so visceral that I can't speak. I don't want to say anything until I'm confident it won't come out wrong.

Just say it.

My eyes snap open. That wasn't a voice I recognize. The machine of Agent 97 and Limerence's hold are gone, and Ishtar's has a definite texture of its own. Could it be that this voice is mine? After a year of searching for it, has my own soul finally found its way home? My heartbeat doubles, flooding my system with fresh confidence and courage.

"You're right," I say aloud. "The emotions that formed the connection aren't going away. This is old magic, the kind that has a will of its own. We're past the point where we can intervene. Even broken hearts can't unravel it now. I tried to explain, but you wouldn't listen." She winces, the accusation landing hard. To soften the blow, I reach out to take her hand, rolling my chair forward until our knees touch. "Trust me, I understand the desire to push away things that make you weak, especially if they're good."

She sighs and leans forward, wrapping our free hands together. A blue spark falls to the carpet and winks out. "If it doesn't matter what we do...," she says, but trails off. Her fingers tighten around mine.

I bow my head to meet her eyes. There are strange emotions there. But the ones I most want to see shine brightest. "Cora, we.... I...."

I have to stop. I'm not sure what to say. I know what I feel, and the bond tells me what she feels. We both know what we want. She's right, though. The closer we are, the easier it is to take advantage of us, at increasingly high probability the deeper Eris' conspiracy runs. But it's going to happen anyway. We're drawn back to each other. We've proved that much in the last twenty-four hours. Is it better to hold our heads high, be what we want, and face the danger of that choice, knowing it could cost one or both of us our lives? I honestly don't know. A year ago, I couldn't process a single emotion; now here I am, navigating dozens, trying to decide if love is better unrequited or boldly given. How things change. How complicated they can be.

Not knowing what to say, I squeeze her hands, so small and rough in mine. She squeezes back and smiles in a way I haven't seen since a faraway morning in a bed we shared for a few hours. Sweet and warm. She pulls herself to me, leaving her chair and sliding into my lap, legs off to one side in the ripped skirt of her emerald dress, then wraps her bare, ash-streaked arms around my neck. My heartbeat quickens. I move to put my arms around her waist, but hesitate. She gives me a subtle nod. I wrap both arms around her and pull her to my chest, one of my hands burying itself in her copper hair. Her head rests in the hollow of my shoulder, and we sit that way for a long time, simply holding each other. Everything we want to say races through our link, pure emotion translated into a magic of its own. Neither of us is fighting it anymore. There are undoubtedly obstacles and danger ahead, but here in this moment, none of them matter. A diffuse cerulean glow slowly fills the room. The magic is sealed, the bond complete.

The office phone ringing throws us both out of the chair.

I start violently, jolting Cora, and she leaps to standing, hands raised like a karate master, eyes darting around the room. Stifling my laughter, I reach over to pick up the receiver.

"Agent Ninety-Seven."

"Jack, you need to get back to the lab right now. You're going to want to see this."

"Be right there, Cid," I say into the phone.

"That was fast," Cora says.

I hang up the handset and stand, smoothing the wrinkles in my suit. Not that it makes a difference on top of the damage it suffered between the evening's monsters. "It was," I say, "which can means bad news. We'd better get down there." I step past her and hold open the glass door of my office. "After you, my dear," I say, feeling absurd and amazing at once.

She smiles cordially but pauses halfway through the door. Her grey eyes glitter mischievously. I want so badly to kiss her then. Instead, I raise an eyebrow and say, "What?"

"You think we'll ever have a normal relationship?"

The bluntness of the question catches me so off-guard that I laugh. "It depends on what you mean by 'normal,' I suppose," I say. Then, more seriously, I add, "Maybe. If we win this—"

"When," she interrupts. "When we win this, Agent 97...," she reaches out to straighten the collar of my shirt and grins wickedly, "I'm going to ruin you." She winks, then starts down the hall.

I stand there, stunned, and at a total loss, caught between the thrill of confirmation and the ache of being denied what we most want.

The chime of the elevator signals me to move again. I rush to lock my office and join her as the doors open, walking on air despite knowing that whatever Cid has found will send me crashing back to earth. I take her hand for the ride down. A short, stolen moment is better than none at all.

TWENTY-THREE

We're halfway down the hallway leading to the lab when Manny comes running up. His expression reminds me of a golden retriever puppy. "Guys, you are not going to believe this," he says, falling into step beside me. I expect him to tell us what Cid's found, but instead he pulls out his phone. "I got a voicemail from Akiko."

He hits play before I can ask why he didn't answer the call.

"Agents, I am alive and well. Agent Ninety-Seven's remaining lycan allies arrived shortly after your departure and swiftly ended the conflict. However, they were not able to secure Seanan Kincaid, whose whereabouts are currently unknown. I am obligated to tell you that I have chosen not to return home at the present time. It is my intention to stay in New York for the foreseeable future to work with Finnegan Kincaid on a solution to the outbreak of *éclat mort*. He believes it is the key to the vampires' idiotic alliance with the chaos goddess, which he has ended in inheriting the role of Dracula Founder. He wishes for you to count him among your friends. I trust you will be in contact with me the instant you have information on the mirror. I look forward to speaking with you again soon. *Arigato.*"

The message ends as we reach the lab, and Manny tucks his phone away as Cid rolls up to us. The quartermaster's face is flushed and his glasses are askew.

I nod to Manny. "Thanks, Forty-Two. We'll get in touch with her ASAP." To Cid, I say, "What happened?"

"I don't know how they did it, boss," he says breathlessly.

He guides us to the back of the room where the antimagic booth is located, speeding ahead in his standing dock. When the rest of us reach him, he's standing next to a huge mirror in an ornate gold frame leaning against the wall. It's fully four feet tall, and the glass is hazy, as if smeared or smoked. Cid waits for us to line up in front of it, then stabs a hand at it accusingly as his words come out in rapid-fire succession.

"This is the same mirror you gave me. The glamour popped off of it about ten minutes into the process. It must've been designed to disintegrate."

"Cid," I interrupt.

"You said you took it out of a vampire haven, right? I don't know how they got this kind of magic or how they got a hold of the damn thing in the first place. It's supposed to be in the Roosevelt archives; I checked it against the logs right away, and it's been missing for months."

"Cid."

"Obviously, it's not Amaterasu's mirror, which sucks. I mean, I don't know why Manny's powers didn't work. Are you sure that's the one you need, anyway? I'd think any magical mirror would do the trick if the prophecy is about reflection. Maybe even this one, but you'd have to get the spirit out first."

"Cid!" I shout.

Finally, the quartermaster stutters to a stop. He winces and scratches the back of his head, embarrassed. "Sorry, Ninety-Seven. Got carried away. There's a lot going on here. Stuff I've never seen before."

"It's fine," I reassure him, "but I need you to tell me what it is."

"Ah, right." He eases his dock over so he's in front of the mirror, then he clears his throat dramatically and says, "Mirror, mirror, on the wall. Get out here and tell Jack what this is about."

There's a shimmer inside the glass and the haze begins to fade like a developing Polaroid. After a few seconds, it reveals not the disembodied head of Snow White's looking glass that I was expecting, but a full-sized person. Cora and Manny gasp when the girl appears, but I sigh heavily and cross my arms. This won't be good.

"Mary, what are you doing in there?" I ask.

The ghostly teenager puts a hand on her bloodstained hip. "Hey, don't talk to me like that,

321

Mister. You try being locked up in here with Mr. Dreary Head for weeks on end and see how you like it."

"Mary?" Cora says from beside me. "Like, Bloody Mary?"

"Yeah, what's it to you?"

Cora opens her mouth to retort. I wave her off. I've been around with Mary before. "Don't. She'll win." Cora looks offended but subsides. To Mary, I say, "How did you get locked in there? I thought spirits couldn't share objects."

She shrugs. "I was just passing through. Mirror, Mirror and I like to hang out, shoot the shit, gossip, you know. I bring him the news since he can't move around and I can." Then she scowls. "But then this fur-faced asshat comes along and starts chanting while we're out of frame. The next thing I know, everything's tiny and BAM, I'm stuck."

"Must've been when they put the glamour on," Cid says. "Changed the mirror's size and locked it against magic, so Mary couldn't leave."

"Who was the magician?" I ask.

Another shrug. Teenagers. "No clue. He was talking some language I ain't never heard before."

"Werewolf?" Cora suggests.

I shake my head. "They don't have external magic like that."

"An animal god?" Manny tries.

"Could be. Tough to pinpoint without knowing the geographic area."

"Hey, can I go?" Mary says. "I'm way behind on appearances, and I swear to fuck that if those idiots in St. Louis don't knock it off, I'm going to kill them all."

I narrow my eyes at her. "Yes, you can go, but you're out of warnings. Last time you interfered with that coven, you spent three weeks in the Roosevelt. Next time, it'll be a permanent stay. Or worse."

She seems momentarily frightened but covers with attitude. "Yeah, yeah, whatever. I'll be good. See you later, squares." Then she walks out of frame and the glass clouds over again.

"Well, isn't she a little ray of sunshine," Cora says acidly.

"What do you expect from Bloody Mary?" Manny says. "She's been on the SCD payroll as an informant for a while, though. Does good work when she's not being a heinous bitch. Or digging out people's eyeballs." He shudders.

I turn to Cid. "So, we've got the Snow White mirror?" He nods. Then I turn to Manny and say, "How did this happen?"

Forty-Two bows his head sheepishly. "Wish I knew, boss. My powers are based on serendipity, far as I can tell. I've been working on conscious control for like three years. It's better odds, but not perfect. There's always a chance things just go normal. Or, in this case, wrong." He grimaces. "Sorry, dude."

I take a deep breath and hold it as I process the implications, trying to come up with a way to address this egregious error without yelling. Thankfully, Cora chimes in, sparing me the pain of laying out the direness of the situation.

"So, if we don't have it and Akiko didn't mention finding it in her message, we have to assume Kincaid has Amaterasu's mirror," she says. "The vamps can't use it to make themselves into daywalkers, but that doesn't mean he won't give it to Eris. That'll give her two of the three relics she needs for the apocalypse ritual." I nod. "And," she adds, "we haven't accounted for what's going on with Patel."

At the mention of Agent 99's name, there's another shimmer in the glass of Snow White's mirror, this time revealing its true occupant. A large, disembodied theater mask emerges on a backdrop of green and black flames. We all turn to look.

But the voice that booms from Mirror, Mirror's mouth isn't his. It's Samir Patel's.

"Agents of the Supernatural Cases Division. If you have discovered this message, it means you have fulfilled your role in the game. Without your tireless efforts and willingness to obey orders, we could not have come so far, so fast. The sword is ours. The mirror is ours. The apple is within our grasp. The war has begun, and the key to humanity's salvation is in our possession. The Gauntlet will fall. The worlds will be united. Mortals will once again serve supernals, as is natural and right. There is nothing you can do to stop it. Lady Eris and I thank you for your assistance, but your services are no longer required. Farewell."

Message conveyed, the mask fades, leaving the glass empty and the room echoing with fatal pronouncements.

"What. The. Hell," says Cora, voice shaking. Her anger stirs my own, threatening to sweep me along with it. "Did that motherfucker seriously just admit, balls-out, that he's with Eris? And that he played us?" She wheels to face me. "And what did he mean by 'the key to humanity's salvation'? Is there more to the ritual than Tithonus told us?" She grimaces and stomps her foot in frustration, making Manny flinch. "Shit, is the Lorekeeper a bad guy, too?!" she yells. "What the supernatural fuck is going on here?"

I grab her shoulders and hold her steady, despite the gnawing in the pit of my own stomach. "Cora, stop. We have to keep our heads clear." I lock her eyes and try to pour as much reassurance into my voice as possible. "We can deal with this. One thing at a time. Besides, we already knew Ninety-Nine was compromised."

"Uh, I didn't," says Cid, waving a hand for attention. All the color has drained out of his face. If he weren't strapped into his standing dock, I think he'd fall over.

I release Cora as I turn to study the mirror. Details and data swirl through my mind, interlocking into a coherent picture. I let myself process out loud. "He must've recorded that right before we left on assignment. He sent us on purpose. Chose us, specifically." I turn to the agents I brought back from New York. "Manny to find the mirror. Me to bring the ambassador. And Cora...." I hesitate. How could he know Cora would get involved? The answer arrives like a bullet in my stomach. "And Cora to find him out."

Her eyes widen as she picks up my train of thought. "He knew about our new powers, so he had to know about the bond. He knew I'd run straight to you with the news about One Hundred. That scumbag wanted me in New York to make sure you did something stupid enough to get yourself killed, like confront a pack of werewolves or run into a nest of vampires."

"And give him time to get away."

Five full seconds of silence pass. Then Manny says, "Dude. That's heavy."

I press my hands to the steel lab table to cool my rising rage, drawing on the last of my exhausted willpower to remain calm. This man was my mentor since the day I set foot in the agency. He watched over me, disciplined me, encouraged me, grew me, drove me—for ten years, a father where my own father was not. And now this. I've been manipulated, moved across the board as a pawn and sent to be sacrificed when deemed no longer useful. I grip the edge of the table until the metal complains and begins to buckle.

"Jack." It's all she says.

I stifle a growl of frustration and turn to face the group. "Okay," I say. "I'm okay." It's more to convince myself than them. "If Ninety-Nine is this far ahead, we're going to have to come up with a new plan. He knew everything about us and our investigations before, but now that he's declared his side, he won't. Things will be different. We just need to find somewhere safe so we can form a plan."

Cora's phone rings as I speak the last word. She digs it out of her pocket apologetically. Her face lights up when she looks at the screen, and she answers right away. "Hey! I was getting ready to call you. How—"

Her face falls and pales dramatically. Without a word, she lays her phone down on the table. The caller ID says *Mamma Bear*. She touches a button on the screen, then leans back, chewing her thumbnail.

"Did you put me on speaker, cher?" says the voice from the other side.

My heart tries to stop. Anything but him.

"Wex?" I manage.

"Hello there, Jackie boy," he says amiably. "How're you feeling? Back holding up okay?"

"Cut the shit, Wex," Cora spits. "What do you want? Where's Sofi?"

"*Tsk, tsk.* Such language." There's a pause, then a rustle. "Your girlfriend here has quite the mouth on her, too. She must've learned it from you."

"Cora? Jack?" Sofi's voice is ragged and dry.

Tears leap down Cora's cheeks. "Soph? Are you okay? I swear to god if that motherfucker touched a hair on your head—"

"I ain't touched nothin', cher. Yet."

"You stay away from her, you bastard!"

"Too late for that, I'm afraid. Now you back up

off the phone and let the grownups talk, alright?"

Cora reaches for the phone, but I snatch it up first. I hold it in the palm of my hand so everyone can hear.

"What do you want, Wex? You know I'm not about to negotiate with you."

"Oh, I think you'll have a change of heart when you hear what I'm offering."

"Doubtful."

"How about a sporting shot at finding the last relic? You know that apple is down here in Johnny's orchard."

I hesitate for half a second. "Appleseed's final planting was never verified. Why should I believe you?"

"You already do." The half-second was too long. I can hear his grin. "All you gotta do is bring you and that pretty little miss of yours down here to the desert. I'll even give you a head start and your feral pet back."

"Out of the goodness of your heart, I'm sure."

"Why, of course. Just because I'm going to be an actual-factual god soon doesn't mean I've forgotten my Southern roots. Consider this a gentleman's wager. You and your crew of adorable misfits against me and mine. Winner take all."

"You have two of the three relics already. If you were smart, you'd grab the apple and run. Bringing us in to make it interesting surely isn't good for your Mistress' plans."

"Isn't it deliciously chaotic, though, cher? She'll love it." If he were standing in front of me, he'd be winking.

The others are staring at me with expectation. They want me to make the decision. With horrible clarity, I realize that there is literally no one above me anymore. I'm the top agent. This is not the way I wanted to achieve that goal.

"Guys?" I say to them.

One by one, they nod. I nod back.

"You're on, Wex. When and where?"

"Oh, let's be generous and say six hours from now at 34.0790 north, 107.6184 west. That's the asshole of New Mexico, if your geography is rusty."

Cora jumps in. "Six hours, are you fucking kidding? How are we supposed to get all the way across the goddamn country in that time?"

A rich chuckle. "I'm sure you and your secret agent lover man will figure out a way. See you soon, Jackie. Ta."

The line goes dead.

Mastering my desire to crush the phone, I wordlessly hand it back to Cora.

"What is this, Bad Guy Monologue Hour? Shit," she mutters. Sniffing, she stows the phone and wipes at the tears on her face.

Her distress collapses my attempt to compile logistics for getting to New Mexico by daybreak, telegraphing too strongly through our bond at close range. I pull her to me, not caring what the other agents think.

And then the sirens start.

"Seriously, what the fuck now?" Manny yells in the cacophony.

Red light spills over the lab as the automated system kicks online and the PA broadcasts a pre-recorded message. "Code 433 in progress, priority one. Location: RCCC. Levels: administration, archives, library, maximum security, minimum security. Emergency systems offline. Lockdown procedures disabled. Evacuation plan Alpha Six-Oh-Alpha."

"What does that mean?" shouts Cora.

I'm already running as I shout over my shoulder, expecting them to follow.

"The Roosevelt is burning."

And so ends this episode of the *Forgotten Relics* series!

But there are so many
unanswered questions!

Where is Kincaid?
Why did Manny's luck fail?
Is Sofi okay?
How will Cora and Jack get to
New Mexico in six hours?

Stay tuned to find out in
The Apple of Chaos

Visit EllieDi.com
to keep in touch

ACKNOWLEDGEMENTS

First, I'd like to thank everyone I met during my tenure in the Camarilla, LARPing it up in *Vampire: The Requiem*. I could write an entire book about our adventures, what you taught me, and what I'll carry with me always. In particular, thank you to the South Central for opening your hearts, for sharing the cheese, and for every moment of the God Squad; thanks to the players/characters hat-tipped in this book, who I'd name individually, but it's more fun if you guess; and thanks to Brent Collins, who gamely lent his nerd-avatar for this book's villain, among many other kindnesses he's shown me—thanks for being my Huckleberry.

Thank you to my beta readers, Megan Fair, Katy Rose, Dave La Rush, and Kyeli Smith. These books would suck without you; thank you for making me look good.

Thank you to Desiree Kern, my cover artist, who works with me even when I'm unreasonable and whose loveliness graces more than canvases.

Thank you to Lino, who is confident, against all evidence, that I'm not completely insane, and continues to love and feed me in myriad ways as I stumble along my path.

Thank you to Maureen Hurley for giving me a rigorous Irish Gaelic lesson on Facebook so I didn't muck up two words out of the 78,000 in this manuscript.

Thank you to Eddy Webb for holding my hand through the sticky anxiety of stealing like an artist.

Thank you to everyone who gave their hard-earned cash to crowdfund Desz' well-earned artist's fee: Candace Buck, Megan Fair, Sharon Harris, Debbie Ingersoll, Agnes Jankiewicz, Jasmine Jobe, Katherine King, Steve Kornic, Barbara Locker, Margie Markevicius, Helen Morris, Shelby Olrich, Elizabeth Patt, Joy Robertson, Joel Sullivan, Dianne Sylvan, Daniel Tan, Jennifer Wilding, Aaron Wilson, and Tabitha Wilson.

And finally, an extra-special "thank you" to the ridiculously generous members of Team Patreon who throw money at me to tell pretty lies: Nikki Colborn, Karen Coverett, Tori Deaux, Zachary Eskins, Megan Fair, Jo Gough, Shenee Howard, Agnes Jankiewicz, Jessica Lee, Michelle Nickolaisen, Shelby Olrich, Liz Patt, Laura Simpson, Leela Sinha, and Daniel Tan. Thank you for believing in me. Mwah.

ABOUT THE AUTHOR

 Ellie Di Julio is a nomadic writer currently living in Hamilton, Ontario with her Robert Downey, Jr. lookalike husband and their two cats. Between nerd activities like playing *Final Fantasy IX* or watching *Top Gear*, she enthusiastically destroys the kitchen and tries to figure out what it's all about, when you really get down to it. She also writes urban fantasy novels and short stories riddled with pop culture references, peculiar memories, and sexy secret agents.

Questions, comments, funny stories?
Reviews, interviews, guestposts?
Get in touch!
ellie.di.julio@gmail.com

FORGOTTEN RELICS

Inkchanger (Forgotten Relics #0)

Zara Carter has never fit in at in Runaway Heights, a secret community of teens hiding from their own personal hells. No one has been worth the risk of opening her heart. Things would've stayed that way had it not been for the inkpen, a device that pushes Zara's artistic talents into the realm of magic. The tattoos she creates come to life, and each design gives her a taste of her deepest desire: a heart filled with hope and love.

But power like that doesn't go unnoticed. Assigned to the classified Supernatural Cases Division, Agent 97's feelers are out, searching the decaying industrial town for a wild girl with a remarkable talent.

If only he could catch her.

FORGOTTEN RELICS

The Transmigration of Cora Riley (Forgotten Relics #1)

After thirty boring years, nothing about Cora Riley's life has measured up to her childhood dreams of being truly extraordinary. It's too bad that the night she decides to seek out her specialness she crashes on a rural highway.

Cora wakes in the clutches of the Mistress of the underworld who sets her a seemingly impossible quest. If she wants a second chance at life, Cora must find her way through the dozen heavens and return to the castle in three days.

With the help of an unusual guardian angel named Jack and a little boy named Xavier, Cora navigates the afterlife doorfield and quickly learns that gods and monsters are very real indeed. Terrifying and tempting obstacles litter her path; only the power of belief – in the Otherworld, in her companions, and in herself – will return her to the land of the living.

FORGOTTEN RELICS

The Sword of Souls (Forgotten Relics #2)

Second chance at life? Check.
Ultra-rare magic powers? Check.
Badass new job? Check.
Saved world from evil goddess? Not so check.

Cora Riley assumed when she joined the FBI's Supernatural Cases Division that she'd be dismantling Otherworld treachery alongside Jack Alexander, the storied Agent 97 who guided her through the underworld. Instead, she's filing reports for Sofi Strella, a smart-mouthed agent ten years her junior.

When Jack finally does make contact, it's not for sidestepper training, a quiet drink, or even an apology; it's to investigate a magical narcotic that's boosting supernatural belief to dangerous levels.

The case leads to the realm of Faerie, where Jack encounters an old flame and an even older enemy, both demanding his allegiance. As he battles the entanglements of his past, Cora continues the mission, ultimately facing the eerily-familiar Queen Mab, who wields a legendary blade in the name of Eris, the mad goddess of chaos.

FORGOTTEN RELICS

Confidential: 12 Unredacted Reports from the Supernatural Cases Division

This collection of canon-approved short stories delves into memories and history, adding depth and mystery to what you know about Cora, Jack, and many other characters in the primary novels. (Kindle only.)

STORIES INCLUDE:

- Cora's First Sighting
- Jack's New Assignment
- The Gods' Own Creation Myth
- Ambrosia Makes Fools of Us All
- Nix the Pity-Party
- Hel's Dying Star
- Faerie Halfling Seeks Southern Woman
- The First Day of the Rest of Her Life
- Handle: 5tilt2k1n
- A Bloody Office Romance
- A New Tradition
- Memo on the Holiday Conflict

www.ingramcontent.com/pod-product-compliance
Lightning Source LLC
Chambersburg PA
CBHW020225180626
46810CB00006B/2053